10

6/21

CRACKSMAN ON VELVET

CRACKSMAN ON VELVET

FRANCIS SELWYN

STEIN AND DAY / *Publishers* / New York

First published in the United States of America in 1974
Copyright © 1974 by Francis Selwyn
Library of Congress Catalog Card No. 74-78535
All rights reserved
Printed in the United States of America
Stein and Day/*Publishers*/Scarborough House,
Briarcliff Manor, N.Y. 10510
ISBN 0-8128-1729-X

1

THE McCAFFERY DODGE

I

McCaffery's part in the plan was over, even before he knew the details of the plot. In a few more minutes, in the barrack field near Meerut, the chaplain of the garrison would begin to read to him his own burial service. Precious moments passed and still he could not collect his thoughts properly.

The gold fringes on the epaulettes of the mounted officers jiggled to the horses' walk and the wine-red of their sashes glowed richly against the bright scarlet of their tunics. Both the riders and the foot escort were clear of the town already, leaving behind the strange cluster of buildings which made up the principal British garrison town in the Punjab. Beside the Indian temples and the native bazaar stood airy bunga-lows, the military bandstand, the polo grounds, and the new Victorian church of St John, a gothic building which looked as if it had been snatched up from Knightsbridge or Cheltenham and set down on this hot, windy plain.

They had led McCaffery from his cell at daybreak, and the morning light began to catch in quicksilver flashes on the men's bayonets and the officers' drawn swords, like sun on a moving river. A few white-robed palanquin-bearers and coolies watched the detail, in its tall fur shakos, red serge tunics with white webbing, and blue trousers, as it marched to the slow, dying beat of a muffled drum. Both regiments of Native Infantry had been confined to their quarters. Colonel Collins believed it bad for discipline on both sides for the execution of a British soldier to be witnessed by the subject race.

Even in the early morning, the April heat of the Punjab made the sweat start and prickle like a rash under the red serge of the men's tunics. At the head of the little column, the perspiring bandsmen filled their cheeks and blew the opening notes of the army's favourite funeral dirge, "The

Dead March from Saul," on gleaming silver instruments. To the men stationed in Mecrut in the oppressive spring of 1857, the notes of the slow march had only one meaning.

McCaffery.

McCaffery sauntered in the centre of the detail, almost as though the proceedings were no concern of his. His head was bare, even of a forage cap, and his brown hair was dishevelled. His red tunic hung open. They had cut away his buttons after the court-martial finding was confirmed. There was no need to strip him of medals or rank; McCaffery was not the sort to win medals or earn promotion. As he walked, he rubbed his wrists from time to time, where the manacles had left a red indentation.

Some of the newest recruits, little more than boys, seemed dazed with fright at what they were about to witness. The older privates and NCOs, with their mutton-chop whiskers and sun-reddened foreheads, stared impassively ahead of them. It was a bad business when a man had to be shot to death by a file of muskets, but many of them had seen wholesale death, and mutilations worse than death, in the Afghan campaign or the Sikh wars of the 1840s. Some had watched their comrades blown into butcher's meat by the Russian mortars on the Sebastopol ramparts. All had paraded regularly when a man was stripped and lashed to the triangle. Two drummers laid it on from either side, their thongs slicing open the man's back until the flesh shone with blood and the flies clustered hungrily round the wounds. The men of the regiment might pity a condemned comrade, but they had taken the Queen's shilling. They took it for bread and beef twice a day, for gin in the regimental canteens, and for the golden-skinned Indian girls in the garrison knocking-shop. In return, they accepted the savagery of war and the harsh discipline of peace.

Several subalterns, with smooth cheeks and trim moustaches, rode forward on smartly brushed and glossy bay geldings. To them, too, it was a disagreeable business. They wanted it over, so that they might return to the comforts of the sofa, with cigars, hock and seltzer, talk of polo matches or tiger shoots, and rumours of the latest regimental adulteries. It had become a damned bore, the way that no woman in Meerut would talk of anything but McCaffery. Not only had the confounded man deserted his post and shot Private Spurgeon, he had raped a delicious Anglo-Indian girl into the bargain.

Bearded and lantern-jawed, McCaffery walked lankily between his guards. He was not going to give way to fear now, to be dragged there, as some were, crying for respite, having to be tied into a chair and despatched sitting down. He had promised the padre to "act like a man," and he would. It was only to suffer a little pain, less than a cut with a razor. He had felt worse in many a Saturday night brawl off the Waterloo Road, in the Brill or the dark side-streets. In any case, it was not going to happen yet, they had not even reached the barrack field.

Just before they had left the cell, he was invited to make any final requests. He had one, though it was not one which anybody there could fulfil. He wanted to know why the girl, Jolie, had lied.

McCaffery knew, of course, that girls told lies. He had once been in the way of making a dishonest pittance by it in Blackfriars. But why this one? Why Jolie? The regiment would have shot him for desertion and attempted murder, whether or not he had raped the girl. Why had she sworn to it when it never happened? She had gained nothing, not even his execution, which would have taken place anyway, and she had destroyed her own reputation. Why?

Each night McCaffery had pictured her in the darkness of his prison cell. The profile and colouring of a young Egyptian princess. A body that was slender but well shaped. He remembered the dark, scented hair coiled in an elegant coiffure, the delicate moulding of her ears and the nape of her neck.

It began when he was sent with Sergeant Pickles to deliver copies of garrison commander's orders, and had been left to make his own way back to his billet. In the warm dusk, the girl had approached him, close to the native bazaar. He would have taken "a shillings-worth of greens" from any woman that night, the mood he was in. But even by the lamplight he knew that this was not one of the local whores, kept more or less free from pox to provide comforts for Queen Victoria's army. This one was an officer's doxy, sure to be. Probably out to make a little spending money while her usual protector was on secondment at Bombay or Cawnpore. Better still, perhaps she had been left for weeks and was desperate for a man. Who better to oblige her than Thomas McCaffery? It never occurred to him to be frightened. After all, he had his "Brown Bess" with one round for the spout.

The house they went to, on the edge of the Indian quarter, was no ordinary brothel. In the twilit room, McCaffery had never seen such expensive undergarments on a girl, not even in England. Candy-pink petticoats slid to the floor, and then Jolie displayed herself in bodice and in silk drawers that fitted tight as a ballet-girl's fleshings. Turning out the single lamp, she posed on one knee on the chair, her back arched to increase the tilt of her little breasts and the full rounds of her rear cheeks.

"Well?" she said, in a voice that owed more to the Ratcliffe Highway than to the Punjab, "Unlace me, then!"

McCaffery was no lady's maid and, in the gloom, he began to fumble chaotically with the strings of her drawers. He fingered her thighs and backside roughly through the awkward material, as she seemed to push her body harder into his hands. He breathed the perfume of her hair and then, in a fit of frustrated desire, began to tear at the tangled laces. To his utter dismay, a few seconds later the girl started to scream.

"Hold on, can't you?" he said irritably, still not understanding.

Her nails flew in his face and he hit back methodically, punching her on the arms and legs, which was his habitual way with an awkward woman. It flashed through his mind that as soon as he could knock her flat, he had better snatch up his musket and run, using the butt on any native pimp who might stand in his way. Then there was a babble of

Indian voices outside. The door of the darkened room was kicked open. Its tiny bolt splintered from the frame, and strong light shone inwards, dazzling him. McCaffery threw the girl from him and clutched his musket, equally frightened of having been missed from his duty or of being caught in a native ambush and murdered for his week's pay and the price of his clothes.

Another lamp appeared in the doorway, blinding him completely, and a man's shape hunched forward. McCaffery could see nothing but the girl's face, contorted to a devil's mask as she screamed abuse at him. He crouched in the furthest corner of the room, shouting,

"Halt! Stand fast!"

It had no effect. An Englishman, surely, would have answered the challenge somehow. These were Indians. McCaffery had heard enough garrison tales of the Cabul massacre or the fate of Tippoo Sahib's prisoners, the victims mutilated and cauterised by hot oil. No bastard of a savage was going to take Thomas McCaffery alive.

But he had no wish to answer a charge of murder. So he aimed the muzzle of his rifle at the dark space of the door-way, knowing that any Indian pimp would run like a hare at the first flash of a musket. A jet of flame shot from the barrel, like a miniature thunderbolt, and the very floor shook with the stunning roar in that confined space. But instead of running like hares, two men threw themselves upon him and bore him to the ground. For their courage in facing and overpowering an armed deserter, Sergeant James O'Sullivan and Lance-Corporal Henry Dawes were commended by the garrison commander. Private William Spurgeon lay across the threshold of the doorway, his forage cap gone and a darker red staining the lower back of his scarlet tunic. McCaffery offered no resistance as they led him away, his wrists bound behind his back, but he asked repeatedly,

"Why, for God's sake, did you not speak?"

The incident was what the Liberal newspapers in London called "a tragedy."

McCaffery knew little of military trials, but he had supposed them to be rather grand occasions. His own court-martial was perfunctory enough, even though the presiding officers wore full-dress uniforms, medals and swords. It was held in an empty ward of the garrison hospital, with a single punkah wallah pulling lethargically at his cord to fan the humid air round the heads of the officers.

The proceedings themselves were conducted with the brisk precision of a drill exercise. McCaffery was charged with desertion and attempted murder. The bullet had entered Spurgeon's left side, just above the hip, and exited close to the spine. McCaffery could hardly deny either of the charges and, with something of the petty criminal's sense of fair play, he would have been content to say nothing and take his punishment. Sergeant O'Sullivan told the court how he and his detail had been begged for assistance by a group of terrified Indians on the fringe of the bazaar. As they approached the house, they had heard the girl beginning to scream. McCaffery was sure that O'Sullivan had no reason to lie, and he let the evidence pass unchallenged.

But when they read out Jolie's affidavit, accusing him of rape, McCaffery's sense of fair play was offended. He knew little about the law, but he was wise enough in other matters to know that tumbling a girl and pulling her laces did not amount to rape. Why had the stupid little bitch sworn to it? She had destroyed her own character and gained nothing. Bewildered by such injustice, McCaffery tried to challenge the evidence of Surgeon-Major Fitzgerald. Was the surgeon-major sure the girl had been an unwilling partner in the romp? Oh yes, beyond a doubt. Indeed, the bruises on the arms of the poor "child," not to mention those upon her—er—her upper legs, were additional corroboration of the main evidence of rape. McCaffery had never begun to learn reading or writing and most of the answer was incomprehensible to him. But he caught the final words. Main evidence of rape? Indeed, said the surgeon-major, evidence of—er—criminal connection having occurred, of which the bruising and the discovery of McCaffery were additional confirmation.

At this McCaffery asked plaintively,

14

"Sure, and how can there be evidence, sir, of what I never did?"

Surgeon-Major Fitzgerald permitted himself a thin, dis-approving smile at the man's stupidity.

"If you had not done it," he said crisply, "there would have been no evidence. The conclusion is, I think, obvious."

McCaffery capitulated. The presiding officers failed to see why he should make such a bother over the business of rape. They were not trying him for rape, it was merely part of the circumstantial evidence. Moreover, they wished to spare the girl the ordeal of a court appearance. Several times, the Judge Advocate, a cadaverous, thin-blooded John Company lawyer with clothes like an undertaker's mute, warned McCaffery to answer the actual charges of desertion and attempted murder. For these crimes, men faced a firing party.

McCaffery cared nothing for the actual charges. He had no contradictory evidence, and no means to show that the prosecution witnesses were mistaken. But why had the officer's doxy lied? They would shoot him anyway, without a word of her affidavit.

McCaffery's reverie ended as the detail marched into the barrack field.

"Prisoner and escort, stand fast! Detail, forward march! Quick time!"

The regiment was drawn up on three sides of the field, as the brigade-major began to read out the court-martial find-ing and sentence, confirmed by the commander-in-chief at Delhi. McCaffery had heard it all before. It was irrelevant to his present preoccupation.

Sergeant-Major Hayward finished distributing muskets to the firing party, two guns at random loaded with blank powder, so that no man should bear the certain guilt of murdering a comrade. Then a bearded officer, who was a stranger to the regiment, approached Colonel Collins and saluted. The colonel returned the salute with exaggerated precision and said,

"Your prisoner, sir!"

In the little group that hid McCaffery the provost-sergeant lifted a mug of something warm and sweet to the lips of the condemned man.

"Get this down, lad," he said gently.

McCaffery wanted to refuse, but the contents of the mug seemed to be burning in his throat before he could speak. The actors in the grotesque melodrama then began to move with a brisk punctiliousness. The stranger pinned a little square of white cloth to McCaffery's left breast, like a medal, while the provost-sergeant strapped the man's wrists behind his back.

"Head up," said the officer, with sharp disapproval.

"Be quiet," said McCaffery, fumbling for words. "Be quiet, will you? I want to think."

Another voice, calm but ringing loud, came from a distance.

"Man that is born of a woman hath but a short time to live . . ."

A file of soldiers, who had acted as a human screen, were marched smartly away and McCaffery saw for the first time a white wooden box lying by a short trench. It was not twenty yards away.

"He cometh up and is cut down like a flower . . ."

McCaffery's mind began to wander in the misty stupor induced by the hot rum. Why had the little bitch lied? Quickly! Why? Why? Faster and faster, the padre unrolled the cadences of the living man's burial service.

"He fleeth as it were a shadow, and never continueth in one stay . . ."

Before he clearly understood what they were doing to him, McCaffery was pushed to his knees on the white coffin. Another second and a black band over his eyes closed him from the sunlight.

"Firing party, present!"

From the edge of the field, in an instant of great stillness, he could hear the chatter of sparrows. He swayed as the twelve muskets came up to a level. The signal was the drop of the officer's arm, so that the condemned man should not hear the order and twist out of aim. The arm went down. But in the instant before the volley of bullets came, the men in the barrack field heard McCaffery give a wild cry. Whether it was a final protest, or a curse on them all, they never knew. To Corporal Alfred French it sounded as if, on the verge of eternity, Thomas McCaffery had solved the riddle of a lifetime and had only the fraction of a second to tell the world. The shout itself meant nothing to Corporal French, as it drifted away across the dry echoes of the field, and faded in the hot, distant plains.

"Take her . . . !"

The last reverberations blended with the sharp, sputtering burst of eleven rifles. The firing party looked pale as any sick parade and one of the men had dropped his musket and collapsed. McCaffery's body was knocked sideways by the force of the bullets and fell at full length. The birds were silent, and for a long second not a man moved. Then the anonymous officer marched smartly towards the body, for the hands and feet still twitched in muscular spasms. He drew his Manton pistol, but before he could use it, all movement in the shattered chest of Thomas McCaffery was extinguished.

McCaffery's final cry upset Colonel Collins, who complained angrily in the mess-room of the condemned man further dishonouring the regiment by "screaming like a damned girl when they shot him."

Corporal Alfred French was puzzled by that final cry. "Take her!" Take who? And where? The girl Jolie, presumably.

That evening, French spoke to Charlie Dalby, a gentleman-ranker of ten years' service. More ranker than gentleman, French thought. However, he asked Dalby what had become of the girl in the McCaffery case.

"Too late, Frenchy!" chortled Dalby. "Too late m' boy! Gone to England. Goin' to be looked after by a charitable old couple. Make a pretty little horse-breaker, I dare say. Dammit, Frenchy! Don't mean you fancied the little whore yourself? Eh?"

Alfred French walked slowly away and considered the facts again. Then he considered the charitable old couple. Charitable old couples might send money to India for the relief of distress. But they did not, as a rule, bring raped half-caste girls all the way to England to live in their own homes. French found Sergeant O'Sullivan.

"Yes, Fred French, I recall exactly how we found 'im and the girl. No, Fred French, I ain't going to tell no one the prime bits of the story unless someone is going to moisten my bleeding throat with a quart of that Hodgson's India Pale. Why, 'ow 'andsome of you, Fred French! As I was saying, this bunch of natives tells us about the shindy, like, and off we go. Takes five, ten minutes. Just as we gets there, the poor little doxy starts squealing like she's got a bayonet in her bum . . ."

"It didn't start till you got there? The shindy didn't start . . . "

"Not that we heard."

"Then how did the natives who fetched you know it was going to happen?"

" 'ow should I know?"

"They bloody planned it, that's how," said French angrily. "They faked the whole lay to put McCaffery in the salt box."

"Don't you go saying that, Fred French! Not unless you want to end up head over your heels in regimental excrement! Faked! I saw that bugger McCaffery! Bloody near killed the lot of us! Yes, and you should have seen this lovely little tit he'd got with him! Listen! She'd got her bubbies all tilted up, real ladylike, and she'd got an arse like a marchioness. She had her drawers half off and you could see . . . 'Ere, Fred French! Where yer going, Fred French?"

Alfred French was a slow writer. It took him most of the night by the light of penny candle dips to produce a laboured but faithful statement of McCaffery's case. He read it through for the last time and thought about it. Several years earlier, in the mud and drizzle of the ravaged hillside at Inkerman, a sergeant of the Rifle Brigade had stumbled doggedly through the brushwood and the mist to drag back two wounded men from the Russian bayoneting. One man, a cornet of dragoons, had been so savagely and repeatedly stabbed that he bled to death as his rescuer carried him on his back. The other, Private Alfred French, was less severely wounded and had lived to earn his corporal's stripes after the fall of Sebastopol.

Alfred French decided that a man who would risk his life to save two comrades in that manner was a man to be trusted with McCaffery's case. In slow, deliberate script, he addressed his statement to Sergeant William Clarence Verity, late of the Rifle Brigade and now of the Private Clothes Detail, Metropolitan Police "A" Division, Whitehall Place, London.

2

Sergeant William Clarence Verity of the private clothes detail, Whitehall Office, presents his compliments to Inspector Croaker. Sergeant Verity has the honour to request that Mr Croaker will read the attached paragraph from the Morning Chronicle *of the 11th inst., "Military Execution in the Punjab," and the enclosed letter from Alfred French, Corporal of Her Majesty's 77th Regiment, now under orders for Allahabad.*

Sergeant Verity has the honour to request that Mr Croaker or his superior officers may authorise a further investigation into certain circumstances attending the death of Private Thomas McCaffery. The man McCaffery had, to Sergeant Verity's knowledge, served two terms in Horsemonger Lane gaol for picking pockets. Both sentences were attended by hard labour upon the treadmill. Last autumn, previous to going for a soldier and sailing with his regiment to Bombay, McCaffery had been a companion of Edward Roper, a person of a criminal reputation.

Ned Roper is known to Sergeant Verity as a man once prosecuted, but acquitted, on charges of receiving. Until last year he was the proprietor of a betting office in Fitzroy Square and known on racecourses as one of the Swell Mob. He has been engaged in the management of houses of ill-repute in the neighbourhoods of Regent Circus and the Waterloo Road. He is spoken of among low women and gamesters as "one of the flyest flats in the village." He acts for the putters up of robberies who can thus remain outwardly respectable.

Sergeant Verity hears that Ned Roper has several times boasted to street girls of making £500 in a year by criminal conspiracies. He is thought to have benefited by £200 or £300 as an accomplice in frauds upon insurance companies perpetrated up to 1850 by Walter Watts of the Olympic Theatre.

During the last summer, Roper associated with McCaffery and was liberally supplied with money from an unknown source. After a drunken argument in the Grapes public house, Southwark Bridge Road, McCaffery swore that he and Roper had been paid to commit the greatest robbery of modern times. Two weeks later, after a similar affray, McCaffery boasted in the presence of a constable that he and his friends had a plan to rob the Bank of England and every bullion merchant in the City of London, which plan must infallibly succeed.

McCaffery, when sober, denied this boast. He was taken into custody and committed to Clerkenwell prison for a short period for disorderly conduct. While in the House of Detention, he exhibited great fear for his life. It appeared that he had betrayed the confidences of his associates and that they had promised to revenge themselves upon him. After his release, he was not noticed by the police again and it was later learnt that he had enlisted at Gravesend in a regiment which was already under orders for India.

Sergeant Verity also begs to state that a young

*woman of a bad reputation, answering both the name
and description of the girl Jolie, was taken up in Langham Place in March 1856, upon a gentleman complain-
ing of her to a constable.*

*In conclusion, Sergeant Verity is of opinion that a
crime of considerable significance may be in contemplation by conspirators of resource and experience. If
such men contrived the death of Thomas McCaffery
in India, Sergeant Verity believes the proposed felony
must relate to property of the greatest value. Sergeant
Verity therefore respectfully begs that orders be given
for the pursuit of fuller investigations.*

*Sergeant Verity has the honour to remain Inspector
Croaker's obedient humble servant.*

W. Verity, Sgt.
25th of May, 1857.

*Inspector Croaker presents his compliments to Sergeant
Verity, and is in receipt of Sergeant Verity's request of
25th of May instant.*

*Mr Croaker cannot help expressing surprise that
Sergeant Verity should think fit to address his superior
officers in a manner as if he knew the business of the
Division better than they. It appears to Mr Croaker
that Sergeant Verity would best serve his own interest
by satisfactory completion of those duties already
allotted to him. Upon consulting the defaulters' sheet,
Mr Croaker observes that Sergeant Verity has been
paraded twice in the past twelve months, once for
insubordination and once for an assault upon a member of the public. Mr Croaker hopes that Sergeant
Verity will reflect upon this.*

*However, Mr Croaker has carefully perused the letter
from Corporal Alfred French and the paragraph from
the* Morning Chronicle. *This is not a paper which Mr
Croaker normally has the pleasure of reading. Mr
Croaker is bound to say that, even were it his privilege
to do so, he could find no fault whatever with the*

verdict and sentence in the case of Private Thomas McCaffery.

McCaffery was not convicted in respect of any offence against the young woman, Jolie, nor was the girl a material witness. However, Sergeant Verity must be aware that her evidence, such as it was, appeared abundantly supported by Surgeon-Major Fitzgerald. No positive proof exists to identify this unfortunate young woman with the street-walker to whom Sergeant Verity refers. Even if there were such proof, a common prostitute in a case of violence is no less entitled to the protection of the law. Mr Croaker trusts that Sergeant Verity will remember this in future.

Mr Croaker is disturbed at the apparently easy terms upon which Sergeant Verity associates with low women and others of the criminal class, and the reliance he seems to place upon their evidence. The man Edward Roper is a person whose earnings may possibly accrue from gaming or prostitution. He stands convicted of no crime, however. Mr Croaker is dismayed that Sergeant Verity should regard a threat by Roper or McCaffery to rob the Bank of England as anything but a drunken boast.

Mr Croaker must solemnly remind Sergeant Verity that the use of a plain-clothes detail is confined to detecting crime and is not to extend to espionage upon men who may be in contemplation of a crime. This limit is imposed by the good sense of the Home Office. If Sergeant Verity feels unable to perform his duties within this limit, Mr Croaker will expect to be informed at once.

If Sergeant Verity should possess knowledge of a crime to be committed and should allow such crime to be committed for the purpose of apprehending the criminals, he will be in danger of being charged as accessory before the fact. Mr Croaker hopes that Sergeant Verity will think of this.

Mr Croaker takes this opportunity of returning

Sergeant Verity's enclosures and begs to remain his obedient servant.

H. Croaker, Inspector of Constabulary,
26th of May, 1857.

3

Below the level of the pavement, William Clarence Verity sat on a tall counting-house stool and finished posting up his books. The air of the warm Saturday evening filtered a pervasive smell of horse dung and soot through the open window above his head, while the crash of cartwheels on cobbles was drowned only by the occasional hearty cursing of a drayman.

Sergeant Verity was a portly, youngish man with a pink moon of a face, well-flattened black hair, and moustaches lightly waxed at the tips. The little room seemed all the smaller for his bulk and the tall stool on which he perched at his desk appeared in danger of collapsing like dolls' furniture under his tightly-trousered buttocks. With a little groan of satisfaction he dipped his quill judiciously in the ink-well and laid it on a scrap of paper. Then clenching his plump fist round a cylindrical ruler and holding it like a truncheon, he ruled the final line under a faithful record of his week's work.

Beyond the little window above his head lay Sergeant Verity's Westminster. A curious mixture of the verminous courtyards and alleys of the Devil's Acre, and the airy Gothic palace, newly rebuilt for Britain's Imperial Parliament. It took every effort of the Whitehall Police Office to protect the silk hats and gold hunter watches of parliamentary gentlemen from brutal attacks by starving ruffians, or from the nimble fingers of street girls, educated only in selling their thinly-clad bodies for two or three shillings a time.

Sergeant Verity shut the ledger, closed the little window,

adjusted a tall stovepipe hat on his head with the aid of a cracked mirror, and drew on his gloves.

"And now, sir," he said cheerfully. "Damn your eyes, sir!"

The eyes to be damned were narrow, glittering ones belonging to Inspector Croaker, with his frock coat buttoned up to his leather stock, and his face the colour of a fallen leaf. The Inspector sat in a more spacious office, above Sergeant Verity, while Superintendent Gowry sat higher still, in celestial opulence, high above the horse dung and the soot. Whitehall Police Office had once been a gentleman's house and even in the 1850s it still retained a proper distinction between those who lived above and below stairs. Inspector Croaker lived above stairs. What could he be expected to know about men like Ned Roper? Croaker was an ex-artillery lieutenant who had never so much as been in the same room as a gonoph or a magsman. Who was Croaker to send disparaging memoranda to Verity?

"No one," said Verity aloud. "No one whatsoever, sir."

He patted his smooth red cheeks with an even redder handkerchief and climbed the stairs from his dungeon.

In the front office, Swift, the night inspector, sat preoccupied with his own ledger, apparently deaf to the screaming weekly delirium of old Carrotty Jane in the cells. Verity reported for permission to go off duty. The night inspector consulted a roll of names.

"A warm evening, sergeant," he said, looking through the list again.

"It is warm, sir, yes," said Verity sincerely. "Warm for May, that is."

"Yes," said the night inspector, nodding and putting away the list. "The river stinks tonight. You can smell it the length of Parliament Street away."

"So I believe, Mr Swift, sir," said Verity respectfully.

"And the streets!" sighed the night inspector. "Forty-two pounds of horse dung every day from each cab horse! Did you know that, Sergeant Verity?"

"No, sir, I cannot say I did. Not know it as a fact, that is."

"Ah!" said Inspector Swift. "You should read a little

more, sergeant. There's no knowing what a man may do, if he'll only read."

"I believe that is very true, sir," said Verity, fingering the brim of his hat, which he had removed on seeing the inspector, and lowering his head a little in a gesture of humility. Then he wished the inspector a good night, put his hat on his head, and set off in his usual manner, shoulders bowed and hands behind his back, one resting in the palm of the other. Swift watched him go. Verity's rotundity gave him an air of prosperity which his threadbare frock-coat and shiny black trousers denied. He looked to Swift like a dubious man of property who had disguised himself as a clerk in order to accost young women in the Waterloo Road or along the Ratcliffe Highway.

The evening air was oppressive, even for the end of May. Every stretch of pavement from Westminster to Trafalgar Square, and on to St Giles's Circus, was hot and gritty under the worn soles of Sergeant Verity's boots. The smoke of the day's fires had left a deposit of soot in the air, giving the entire city the taste and smell of a railway terminus. Coal wagons drawn by teams of heavy, ungroomed horses, rattled down Whitehall and Parliament Street towards the Whitehall Wharf. Verity soon felt the hard black dust between his teeth.

What he longed for more than anything else just then was a veal cutlet wrapped in a cabbage leaf, such as they sold from the stalls in Paddington Green. And an onion. Saturday was the day for an onion. But this was no ordinary Saturday. He strode past the wine vaults with their faded gilt lettering, and past the bootmaker's with its display of "The Wellington Boots" in a bow window. He walked in a lumbering manner, like a badly trained performing bear. It was just as he was passing the little jeweller's near the turning of Whitehall place, with its discreet notice that "ladies' ears may be pierced within," that he finally decided that Inspector Croaker could go to the devil, if the devil would have him.

Along Whitehall the gas lamps were burning against a

pale blue twilight. Whores in their cloaks and feathered bonnets were sidling like a plague of rats, bearing disease and
poverty from Union Court and the Westminster slums. None
of them approached him. A few even shuffled further away.
They knew a private-clothes peeler as sure as he knew them.
In any case, Verity's habit of beginning to talk aloud to himself was, to say the least, discouraging.

"You do not follow a man all the way from London to
Meerut, and then contrive his death, just because you dis-
like his face. No, Mr Croaker, sir, you do not! You do not
employ an expensive young harlot and carry her to the
Punjab to assist you in the scheme, unless it is a desperate
important secret that McCaffery can give away!"

A ragged boy of nine or ten, with a broom taller than himself, swept a path for Verity across the Strand, whisking aside
the refuse of costers' barrows and the horse dung. Verity
dropped a copper in the boy's hand. The copper was not for
the sweeping but for information regularly received. Down
the Strand, towards Exeter Hall and Southwark Bridge was
a confusion of carts, cabs, twopenny buses, barrows, and
coffee stalls. A pair of horses pulled a huge portable placard
on wheels, advertising a new waxwork show, a firework display at Vauxhall, a Derby night supper at the Cremorne
Gardens, and a masked ball at the Holborn Assembly
Rooms.

Verity threaded his way through the top-hatted crowds
outside Morley's Hotel and St Martin-in-the-Fields.

"The Bank of England," he said firmly. "They meant to
rob the Bank of England. And now that McCaffery is in his
six-by-two, by God they will do it. But how?"

Several heads turned and looked disapprovingly at the
man who was talking to himself. Verity shook his head,
puzzling over the problem, and turned north towards the
great criminal "rookery" of Seven Dials. He was a walking
self-advertisement, whose behaviour was so odd that he had
twice been arrested by the uniformed constables of other
divisions before he could prove to them who he was. Small
wonder if Ned Roper and his friends were certain that they

could "cook Verity's goose for him," as Roper called it, whenever they chose. But wiser brains than Roper's had decided that the chosen time had not yet come. "The quality of vengeance is not strained," one of the abler brains had said. Ned Roper did not know precisely what this meant, but every time his able friend applied it to Verity, Ned Roper laughed even louder than fat old Mother Martileau, who kept the "French Introducing House" off Soho Square.

Saturday night street-markets stretched north along the Tottenham Court Road and south towards Charing Cross. Stalls were packed into every adjoining alley and courtyard from St Giles's Circus onwards. At pay-time the area was thronged like a fairground. The white glare of self-generating gas lamps on the cake stalls faced the red flare of grease lamps on the fish barrows. Hot coals shone through the gaps of the roast-chestnut stoves. Verity sniffed at the misty air, as the soot of the great city was overlaid by the aromatic scent of roasted nuts and hot nougat. Candles stuck in a haddock or turnip on the vegetable stalls competed with the butchers' open gas-lights, streaming and fluttering like flags of fire.

Picking his way fastidiously though the crowd, Verity pushed aside the starved urchins who held up bunches of onions and begged him, in whining tones, to buy. On every side rose the babble of the Saturday night markets. "Eight a penny, stunning pears! Now's yer chance!" " 'aypenny a skin, blacking!" The woman at the fishmonger's stall plucked his sleeve, brandishing a Yarmouth bloater on a toasting fork. "Come and look at 'em! Here's toasters!"

He shouldered his way determinedly towards the ground-glass globes of the tea dealer's shop and the dazzling row of gas-lamps outside the bootmaker's. An old man stood in the glare, which was no inconvenience to him, since he was blind. He held a bamboo flute to his lips and played "Villikins and his Dinah" in a mournful tremolo. Verity had no need to touch the old man's sleeve. The beggar, sensing his presence, lowered the flute and turned up the whites of his eyes.

"Can you tell me," said Verity, breathing heavily and

confidentially over the man's ear, "where Miss Ellen Jacoby does business tonight?"

The old man's mouth twisted, as though he were gathering saliva to spit.

"Ellen Jacoby, you mean," he said.

"Just so," said Verity humbly.

"She don't do business at all," said the beggar. "Least, not in the Dials. You want her, you go to St James's Street with five or ten sovereigns running loose."

Verity sighed heavily and dropped two pennies in the cap. The chapped hand slid down, examined them, and then withdrew. The beggar nodded.

"That's not to say," he continued thoughtfully, "as you mightn't find her in the palace. Not that she does business there, but more as she might oblige a friend."

Then, gathering up the saliva in a final twist, he spat accurately past Verity and into the gutter.

The lights of the market fell away behind him as Verity entered the first of the twisting alleyways which led to the heart of Seven Dials rookery. The narrow path was unlit and, for all the warmth of the day, a stinking moisture lay in a film over the footway. Tall, rat-ridden houses overhung the alleys, monuments to two hundred years of relentless decay. The sharper and the cracksman, the magsman and his poll, lived in uncongenial squalor behind the boarded windows and cracked masonry. At some points the houses clustered so close together that a man of Verity's bulk had to squeeze sideways to pass between them.

Shadows and quick footsteps moved along the edges of the ill-lit alley.

"Why, Mr Verity," said a voice from the darkness. "You're a way off your beat, ain't you? All alone, as well!"

"It won't do, Jack Flash," said Verity magisterially. "Don't try it!"

"I bin in stir afore for muzzling a peeler." The voice was closer.

"Hook it, sharp!" said Verity, plodding onwards.

"What am I a-doing, then?" asked the voice indignantly

"I'll let you know pretty quick, if you don't hook it!"
answered Verity softly.

Other voices came from the dark, in derisive imitation of
his own.

"Hook it, Jack Flash! . . . Why don't you hook it nicely,
when Mr Verity tells you? . . . Oh, I say, Flash! Do hook it
when Mr Verity says so!"

The voices fell silent and the alley was empty again. Its
dark passageway opened out abruptly into an irregular
cobbled square, crowded with porters and street women, and
blazing with the great ornate gas lamps that hung on iron
brackets the length of the gin palace. French and Irish voices
mingled with cockney. Here at last was anonymity, even for
Verity. In the angle of two streets stood the most splendid
building in all the Seven Dials, the fairy palace of gin. The
brilliance of its lamps streamed out through plate-glass
windows, between marble pillars and gilt mouldings. Verity
chose the doorway whose lettering on frosted glass promised
"The Wine Promenade."

The floor was thickly carpeted and a bar of polished
French mahogany ran the full length of the building.
Behind this, two plump young women and a stout, unshaven
man in a fur cap busily dispensed "combinations of gin" to
the impatient crowd. Voices called out for "The Real
Knock-Me-Down!" "The Reg'lar Flare-up" and the "No
Mistake."

At the end of the mahogany counter was a tall girl in
black satin. She was not particularly pretty, her blue eyes
were a little too vacant and her lips a little too thin. But her
height gave her a handsome length of leg, and her hips
seemed all the rounder for her close-waisted jacket. The
jacket followed the inward curve of her back, emphasising
the erotic swell of her buttocks under smooth black satin.
Her blonde hair was pulled back in a chignon held by a black
velvet bow. It was too short to fall in a "horse's tail," and
Verity, admiring her broad hips and long legs, was reminded
of a restive mare with her tail docked. The brushing of her
restless thighs, the impatient movements of her bottom

under the long black skirt, seemed a permanent sexual challenge to every man in the room.

Verity crossed the bar towards her, watching her toss back the last mouthful in a glass. She was easy, this one. She had been arrested once too often as a common whore. The next time, she knew what to expect.

"Ellen Jacoby," he said, standing just behind her, "Miss Ellen Jacoby."

"Ellen Jacoby." She turned on her elbow, wrinkling her nose in tipsy contempt. "Mrs. Ellen Jacoby."

"Ah," said Verity respectfully, "wrong on the charge sheet last time, was it?"

Then she turned to face him properly, pushing her skirts back in a gesture of bravado.

"You've got no call to roust me. I ain't done nothing."

"That makes me happy," said Verity in a gentle voice. "Will you take a glass of something?"

"Don't mind then," she said, shrugging and automatically smoothing down the front of her dress to outline her breasts more clearly. "Drop of summat short, miss!" she called to the barmaid.

"Now," said Verity, "you can oblige me if you will."

She half smiled and bent her knee forward until it just played against his.

"I oblige those I choose to oblige, that's all. I oblige one or two jacks in the "C" Division, and they returns favour for favour. If you take my meaning."

Verity nodded. He had heard enough reports of the corruption in "C" Division, where constables in the pay of Haymarket brothel keepers stood guard over the establishments, protecting them from law and competition alike. It was no secret.

"I want to find a girl," he said simply, "name of Jolie. Darkish. Expensive. Used to work for Mr Roper."

"What you want her for?"

"I was recommended," said Verity. "They say she's a real artist."

"That's all gammon," said the girl. "Another bloody little shickster, most likely."

30

"You know her, then?"

"Never 'eard of her."

"Nor of Ned Roper?"

"Who's he?"

Verity took off his hat. Very slowly and lovingly he began to polish the worn brim on his sleeve. Ellen Jacoby half turned away from him.

"Cross me once more, Ellen Jacoby," he said pleasantly, "and I'll have such things done to you that'll break your heart clean in two."

Then she turned back, lips narrower than ever, looking like a cat about to spit defiance. Her eyes moved quickly and angrily over him.

"It'll take a considerable bigger man than you to touch me," she muttered. "I'm that handy with me mauleys, it'd take you and six more to get me through that door. And I got friends in certain places."

"Not in the workhouse, you haven't," said Verity softly, "not in the dear old spike."

For the first time he saw the self-assurance ebb from her eyes.

"Go on with you," she said feebly, tipping back her gin.

Verity picked up his own glass of shrub, the gin hot and the pineapple cordial pungent.

"You'll pick oakum there, my girl, till those pretty fingers are raw. You'll cry at night to see the blisters and the corns."

"Won't scare me," she said bravely.

"Not even the Hoo Union?" Verity inquired. "Because it'll be the Hoo Union for you, I give you my word. Mr Miles's little house of sorrow."

Now she was frightened. As a girl of fourteen she had been in the notorious Hoo workhouse. She had known James Miles, the workhouse master, who ruled girls by the rod and loved his work.

"You got no right . . . " she said hopelessly.

"With a known whore, I have special rights at all times," said Verity placidly. "Not all the jacks in "C" Division can help you there."

31

"I've done nothing. It's Roper who carries the cash for the girls."

"Mr Miles remembers you," said Verity cheerfully, "and those afternoons you spent kneeling over the block in nothing but a pair of stockings. But with such a fine young woman as you've grown into, why, he'd wear out four or five birches on your backside and think nothing of it. If the justices send you to the old spike, Miss Jacoby, it'll be the Hoo Union for you. Why, Mr Miles would never forgive me if I let a strapping young doxy like you slip away from him!"

"All right," she said venomously, "Monmouth Street. You might find that little shickster in the gaff there. But she won't talk to you."

"And why not?" asked Verity, his face a study in plump, angelic innocence. Ellen Jacoby tipped back the last of her gin.

"Why not? Because she thieved some codger's watch and clothes and spouted them for all she could get. Bloody near put Ned Roper in quod. Now she wears his mark to remind her."

"What mark?"

Ellen Jacoby put her hand under the chignon of blonde hair at the back of her neck.

"Just there. Took two men to hold her down while he did it. Put a great cross there with a knife-blade heated twice. That bitch won't ever wear her hair up again. She hates Roper like a dose of poison, but she's a hundred times more scared of him than she'll ever be of you."

Verity finished his shrub, watching Ellen Jacoby move away from him across the room. He felt warm and content.

He had heard of Roper's ways with his girls, but now Jolie, scarred for life by him and hating him, would be easy to talk round. She might even inform against him on her own behalf, for grievous bodily harm. At the very least she would turn Queen's evidence over McCaffery. Not at first, perhaps, but when Verity had talked to her about the death cell and the last morning, and the suffering of a bungled hanging. It seldom failed with young women, who would generally do anything to stay alive. It never failed when they would otherwise face death to shield a man they hated. Roper was stupid as all of them, in the end. To mark a girl like that and then turn her loose, knowing what she did!

In his mind's eye, Verity saw himself standing before Inspector Croaker on Monday morning and, with an air of effortless superiority, laying the conclusive evidence before him. For the present, he eased his way through the crowd towards the door. As he passed by Ellen Jacoby, he allowed his hands to travel over the black satin which covered her strong hips and the softness of her thighs. How warm, he thought wistfully, and how smooth. Then the glass door closed behind him and he disappeared once more into the darkness of Seven Dials, heading towards Monmouth Street.

4

Drab and ill-shaped coats or dresses hung in rows before the second-hand shops which lined the narrow street. In front of the cracked and boarded windows, the costumes of dead men and women, the only legacies of the poor, drooped from long rails. The shopkeepers, whose own dress seemed even more worn than their stock, leant against door-posts and smoked their short clay pipes. Ragged children sat cheerfully on the pavement edge and watched paper boats race down the gutter. Beyond the darkness of the street, Verity saw the penny gaff, its glare of gas light streaming out into the thick night air and glittering on the grimy windows of the houses opposite. There was a babble of voices and the cracked sound of an old piano playing "Oranges and Lemons."

The shop front had been taken out to make an entrance to the improvised theatre, where a crowd of a hundred or more young men and women pressed forward with their pennies towards the money-taker in his box. Girls in cotton-velvet dresses with feathers in their pork-pie hats danced noisily with one another in the middle of the street. Among the crowd were several young dragoon officers and a number of elderly gentlemen who would have looked more at home in the United Service Club. The gaff was close enough to Pall Mall to attract the occasional swell.

Verity pushed his way past the groups of costers, lounging against the walls, smoking and shaking handfuls of coppers in time to the music. As he handed his coin to the money-taker, those already in the gaff began to stream out through a doorway in the canvas partition, as the first performance ended. In the warm evening the smell from the unventilated auditorium was nauseous. The crowd surged out, laughing and twisting, girls screaming convulsively as boys behind them fumbled, tickled, or jumped on their backs. A young woman, stupefied by drink, carried a sickly child with a bulging forehead, while two boys behind drove her forward.

Verity drew a red handkerchief from his sleeve, dabbed the sweat from his cheeks and neck, and shuffled forward with a heavy groan. The auditorium was a small warehouse with plain brick walls and a platform at the far end. Black curtains were painted on either side of this makeshift stage, where double gas-jets flared with a harsh brilliance to provide a form of limelight. Costers in cut-away jackets and small cloth caps monopolised the front benches, bawling, "Port—a—a—r! Port—a—a—r!" as they passed dark flagons of Allsops India Pale Ale among themselves. Others munched chestnuts or oranges, spitting husk or pip nonchalantly into the dark corners.

Already the heavily ringed fingers of "Professor Robinsini" at the broken-down Broadwood had struck up a rattling drum-roll. From the costers there was a roar of derision to greet the "comic singer," a drayman in concertina'd hat, false nose, and a monstrous red cravat which drooped to his waist. The gas dwindled to tall undulating flames, leaving all but the stage in semi-darkness. The singer glanced left and right, cocking a foot up behind him and shielding his eyes, like a sailor sighting land. The audience roared for "Flash Chants!" "Pineapple Rock!" and "Port—a—a—r!"

He glanced down at them, grinning self-consciously.

"'old yer jaws!"

The "Professor" struck a single accompanying chord and the singer followed, loudly but off-key:

> *"I've just dropped in, dear ladies fair,*
> *I 'opes it won't yer shock.*
> *I'll sing you a song, and it ain't too long,*
> *It's about my long-tail jock!"*

He flipped up the dangling red cravat with a knowing grimace, and even Verity was shocked to hear that the girls screamed loudest with laughter.

"Whatcher waitin' for, then?" roared the singer, "Chorus!"

> *"Just look at my long-tail jock!*
> *Oh, how do you like my jock?*
> *I'll sing you a song, and it ain't too long,*
> *It's about my long-tail jock!"*

Through the half-light, the features of the brick interior grew dimly visible again, like Thames landmarks in a December fog. There was a curtained doorway to one side of the platform. Verity wondered to what, and to whom, it led. The comic singer reached a crescendo:

> *"I sailed to the city of Washington,*
> *Of pluck I'd got a good stock,*
> *I went to President Jackson's levee,*
> *And there I showed my jock ..."*

The audience at the rear of the gaff consisted mainly of counting-house clerks in stovepipe hats, and clubmen with a taste for adolescent coster girls. An elderly man with military whiskers and check trousers breathed port wine and cigar in Verity's ear.

"Ruffians, sir! Out-and-outers! Some deuced pretty horseflesh showin' off in these places, for all that!"

"Go to the devil, sir!" said Verity, jowls quivering indignantly at the intrusion. The elderly man sat at attention, hands clasped on the knob of his cane, as though he had never spoken.

The "Professor" was now skipping though an imitation of flute and tambourine in an Arabian dance. When inspiration failed, he fell back on half-remembered scraps of Mozart's Turkish Rondo. Verity emitted a long, contented whimper of satisfaction, causing the elderly man to look sharply at him with a censorious sniff. But now he knew he was right! There on the stage was McCaffery's young Eastern princess, her hair worn thick and glossy to her slender shoulders, the oriental elipse of her eyes, and the exquisite features more mysterious than the harem veil she wore.

Verity knew that she must be wearing her hair so unfashionably in order to hide Roper's mark by letting the tresses fall loose to her bare shoulders. There, on the girl's skin, was all the evidence needed to bring Ned Roper to justice.

Though the costers roared their approval of "Miss Jolly," her expertise as a ballet-girl would not have got her on to the stage of the most easy-going music-hall in Southwark or Blackfriars. Yet her dance and costume was everything a Saturday-night crowd in a penny gaff could wish. Her pretty lips were just visible through her veil, and her ankle-bells sent out ripples of dainty sound with every movement of her limbs. A low-cut band of emerald silk supported her neat breasts sharply, leaving her shoulders and brown-white belly bare. There was total silence as her hips and thighs began a snake-like undulation, and then as the music rose, the flower-like little navel began to open and close rhythmically in her lascivious belly-rolling.

To the delight of the costers, she had shown herself "game" by wearing no tights under the thin silk of her slave-girl trousers. The light shining through the filmy gauze showed the slender rotundity of her thighs and the palest gold sheen of bare flesh. When she arched her hips forward and writhed her breasts in their taut silk halter, there were subdued murmurs of approval. It was the height of professionalism in a penny gaff.

Above the veil, her eyes watched them knowingly. Her

raised arms twined and caressed one another suggestively and, while she fondled herself in this manner, she turned slowly and undulatingly round. The insistent belly-movements were hidden as she edged her bottom to face the audience, arching the full cheeks under the thin silk and squirming them invitingly. Hollowing her back until the translucent silk was skin tight across her buttocks, she bent slowly forward, her backside broadening until she presented her complete rear view to the costers and their girls. There were growls of sexual menace from the boys and shrieks of amusement from the girls, who seemed no less eager than their escorts to view the young ballet-girl's anatomy. She remained motionless for a long perspiring moment in the gaff, as though carefully watching the effect of her posture upon those who saw it.

Slowly she straightened up, turning again, arms twining above her head, and thighs squirming sinuously together as though trying to hold some slippery and elusive lover between them. The rhythm of the music increased, her hips swaying faster and faster, until there was a crash, a drum-roll, and the tension seemed to fall away from her body. Her knees bent slowly, and she sank to the floor in a gesture of grateful sexual fulfilment.

After such a performance, an information laid by the top-hatted Society for the Suppression of Vice would have brought the girl and the management of the gaff before the Bow Street magistrate on Monday morning. But the Vice Society angled for bigger fish, and so did Verity. As the girl scrambled up and ran from the stage, to the stamping and cheering of the costers, he slid from his place and walked, unnoticed, to the entrance. There was no way out except through the front of the gutted shop. That was the way the girl must come.

In the street, waiting to catch the customers as they poured from the gaff, a running patterer, in a shabby coat and threadbare hat, stood with his penny pamphlets. He announced them in a rapid, mock-educated chant.

"A Woice from the Gaol, being the story of William

Calcraft, public hangman! Let us look at William Calcraft in his early years. He was born of poor but industrious parents . . . "

Verity joined the group of spectators, placing himself to watch the entrance of the gaff.

"Alas!" droned the patterer, "alas for the poor farmer's boy! He was never taught to shun the broad path leading to destruction! His secret debaucheries soon enabled the fell demon of vice to mark him for her own! He is tortured by remorse heaped upon remorse! Every fresh victim he is required to strangle . . ."

Verity saw her. She slipped from the shadow and away towards St Martin's Lane, scurrying along the pavement. She wore a plum-red merino gown and a pork-pie hat with a waving white feather. With one hand she gathered up her skirts a little, holding them clear of the moist film that seemed to ooze at night from the very paving and cobbles. With small, hurried steps she was returning to whichever part of the streets Roper made her walk.

Verity hung back. It was enough to keep her in sight as she came out into Trafalgar Square, where the moon shivered on the surface of the pools and the silhouette of Nelson rode high against a pale flush of starlight. She crossed the great space and made for Cockspur Street. Verity had no doubt that she was one of Roper's high-class girls. The beds that Jolie now shared were those of Pall Mall gentlemen, not of common soldiers like McCaffery.

In Cockspur Street the omnibuses for Hammersmith and Kentish Town were drawn up. Their horses stamped or snorted clouds of warm breath into the damp air; the oil lamps flickered as the driver lounged on his perch, his whip askew and his hat tipped forward over his eyes. The girl flitted along the pavement into Pall Mall East and Verity closed on her a little.

Outside the lofty classical portico of the United Service Club, she slowed down to a leisurely hip-swinging stroll, staring enviously through the tall windows at the brightly lit mouldings of ornate ceilings and the heroic full-dress paintings of Waterloo generals. Verity hurried after her as she passed the private carriages, waiting in the white light of gas globes on the wrought-iron pillars, and turned the corner into Waterloo Place.

By the time he saw her again she had been cornered by two troopers of the "Cherry Bums," the 11th Hussars, in their tight scarlet trousers, royal blue jackets laced with gold, and fur caps. One had her trapped against the wall, leaning his palms on the stonework on either side of her shoulders. The other, brushing up his ginger moustaches impatiently, said something which Verity could not hear. Nimble as a squirrel, the girl ducked down under the other hussar's arms, and hurried across Waterloo Place with frightened little steps. The two soldiers let her go, knowing that she was beyond their price. Once safe from them, she began to walk slowly up and down a short stretch of the paving, her allotted and shadowy sentry-go.

When Verity approached she turned her back to the wall and cocked the sole of her boot against the masonry behind her.

"Won't you be good-natured to me?" she said softly.

"To you, miss?" said Verity cheerfully. "I could be. I'd be a sight better natured than Ned Roper ever was to you. I'm not one for spoiling a pretty girl's skin with a hot iron. Not my style."

Jolie's voice sharpened, and a faint reflection of moonlight caught the whites of her eyes.

"Who the hell might you be?"

"I might be your friend," said Verity, patting the belly of his waistcoat significantly. "I might do a lot for you, miss, if we were to have a little talk."

"You're a bloody jack!" she said indignantly. "I ain't talking to a jack in the middle of the street for Roper and his bullies to see! I ain't that fond of a beating!"

"You have a room, though," said Verity, moving a step nearer the girl and breathing over her. But it was too dark to see properly, even if he had turned her hair up there and then.

"I get paid for something more than talking when I take a man to my room," she said. "I got my own room in Panton Street now, not in Roper's dress-house."

"I don't pay," said Verity calmly, "but you'll find it worth a shilling or two to pay Roper out for what he did to you. We know about it, you see. And we know about McCaffery."

The girl shrugged.

"You know more than I do, then," she said sulkily. "But I ain't fussy who I take back to Panton Street, so long as they pay."

Turning and gathering up the skirts of her plum-coloured gown again, she hurried before him, leading the way between the horses and hansoms of Pall Mall towards the Haymarket. It seemed to Verity that, like so many whores, she was playing her owner a double game. Ned Roper ran dress-houses where the very clothes on the girl's back were his property. The girls were allowed out only to solicit clients and were often watched by Roper's bully. All the money went directly into Roper's pocket, until a fly bitch set herself up in a room of her own. Oh no, thought Verity, there was no love lost between this one and Ned Roper. Moreover, now that he knew of the secret apartment, he needed only to mention it to Roper for the man to have the skin off her back.

Sergeant Verity hummed a little tune in the darkness. Why, the mystery of McCaffery's death would be explained by midnight. Once it was a question of hanging, then Jolie would betray Roper, and Roper would betray his mysterious benefactor. When the constables came to escort their charges from "C" division lock-up to Bow Street, on Monday morning, Ned Roper's crew should have the honour of leading the dance.

The Haymarket was thronged with girls of all ages and conditions, bartering their bodies with Regent Street swells and mustachioed clerks. Verity followed the flitting figure of the girl, past the steam of the coffee-stall with its tall, simmering urns, through the rustle of silks and laces, where the air hung heavy with the scent of penny cigars. Several of the Panton Street houses had their blinds drawn, lights burning low, and notices over the door promising that "Beds may be had within."

Ignoring all these, the girl turned a corner, and slipped into the shadows of an ill-kept house, built in yellowish London brick and drab as any slum. An iron stairway with a loose handrail led up to a gallery that ran round the four sides of an inner courtyard with a shabby doorway leading off at each little corner-landing. The girl stopped at the last landing but one, by which time Verity had a familiar pain in his right abdomen and was breathing like a winded drayhorse.

"In here," she said expressionlessly.

It was only when she set a match to each of the mantles that he saw how sumptuous the room was by contrast with its surroundings. There were comfortable Coburg chairs and a sofa, a small chandelier, pier glasses, and heavy green curtains across the windows. He turned to the girl, taking in the almond slant of her eyes as her glance flicked towards him and away again, almost feeling the warmth of her slender waist under the silk. She held out a small hand determinedly. Verity sighed and deposited two shillings in the palm.

"A paying concern, miss," he said, lowering himself heavily into one of the chairs, "that's what you've got here."

"Don't do so bad for a distressed milliner, do I?" She drew up her skirts. "I got nice boots, ain't they. You don't get them working in a slop shop. Walk three miles there and back every day for four bloody shillings a week? I'd a sight sooner starve!"

Verity grunted.

"Did they starve you in India?"

"India?" she repeated with unconvincing disinterest. "East India Dock is the nearest I'd ever get. Don't you feel frisky then?"

The sofa was between them.

"Come over here and sit down," said Verity innocently.

She kept her eyes on him like a Siamese cat on its prey, and

began to unfasten her gown. It fell to the floor in a whisper
of cloth. Gaslight shone on her bare shoulders as if on pale
gold satin.

"Dress yourself!" said Verity sharply, half hoping to be
disobeyed.

She ignored him. Her bodice came away and she laid it
down carefully, turning her firm, uptilting little breasts
towards him, and looking him straight in the eyes. Verity
stood up hastily, but she moved round again so that the sofa
was still between them. There was a quick rustling at her
waist and her petticoats joined the discarded gown on the
carpet. She stepped from behind the scroll of the sofa-end,
into full view, her flat brown belly narrowing to a shading
of dark hair between the thighs.

"Damn you, miss!" said Verity, perspiring. "Come here!"

She ran to the farthest chair and slouched down in it,
opening her knees wide.

"Is that it?" she asked derisively.

Verity lumbered forward, but the girl jumped up and
dodged round the sofa again, the light catching the gloss of
her smart black boots and black silk stockings, the only garments she still wore. Facing the other chair, she hollowed her
stomach in and bent forward. Leaning on the chair arm, she
rounded the cheeks of her bottom, watching him tauntingly
over her shoulder.

"Is that the sort of thing you prefer, eh?"

The momentary ache of desire on seeing her naked had
passed. Verity was possessed by righteous anger that he,
representing the majesty of the law, should be treated in such
a manner by an impudent slut. He ran the sofa aside with a
crash, overturned the chair and managed to catch her by one
wrist. The girl fell under him, wriggling and panting determinedly. She twisted a hand free and her nails drew four
parallel furrows across his cheekbone. It was not how he had
imagined their encounter and, as she twisted half over on top
of him with her thigh against his face, he fleetingly thanked
God that Inspector Croaker could not see him.

At length he pinioned her face-down and reached for the

hair at the back of her neck. She twisted her head clear each time until he had hit her with his open hand twice across the bottom and, when that failed, across the face. Then she lay still and allowed him to turn up the soft dark hair, to examine the mark which Roper's hot iron had branded there. Verity pushed the hair back and swore an oath at what he saw.

The skin from her shoulders to the crown of her head was smooth and without the least blemish!

The McCaffery dodge! Sergeant Verity caught in the act of beating up a naked girl! He scrambled to his feet, while Jolie, having recovered her breath, began to scream loudly enough to be heard in the street outside. Thank God, thought Verity, for Fred French's letter. The McCaffery dodge had worked in the Punjab—but it should not work in Panton Street! He pushed his way past the overturned chair and the sofa askew across the room. There were voices and lights already in the courtyard below. No going down! He must go up to the top landing and slip down when they were busy elsewhere.

Verity was not the most agile of the detective police, but no man was more adept at melting into the shadows. From the darkness of the landing above the girl's room, he watched three men hurrying up from the courtyard. One was Ned Roper, the second was a stranger, probably one of Roper's bully boys. The third man's face was hidden, but the tall hat, long belted tunic, and the bull's-eye lantern was enough to identify him as one of Roper's tame constables from "C" division.

The McCaffery dodge, thought Verity, and they had damned nearly had him with it. Yes, sir! They damned nearly had! From the room below he could hear the tone of the voices but not the words. Jolie was tearful but vague, now that the dupe had escaped. The constable was sympathetic, inquiring, but, in the end, inconclusive. The three men came out again.

"Got down the stairs while we were in there, or just

before," said Roper. Their footsteps faded down the iron stairway and into the street. Verity waited.

It was hardly five minutes before Roper returned alone to the girl's room. He opened the door and said,

"You dull-witted little bitch!"

The door closed. Verity heard the girl's shrill whine of protest and then the sound of a hand striking in a series of sharp, explosive slaps. He edged his way cautiously down the iron stairway, past the light that showed beneath the locked door. He had almost reached the foot of the stairs when a man with shoulders like a stud bull stepped from the darkness. Verity guessed it would be Tyler, Roper's companion bully boy, who had been waiting there patiently ever since the whole charade began.

Verity did not enjoy brawling but he accepted what was inevitable. He clamped his teeth hard together, knowing that a loose jaw more easily becomes a fractured jaw. Then, as Tyler's dark bulk came on, Verity moved to one side, caught the man's right arm in a lock and spun him by his own momentum so that he thudded back against the banister rail with a bellowing gasp and a cracking of wood. He swung back again, eyes glittering and shoulders hunched, fencing for a grip on Verity. Twice he lunged forward, knuckles smacking on Verity's plump cheeks. But Verity knew better than to raise his guard higher and expose himself to worse damage. He waited for the third lunge, went back with it, and then threw himself forward with one knee jabbing into Tyler's groin. Tyler flung his arms back to find support, failed to find it, and crashed down in a salvo of buckets and pots.

Verity was upon him as he sprang to his feet, and carried him down again with his own weight. Tyler snatched at the stair rail as he fell, tearing it away from its struts and leaving it dangling vertically from the first landing. He kept hold of a loose strut and drove Verity back until Verity, with a heavy wooden peg, sidestepped and aimed a blow to Tyler's head which carried him through a ground floor doorway that burst open under his weight.

In the confusion of the brawl, Verity could hear dogs barking, a woman screaming, and the crash of bottles as he and Tyler went sprawling over a crate of flagons. But he had matched Tyler, he knew he had. Hold him for a few minutes more and he would be blown.

Then there was a soft explosion deep inside Verity's head, and a pain that seemed to swell like a balloon across the back of his neck. He broke away from Tyler, stooping and vomiting. The man whom he could not see, hit him again, and he sank to his knees in a bright dazzle of nausea. He heard them speak but could not catch their words. He heard, rather than felt, the first boot that sent a remote pain from the base of his spine. The thudding ache sprang up along his legs and his back, the first blows spreading pain like an anaesthetic, so that he hardly felt the later ones. His mouth was full of salt. They must have hit him in the face but he had not really noticed it at the time. There was one more dazzling spasm in his head. And then nothing.

The house had gone. He could see open sky above him. But the dogs were still barking. Men and women were walking past him, their feet not more than twelve inches from his head. They paid him no attention. A fat drunkard lying in the Panton Street gutter must find his own salvation.

Verity eased himself first to his knees and then to his feet. He staggered a little, but steadied himself against the wall. Passers-by avoided him in a wide semicircle. There was a tear from the armpit to the waist in the left side of his coat, the right knee of his trousers had gone in a triangular rent, and there was no sign of his hat. His clothes shone with wet smears of that insanitary moisture which the colder night air had drawn out on the warm paving. Very carefully, he let go of the wall and hobbled forward on bruised legs. At the first step he swayed sideways into a young woman in a crinoline. The girl gave a little cry, gathering her skirts away from him, while her male escort's eyes bombarded Verity with hate and unspoken threats.

Steadier now and with growing determination, he shuffled

from Panton Street into the Haymarket, following the line of the gutter among beggars and vagrants.

"Why, Mr Verity! Oh, my poor Mr Verity! What *has* happened to you?"

Verity stared at the neatly-cut fawn suit and matching top hat, the blue silk stock and the almost ladylike boots. The moustache was palest ginger and the eyes an almost equally pale blue. Ned Roper. Verity stared again, hardly believing that the man could dare to confront him.

"My dear Mr Verity!" It was the voice of the racecourse confidence trickster. "My dear sir! Who has done this to you? Take my arm, please. We must find you assistance at once. Permit me to send for one of your other officers. For Mr Croaker perhaps?"

Verity gave a gasp and then followed this with a frog-like bleat from the throat.

"Roper!"

"My poor Verity!"

"Stand out of my way, you son of a whore!"

"My dear fellow! I shall at least call the constable for you."

"I will break your foul neck, Roper, before I have done with you!"

"Constable! Constable! This way! And smartly, if you please!"

Verity recognised the newcomer without knowing his name.

"Why!" said the man. "It's Sergeant Verity!"

"Leave me be," said Verity softly.

"Best give you an arm," said the constable.

"No!"

Roper continued to stand insolently in Verity's way

"Someone's done you villainy and no mistake. You ain't been robbed have you, old fellow? Best see you've not lost your watch."

Without taking his eyes off Roper, Verity checked his own pockets. Watch, pocketbook, and keys remained. Even his handkerchief and loose change. Only a single piece of paper was missing. Inspector Croaker's reply to his request for fuller investigations into McCaffery's death. How could he have been so damnably stupid as to put it in his pocket and carry it from the Whitehall office?

"Nothing gone, then?" said Roper softly. "Quite sure?"

"Strikes me," said the constable slowly, "the same villains that beat the young lady in Panton Street just now have worked off their spite on Mr Verity too."

"Stand out of my way!" said Verity again, and this time Roper stepped aside.

"Call on my assistance, Mr Verity, at any time. Should Mr Croaker want a witness to what you have suffered, I'm your man."

There was one blemish on Ned Roper's happiness. For safety's sake, he had to walk all the way to his expensive brothel in Langham Place, and wait until Tyler had bolted the door again, before he could release a series of thunderous guffaws which were heard all over the house, except in the pair of specially sound-proofed rooms. He flung open the door of his own private apartments and sat down, cross-legged, on the sofa, flourishing his silver-topped stick like a drum-major. In front of him, Ellen Jacoby stepped out of her black satin skirts and loosened her bodice. The sight of the tall blonde girl, with her thin smile, energetic hips, and long thighs, sent Ned Roper's hat skimming away like a top. His fawn coat and trousers followed it. On the velvet sofa, the girl's white skin shone brightly against the black pile. Roper's tongue flicked her nipples and his fingers played remorselessly between her thighs. Her head thrashed to and fro, eyes closed, teeth clenched on her lower lip. Her legs began to squirm and her hands gripped the sofa edges frantically. Ned Roper watched her for a moment and then grinned.

"And now, my love," he said softly, "here's a reward for a good, clever girl!"

"Why, Mr Verity!"

Bella stood in the doorway, regarding her father's lodger

with wide blue eyes and her charming mouth open in amazement.

"Leave us, Bella!" said Mr Stringfellow, dabbing a wet flannel over Verity's swollen face.

"Oh, Mr Verity!" cried the girl, scurrying forward into the room.

"Clear out, miss!" roared Stringfellow. "Get upstairs this minute, or I'll have the strap off my wooden leg and leave the leather of 'un on your hide!" He pointed meaningly to the thong which secured a wooden stump that had served him as a left leg since the siege of Bhurtpore. The girl looked quickly and longingly at Verity, and then ran from the room, sobbing.

"They meant you some 'arm, chum!" said Stringfellow, dabbing thoughtfully at Verity's jaw, "no mistaking that."

"Walked into it," Verity mumbled. "Got took for a gull by a pair of whores, like any yokel from the shires."

"Not you!" said Stringfellow. "They laid a snare, the whole lot of 'em. Superior numbers, Mr Verity. And what's a military man to do against superior numbers?" He looked at the torn coat, and added cheerfully, "Bella can do something for that."

"Good of her," muttered Verity.

"Good!" said Stringfellow. "That ain't the word for it!" He helped Verity off with his shirt and regarded his back in silence.

"However," he said at last, "in the event of an alliance between Verity and Stringfellow, what's to happen when the lord and master of the firm comes home at night in this state?"

"Rifle Brigade was worse than this a dozen times before Sebastopol," said Verity calmly.

"Maybe," said Stringfellow, wetting the sponge again, "but Paddington Green ain't Sebastopol and Miss Bella ain't Miss Nightingale. Not by a long chalk."

"I've half a mind to give it up," said Verity. "They took one of Mr Croaker's letters from my pocket. God knows I couldn't have made a worse mess of it. I've a good mind to give up the police, and find a little inn somewhere."

"There again," said Stringfellow philosophically, "little inns have their ups and downs, likewise."

"Why, Mr Verity!" said Sergeant Samson with a broad smile. "You ain't struck it rich, 'ave you?"

"No," said Verity shortly, "I 'aven't."

"Special job, then? Coming in your Sunday best, and all?"

"No."

"And 'oo changed your face about like that?"

"Fell down the stairs."

"I'll say!" Samson thumped him on the back, causing Verity to gasp with pain, even after two days, " 'oo pushed you? Eh?"

"Mr Inspector Croaker," said Verity grimly, bracing himself for the next comradely thump.

"Why, Mr Verity!" said Bella. "It can't be such a bad thing as all that!" She pressed closer to him on the sofa until he could feel the warmth of her thigh penetrating to his own. He politely drew away a little and she closed on him again.

"It was a very bad thing," he said, "very bad, Miss Bella."

"But you didn't mean to do wrong?"

"No."

"Oh, Mr Verity, you did what was right!"

She looked up at him, her eyes shining with admiration.

"Yes," he said modestly, "I thought I did right."

"Was it like facing the Cossacks?" she asked eagerly. "For Old England and the Queen?"

Verity thought for a moment.

"Yes," he said, "I suppose it was, after a fashion."

"There!" she said. "There you are, then."

She snuggled up closer to him on the sofa and they sat silently for a moment. It was Bella, unable to contain her admiration any longer, who broke the silence.

"Oh, Mr Verity!" she cried happily. "I'm no end proud of you!"

2

VERNEY DACRE

5

Lieutenant Verney Dacre, cavalry subaltern, now twelve years on the half-pay list, stood tall and narrow as a clock-case with his back to the open windows of the hired dining-room. His hands were clasped under the tail of his bottle-green evening coat, as though he were warming himself at a fire. From time to time, he brushed a hand over his limp blond whiskers, or with a silk handkerchief touched the corners of his blue eyes, which seemed to water gently but without respite.

Dacre's beagle sat, alert, at its master's feet, with all its attention trained on his eyes. Very casually, Dacre reached out to the edge of the littered table, at which he had dined alone. Choosing a long spoon which lay between a plate of smoke-grey oyster shells and an empty bottle in a silver ice-bucket, he turned the metal handle over and over in the tall flame of an ornamental candle. Then holding the spoon carefully at the bowl, and without the least change of expression, he tossed it to the far side of the carpet, where it fell with a dull ringing. The dog pounced after it, rebounded with a shrill yelp, and then fretted round it, whimpering with subdued dismay, but not daring to touch the hot metal again with its chops. Presently it left the spoon and ambled back, resuming its obedient scrutiny of its master's face.

"Dogs and women," said Dacre with a laconic drawl, "never teach them any other way, old fellow."

A stocky, shabbily dressed man, who sat at his ease in a wing chair, but who had not shared Dacre's supper, laughed obligingly. Dacre retrieved his glass of brandy and warm water from the mantelpiece.

"Well then, Mr Cazamian, what is it to be?"

The stocky man got to his feet, bringing into full view a dark head of hair cropped almost to stubble.

"I'm your man, sir. Why, I told Mr Roper. I'm your man for whatever it is."

"Are you now? Are y' really?" Dacre's was the voice of a man who had learned the dandified drawl of a cavalry officer, but who had hardly been born to it. He turned to the window and looked down disapprovingly at the Derby Night crowd, which danced and jostled among the shrubs, iron pagodas, and coloured lights of Cremorne Gardens. As the girls in green and blue silks, with feathered bonnets, hung on the arms of their impoverished swells, the band struck up an American polka. A dark-skinned man was taking up a collection among the crowd for two Indian boys in turbans, who were showing off a pair of poodles ridden by monkeys in the racing colours of the Earl of Chesterfield and Lord George Bentinck.

Dacre turned round and looked at the shabbily-dressed man again.

"If you're anyone's man, Cazamian, it's the South Eastern Railway Company's. Ain't it?"

Cazamian shook his head and leant forward, gripping the table edge, as if to emphasise his sincerity.

"Not any more, nor for five years past. When Mr George Hudson and his bloody railway scheme went smash, he took my little fortune with him. When it's all a man has saved for his children, he don't forget easy. Two of them then, and only one now. But, I ask you, sir. It didn't harm that bastard Hudson, did it? No, sir. The railway is a monster as eats its own children. It's brought a curse upon the working man who trusted it. The railway ruined me. But now the working man may take back what he's owed. When it's a war, sir, it ain't robbery to take from the enemy."

Dacre nodded.

"All right, old fellow, there really ain't any need to go the whole animal upon the subject. I catch the drift."

"Why do you think I owe Mr Roper that money?" Cazamian protested. "Only a-cos I would've tried to win back by gaming what I lost through Hudson's smash."

"How much do you owe?" Dacre made it sound of little concern to him.

"To Mr Roper? Forty quid. It might as well be four hundred."

"The lure of yaller goold," drawled Dacre. "By God, Cazamian, you must have backed some lame nags!"

"That's true," said Cazamian ruefully. He rubbed his forehead, grinned foolishly, and then became serious again. "But there's interest too. Mr Roper charges pretty steep."

Dacre appeared to ponder the problem. He said, "Ned Roper ain't the sort to forget a welsher. He'll work it off on you. Not out of spite, but as a lesson to other bilks. At forty pounds, it won't stop short of a broken neck."

"But I'm your man!" There was a trace of moisture on Cazamian's cheeks, drawn out by the warmth of the room, and he dropped his voice to a stage whisper, as though hoping to impress Dacre the more. "I'm your man for the dodge. Whatever it is!"

"Proof, if you please," said Dacre calmly, "that is what I have come here for."

Very slowly, watching Dacre's thin, arrogant face, as hopefully as the beagle's eyes had done, Cazamian reached into his pocket. He pulled out a sheet of paper, wrapped around something hard. Dacre took it and unfolded the paper. It contained a large iron key, and on the paper was a message in Cazamian's spidery scrawl.

> *This is a duplicate key to the Railway Office at Folkestone pier, removed by me on the 31st of May. If it is missed, they will change the lock, but won't for a few days. Charles Baptist Cazamian.*

Dacre sighed, sat down in a chair, hoisted his feet on to a space on the dinner table, and crossed them comfortably.

"Cazamian, old fellow, I am moved by your trust in us. Especially as you don't even know my name, nor never shall."

"Got to trust," said Cazamian philosophically, "ain't I? The mess I'm in, there's not anything worse can happen."

Dacre nodded.

"Sit down. Let me return the trust, but not the key." He took a cigar case from his pocket, chose a cigar and lit it, without offering one to Cazamian. "Now, Cazamian, to the point. I have been robbed. Robbed of a jewel, an imperial diamond worth more than you could earn in the whole of your life as a railway guard."

"And you ain't told the police office, sir?"

Dacre gave a wry twist of the mouth.

"That ain't so dashed easy, old fellow. That bit of devil's glass belonged to my sister's husband. When he died, his family claimed it back from her, saying it was a family heirloom to which she had no legal right. She refused, because she said it was his gift to her outright. So they set the lawyers on her. At which point she died, and I collected the diamond, which she'd given me for safekeeping several months before."

"And if they knew you'd got it," said Cazamian, "they'd be after you?"

"Precisely, old fellow, but I ain't got it. Before I could get it abroad to Amsterdam and have it cut into smaller stones, it was stolen from *me!* But I can hardly go to the police office or advertise a reward for the confounded thing, can I? Wouldn't do, my dear chap!"

"No," said Cazamian thoughtfully, "it wouldn't, I s'pose."

"Fortunately," resumed Dacre, "I know who's got it and what he's going to do with it. In a few weeks from now he will send it abroad to Paris on its way to be cut. He will not take it himself for fear of me following him. It will go in a bullion box on the tidal train from London Bridge station to Folkestone, for the Boulogne packet. I shall know the day: it will be during July."

Dacre blew a jet of greenish-grey cigar smoke at the ceiling and continued.

"Mr Roper tells me that during July you are on the rota as guard of the tidal-ferry train. I require to travel with you in the guard's van from London to Folkestone on the night in question. I shall recover my diamond, I promise you. There will be no questions asked. Why, my thief can hardly go to the police either, can he? And now, Cazamian, are you still my man?"

Cazamian was grinning with relief.

"I am, sir. I am indeed for a trick like that."

"Your reward will be somewhat larger than the sum of money which you lost in Mr Hudson's railway-share swindle.'"

"Oh," said Cazamian, as if surprised, but without being pleased.

"That's justice, ain't it, old chap?" said Dacre peevishly.

"Oh, it is, sir," said Cazamian, taking the opposite chair. "But that ain't it. Don't you know how they carry diamonds and bullion?"

"You tell me, old fellow."

Cazamian shrugged.

"It all comes in heavy wooden bullion-boxes with iron bands round them. Each box is locked, of course, and the bullion shipper stamps his own seal on the wax over the lock. The boxes arrive in the afternoon by a special wagon. The station master, with the railway police, meets them and takes them to his office to be weighed. When that's done, he and the policemen walk beside the boxes while they are wheeled to the tidal train. In the guard's van is an iron safe, made by Chubb, and the tool don't exist as would crack that. It has two locks, the station master has the key for one and the constable has the key for the other. One can't open it on his own. The guard stays in the van with it until the train gets to Folkestone. We only stop once, at Reigate. The safe comes out at Folkestone and two or three of the railway constables there stands over it on the pier until it comes to be put on the Boulogne steamer. On the steamer there's a double guard from our company and the Frenchies. Once it lands again, the agents of the two companies take it through their customs and sit with it all the way until it gets opened in Paris."

"Good," said Dacre, nodding.

"Good? It's anything but good, sir! Even if you could get near the safe, the tool ain't made that would force that lock."

Dacre nodded his agreement.

"And," continued Cazamian, "you ain't going to get the

proper keys unless the station master and the police gives them to you. And even if they did, and you could open the safe, there's the bullion-boxes, which are locked and bound. Why, you might force the locks and the iron bands, but there ain't any way you could replace the seal without the bullion merchant kindly lending you his stamp. The jig would be up as soon as someone so much as looked at the boxes."

Dacre contemplated the cherry-red tip of his cigar.

"And that ain't the lot," said Cazamian decisively, "a-cos even if you was to do all that, they'd catch you with the weighing."

"Weighing?"

"They always do it somewhere, though not usually the same place twice running. They weigh the bullion-boxes to make sure that the weight ain't altered since London Bridge. If one box were to weigh different, the jig would be up."

Dacre smiled.

"Splendid!" he said. "Superb!"

"Is it still a runner, then?" asked Cazamian incredulously.

"Oh, my dear fellow, this one is not only a runner, it's a winner!"

There was a pause, during which Dacre's enthusiasm quietened. He stood up with his thin, pale face a mask of formality once more, in its frame of neat blond whiskers. His voice was dispassionate again.

"You won't see me again, Cazamian, until we meet on the train, when I shall take back what belongs to me. Roper will tell you whatever else you need to know. In a day or two, he will also return the duplicate key of the luggage office to you."

"And when you've got your jewel back?" asked Cazamian hopefully.

"You shall have your reward, never fear. However, for the time being . . . "

Dacre opened his notecase and handed Cazamian a sheet of paper.

*Received from Charles Baptist Cazamian, Esquire, the
sum of forty guineas, in full and complete discharge of
all monies owed to me, and interest thereon. 2nd June,
1857. Edward Roper.*

"Gesture of good faith," said Dacre. "Your debt is settled.
But cross Ned Roper and he'll still have your neck broken
for you."

"Never!" said Cazamian, his hands dry-washing together
earnestly. "I'm your man, sir, you and Mr Roper."

"Well," drawled Dacre laconically, "I do hope so, old
fellow."

He edged Cazamian towards the door and held it open.

"I mean it," said Cazamian sincerely, "I'm *your* man,
whatever the jig may be."

"Obliged, I'm sure," said Dacre. "But one piece of advice,
my dear chap. If you're going to speculate again, horses is a
deuced long chance. Getting down to the pasties on the old
green baize is more the style. Especially if you've got a good
set of fingers for the cards."

It had to come next, but it was the only part of the whole
scheme which left Dacre's mouth dry with fear. He rang for
his servant and entrusted the beagle to him, to be returned to
the house in Albemarle Street. Then, pushing his way
through the noisy, lurching crowd in Cremorne Gardens, he
called a cab off the rank in Cheyne Walk.

"Sealskin" Kite lived near Hammersmith Mall, in the new
"Stock Exchange suburb" which ran north to Shepherds
Bush, and from which professional men could now travel
leisurely to the City by rail. Kite's was one of the detached
villas, large enough to contain a wife, several children, a
governess, a parlourmaid, a kitchenmaid, and a cook. Both
the parlourmaid and the governess were required to provide
certain discreet services for the pleasure of their employer.

Alone among his neighbours, Kite drew his income from
a source other than the Exchange, or the Temple, or rack
rent streets east of St Paul's and south of Waterloo. The turf

had made Kite a rich man—so rich that now he had men who threatened and maimed and even killed on his behalf without even knowing his name. Kite himself was a merchant banker of the underworld, who could turn goods into gold, gold into notes of credit, and notes of credit into goods, bonds, or stock, with flawless dexterity and impunity. It was more than five years since Kite had even seen a racecourse. When he read of a stable-boy beaten half to death for refusing to wound a likely winner, or an awkward book-maker garotted and robbed, he shook his head and wondered as emphatically as his neighbours what the world was coming to.

Kite never begrudged the cost to the parish rates of Poor Law institutions. He subscribed for the relief of "distressed trades" and dropped half a crown into the collection plate of a respectable chapel every Sunday morning. It was no hypocrisy on his part. Kite felt a genuine warmth of heart when helping the deserving poor. For the undeserving poor, and most of all for the petty pilferer and the mean sneak-thief, Kite harboured a disgust that frequently became an irrational fury. He would willingly raise the honest man who had fallen on hard times, and would as willingly have throttled with his own hands a thief who took the humblest man's cherished trinkets. Kite was extremely dangerous, but he was necessary to Dacre's scheme.

Dacre knew what must be done but, for all that, he still had half a mind to turn back as he walked past the railings of the spacious houses. The palms of his white, bony hands sweated and his heart seemed to be beating in his throat. To do what must be done, while facing the penalties of the law, was bad enough. To do it in the knowledge of what Kite or Kite's bullies would do if they caught him, left him almost sick with fright.

In a patch of deep shadow by the railings he unfastened his cloak. At least Kite himself would not be in the house. Not on Derby Night. There were several heavy objects in the lining of the cloak. Dacre chose a screwdriver, two short lengths of chain, and four metal clamps. He screwed two clamps to adjacent railings, a length of stout chain held taut between them. Reaching up, he repeated the operation at a higher point, so that the six feet of sharp-topped railings now had "stirrups" at two-foot intervals.

Dacre took off his cloak, rolled it up and tied it. Then he tossed it cautiously over the railings, where it fell with a muffled impact on the grass. Nothing for it now, the job was on. It took him one stride on to the low wall, two up the railings, two down the other side, and a jump to the grass. He listened carefully, but there was no sound of alarm.

Being a perfectionist, he would have liked to remove the stirrups so that no passing policeman should catch a glimpse of them, and replace them on his way out. But it was dark by the railings, and he judged that it was worth leaving them in position in order to guarantee a quick retreat. The police were not his most feared enemies on this occasion. He stripped off his bottle-green evening coat, and slipped a black Balaclava helmet and mask over his features. He drew from the cloak a roll of canvas containing the tools of his trade. Folding the coat and cloak, he left them together under a laurel bush.

The house seemed to be in total darkness as he crossed the lawn, until he saw a narrow strip of light between the curtains of a ground-floor room at the back. The front then. Not what he would have preferred, but at least it was some little distance from the road.

He chose a window whose curtains were open. The interior was dark and, presumably, unoccupied. It looked like the drawing-room. The first tool from the canvas wallet was an eight-inch iron bar with right-angled projections, pointing opposite ways, at either end. Gently, he eased one projection between the window frame and its wooden surround. The wood squealed and splintered a little as he gradually increased the leverage. Then there was a sharp crack. Dacre paused, listened, repeated the process on the other side of the frame, and then twice more at a higher level. The frame was now loose enough to be prised outwards by half an inch and the sash handle pushed back with a chisel blade. So much for the "New Patent Hermetic Window Fastener." He slid the window up, holding it above himself while he stepped over the sill, and then lowered it without a sound.

Dacre was standing in the drawing-room, certainly not where a man like Kite would keep his private papers and dearest possessions. He tried the handle of the door to the hall and was surprised to find it locked. Standing there with his hand sweating on the china handle, Dacre told himself that "Sealskin" Kite was too careful a man by half. From the canvas wallet came an instrument with a handle like a key, but ending in a fine metal hook. For a minute or two he tried all the usual positions and movements with it in the lock, listening hard all the time. The lock showed not a sign of yielding. In the warmth of summer, Dacre was trembling with cold. He chose a stronger piece, a slender metal tube with carefully crenellated prongs at either end. This time there was more leverage. He found the place, turned the skeleton key gently, and eased the lock back.

For some reason, they had left the hallway in darkness, but there was a distant light shining through a glass door, and this showed him the stairs. He could hear voices, at least two women and a man. One of Kite's retainers, no doubt. Not a stair creaked as he reached the first floor of the house. There was darkness everywhere, except that the long landing was faintly illuminated by light shining upwards through a back staircase. There was not a sound of breathing, the Kite children were presumably beyond the next, narrower, flight of stairs.

Dacre guessed that the main front room on this floor would be Kite's "study," for want of a better term. The door looked solid enough. He tapped lightly on one of the panels. The deadness of the sound was more than the deadness of wood. From the canvas wallet, he took a wooden tube containing an awl, so sharp that it could only be carried in a container. It bored through the panel of the door like a fork going through cheese. Then, after an inch or so, it stopped.

Dacre tried once more, with the same result. The panels of the door had been reinforced by the new insurance fad of sheet metal on the inside. This was Kite's room. To have used the old lag's method of a knife on a large compass arm to cut a circular hole, would have been useless. Nor was this a lock to be picked. If the job could be done at all, it must be done by the cracksman's masterpiece, the jack-in-the-box.

Dacre assembled it quickly. A horizontal stock of solid brass mounted on a horizontal iron cylinder below. Dacre turned the sharp screw which ran through the cylinder so that it bit into the wood of the door, just below the lock, and held the brass stock level with the keyhole. Through the barrel of the heavy stock ran a powerful screw whose point could be turned into the lock. It had a spherical head, drilled through to take a lever on which maximum pressure could be brought.

Dacre inserted the lever and began to wind the heavy brass screw into the keyhole. The jack-in-the-box, properly used, would bring a pressure of three tons against the mechanism of an ordinary lock, and Dacre could feel the tension building up. From below he heard a woman's laugh, and then a man's. One more turn of the lever. There was a rending sound, far greater than the snapping of a lock, and the door burst open under the force of the instrument. Dacre cursed to himself, and listened. The voices below him were silent. However, he moved noiselessly into the room, still alert for footsteps, and went quickly to work.

Closing the forced door behind him, he lit a candle. In the centre of the room was what he was looking for, an escritoire in the bowed shape of a Carlton House table. Two miniatures of a child's face, no doubt one of Kite's dead, had been placed in the centre of it on ornamental stands of chased silver. Dacre picked up the first stand, complete with its miniature, and dropped it into a bag. He took the second miniature from its stand, added the stand to his bag, and then, putting the little picture under his heel, he ground it to fragments. With a fine chisel, he burst open the drawers of the writing-desk, tipping papers in a pile on the floor. From one of the drawers he took what looked like a diamond neck-lace but would, almost certainly, prove to be paste. However, it had no doubt belonged to one of Kite's past loves and, as such, would prove useful. He added it to his bag. Then, for good measure, he selected a bundle of letters from the papers on the floor and took those as well.

A dog barked, outside the house, but not very far from it. Dacre folded the canvas wallet away and moved back to the landing, holding the proceeds of the theft. As he stepped gently down the stairs and across the hallway, he could hear the man and woman moving about at the back of the house. There was activity in front of the house as well, by the gate-way in the iron railings. In the darkness, Dacre entered the drawing-room, gently raised the forced window, and stepped on to the path outside. Two men were walking slowly up to the house from the double iron gate, and the wheels of a cab rattled away into the distance towards Holland Park.

There was a bush between Dacre and the two men. As soon as they had passed it and were waiting for the front door to be opened to them, he sprinted over the soft turf towards the tall railings. The dog was barking again and he sensed that someone had let it loose. Without stopping to look, he retrieved his coat and cloak, stripped off the mask and Balaclava helmet, pitched the garments over the rail-ings, and put his foot in the chain stirrup to follow. There was even time to remove the two stirrups before he walked, slowly and with his heart-beat gradually quietening again, towards the twopenny bus which ran between Hammersmith and Regent Circus.

6

It had been the most successful night of all behind the securely barred door and heavily curtained windows in Langham Place. Ellen Jacoby had presided over the customers, the girls, and the cash with all the aplomb of an experienced *madame*. Ned Roper felt an almost paternal pride in the girl.

Four or five Oxford men, fresh from the Epsom course, had stumbled noisily in and joined the dancing in the large drawing-room downstairs. Undergraduates they might be, but Roper doubted that they would ever graduate in anything but the *Racing Calendar* or *Bell's Life in London*. There had also been several clubmen in evening clothes, from White's, Boodle's, or the Guards'. There was even an elderly captain of a hussar regiment in full dress uniform, which he had been wearing at a regimental dinner, complete with medals bearing the Alma and Inkerman clasps.

Tyler and Coggin stood guard just inside the door to deter unwanted visitors. In their makeshift footmen's livery, they still gave the appearance of muscle-bound coal-heavers. Even when a customer wanted to leave, Tyler or Coggin had to open the stout front door with a key on the inside. The door had no catch, so that it was equally effective for keeping intruders out and keeping unwilling girls in.

In a little parlour just to one side of the doorway, Ellen Jacoby, in black silk and peacock feathers, kept the desk and the cash-box. Beyond her, beckoning the customers forward, was Jolie, wearing a fancy dress which Ned Roper thought was the most stunning Derby Night idea since Eclipse first won the race. Her black hair was tucked up under a jockey cap, she wore a close-buttoned green jacket to her waist, and a pair of close fitting white breeches down to her black boots. Carrying a light crop, she led each arrival to the dancing, jostling crowd in the smoke-filled drawing-room. Roper watched and grinned. He detected from the girl's impatient little movements that there was hardly one of the men whose white-gloved hands did not come into sharp contact with her trimly clad body.

In a bedlam of waltzes and polkas, the other girls of the house, plump, blonde Sarah; Rebecca, the tall graceful brunette; Charlotte, the green-eyed redhead; Ebony, the copper-skinned mulatto, and several more, danced with their partners. The girls' red or blue dresses were carefully arranged to show their breasts to the nipples and their legs well above the knee. At intervals, one of them would come running out to Ellen, followed by her client. A second, much larger sum of money than the entrance fee would change hands, and the girl would lead the way upstairs.

There had been fourteen that night, at several guineas a time, for they all paid for one or other of the best rooms, which cost a guinea extra. In Ned Roper's opinion, it was worth that guinea just to see the best room. The pink silk hangings of the bed matched the shades of the gas lamps, the gilded brackets of the lamps themselves were in the shape of naked girls holding a phallic torch. Then there were the gilt-framed mirrors and pier glasses, arranged so that the man might admire the scene on the bed from almost any angle. There were pastels on the walls, in the style of Fragonard and the courtly painters of the eighteenth century, depicting plump, fair-skinned girls sprawling on pink or pale blue cushions as they submitted coquettishly to every variety of the act of love. Oh yes, thought Roper, it was worth a guinea of any gentleman's money. When Lieutenant Verney Dacre set a man up in business, he did it in the proper style.

The hussar captain, far gone in drink before ever he arrived in Langham Place, had parted with almost twenty sovereigns for wine and girls before the evening was over. Finally, possessed by some fantasy of being the tyrannical owner of a cotton plantation, he had insisted on taking Ebony to the upstairs drawing-room. Ellen had gone too, just to ensure that the charade remained a charade. The room had been carefully sound-proofed, so that nothing which happened there could be heard, even on the landing outside. Ebony, whose skin was closer to the colour of bronze than ebony, undressed and bent over a pair of folding steps, while Ellen secured her wrists and ankles. Both girls were giggling, knowing that the elderly captain of hussars was far too drunk to offer a real threat of violence. He picked up the birch-rod, which lay on the sofa, and paced about the room.

Then, after giving Ebony several half-hearted strokes with it across her bottom, he sat down heavily and complained of his stomach. But best of all, thought Roper, the poor gull was so overcome with remorse at having hurt the girl, for Ebony had suppressed her giggles and obliged him with some truly operatic shrieks, that he had pressed five more sovereigns into Ellen Jacoby's hands, to be passed on to Ebony as a consolation for her injuries. Much hope of that, as Ellen remarked later.

Before two o'clock in the morning, the festivities were over and Roper was able to sit in Ellen's little parlour and count the results of the evening's work. More than fifty sovereigns, and a cheque on Drummond's Bank for ten guineas. Even allowing for the "rent" to Verney Dacre, it was a fortune for one night's work. But just to be on the safe side, Roper took charge of the cheque. That should be his and his alone. Less than two years before, Ned Roper had been so poor that he had pledged his boots for one good meal. That should never happen again.

He was still sitting and contemplating his good prospects in the high-class "doxy" trade, and the glass of hock was growing warm in his hand, when he heard a cabman's cry outside; jingling harness and iron-rimmed wheels fell silent as the cab stopped. A murmur of voices, footsteps on the pavement in Portland Place, and then two sharp knocks on the heavy door, blows which echoed through the silent house as if it had been a tomb.

Roper had a mirror fixed in the parlour, rather on the slant, so that by pulling back the edge of the heavy curtain he could see the reflection of whoever might be outside the door. It was a simple precaution. He recognised the tall, slender figure of Verney Dacre in top hat, evening cloak, and holding a silver-topped cane. Roper took a key from the drawer of the desk, since the door would not open from the inside without one, and went out into the hallway as Dacre knocked again.

"Well, Mr Dacre!" said Roper with breezy insincerity, "rare pleasure and no mistake!"

"I ain't got time for that, Ned Roper," said Dacre briskly, handing his hat and cane to Roper as he would have done to a servant. "The job's put up and it's got to be slippy."

Roper nodded at the stairs.

"Come up. The drawing-room's free."

When they were alone in the sound-proof room, Roper turned to his acquaintance.

"So it's a runner, then?"

Dacre nodded.

"You saw Cazamian?" Roper inquired.

"I did. He's a safe one. I have a key, which Cazamian says will open the door of the Folkestone railway office. More to the purpose I have a note which says that he stole the key. Your Mr Cazamian is an employee of the South Eastern Railway Company and as such there is a very special and a very harsh law applying to him. If that note of his were to reach the wrong hands, Mr Cazamian would be working off a stretch in Botany Bay for the next fourteen years. See that you tell him, Ned Roper, and then see he don't forget it."

"He's our man, then," said Roper. "He don't know your name, however?"

"No," said Dacre contemptuously, "he swallowed the tale about the diamond, but it's part of the game that he doesn't know me."

Roper's thin lips parted in a smile, showing neat and carefully tended teeth.

"He believes the diamond story?"

"Oh yes," said Dacre, "why shouldn't he believe it? It's paid his debts already and it's going to bring him four or five hundred pounds. Who wouldn't believe it at that price?"

"But you ain't got a diamond, as such," said Roper confidently, standing with his back to the fender and his thumbs in his lapels. "Not as such, 'ave you?"

"I'm a careful man, Ned Roper," said Dacre in a long, impatient drawl, "and I've taken the pains to equip myself with somethin' worth more than diamonds or yaller goold itself."

Roper threw back his head and laughed dutifully, but without conviction.

"Oblige me," said Verney Dacre languidly, "by not acting the fool all the time. Fix this in your mind instead."

He sat down on the sofa, leaning back almost sleepily, his long absurdly thin legs crossed, and the blond petulent face holding Roper's ferret-like gaze.

"The bullion-boxes reach London Bridge in the late afternoon. Each one is bound with iron bands, locked, and with the bullion merchant's seal on it, which can't be replaced if the box is opened. The station master and his constables weigh the boxes and see them to the guard's van. In the van is a Chubb's safe, which no tool that you and I can think of would ever open. It has two locks. The station master has one key and the railway police the other, because it seems they can't even trust each other. The bullion-boxes go in, say a ton and a quarter of gold, and the safe is locked. The guard stays with it to Folkestone. Then they take it out and put it under a police guard on the pier until it goes on the boat for Boulogne. They have a double guard on the paddle-boat, French and English, and a double guard from Boulogne to Paris."

"It's not on!" said Roper indignantly. "Even if you square Cazamian, you can't open the safe or the boxes."

"Wait a bit, Ned Roper," said Dacre softly, "it's steeper than *that*. Just in case some dishonest fellow *could* open the safe and the boxes, and replace the seals and lock the safe again, they weigh the bullion every so often to make sure that, even if they can't see it, it's still there."

"Then the jig's up," said Roper, his respect for Dacre no longer obsequiously paraded.

"No, old fellow," said Dacre more softly still, "that's just what it ain't. In the first place, they think everything's so safe that they aren't expecting trouble. And that's important."

"And in the second?"

"In the second place, how do they weigh the bullion on the journey? You can't put a ton and a quarter of gold and an iron safe on to a pair of scales as if it was a pound of flour. They must weigh the bullion-boxes themselves, and to do that they must be able to get them out of the safe. In other words, there's another set of keys on the way, and I'll wager it's at Folkestone!"

"Well then!" said Roper, as though his enthusiasm had never faltered.

"Well then," said Dacre, "being as it's nearly midsummer and London seems such a deuced tiresome place, I shall go to Folkestone for a day or two. You will come when I invite you, *if* I invite you."

"Whatcher mean?" asked Roper, frowning.

"What I mean, my dear fellow, is Sergeant Verity of 'A' Division."

"Oh!" said Roper, relieved. "That stupid bugger! I reckon we taught him a prime lesson! He needed scarin' off. He was getting wise to the McCaffery dodge. You seen the bloody way he was tackling Croaker about it. He knew about that squeak McCaffery, and that little bitch Jolie!"

Dacre paused for a moment before answering.

"I fancy, Ned Roper, that you are a stupider bugger than Verity will ever be. Now, I promise you, I hate Verity and his kind a great deal more than you will ever do. A fat, canting prig! But I know his type. The army's full of Verity and his sort. The more you hit him, the surer he'll come back. The Rhoosians couldn't stop him at Inkerman and nor will you. But I will. I have a plan for Verity that will make the beating you gave him seem like an act of charity by comparison."

"All right," said Roper ungraciously.

Dacre got up and walked round the table, picking up a blue china snuff box and examining it, as if trying to judge its value. Then he looked up at Roper and his eyes narrowed.

"It's very far from all right. Wherever you go from now on, Verity is likely to go too. Wherever the two girls go, he may go with 'em. They're both to be got out of circulation. As for you, watch for Verity. If you see him or any of his sort, take them round the town and then go to ground. They

70

know you, Ned Roper, but I shall take very good care they don't know me."

"Someone must have known you were kicked out of your commission. They knew you thieved . . . "

"I sold out!" said Dacre sharply. "And there is no court-martial conviction recorded against me. Now, you either carry out my instructions, or the whole thing is off!"

Roper smiled and shrugged his agreement.

"What about the two girls?"

"There's something more important than that," said Dacre impatiently: "I want the use of the little bedroom at the back."

Roper led him across the landing and lit the gas in the tiny room. There was a single bed, a washstand with a cracked bowl, a jug of tepid water, and a slop basin. From his pocket, Dacre took a little box and the key which Cazamian had given him. The top of the washstand was an ideal surface for working on. Inside the box was a lump of wax, greyish-green and softened to the consistency of putty. Dacre laid it on the marble surface and pressed the length of the key deeply into it, making a second impression of the other side of the key. One might be enough, but there was no harm in having another. From another pocket, he took his cigar case, empty now, and laid the two wax impressions carefully inside it.

Roper saw him washing his hands and went in just as Dacre was tipping the water into the slop basin. Dacre handed him the key.

"Give that back to Cazamian tomorrow."

"Why give it back?" Roper demanded.

"Do as I say."

Roper grinned and shrugged again.

"And what about the two doxies?"

"Ah!" said Dacre, relaxing a little. "I was coming to that. Where are they?"

Roper led the way down to the first-floor landing, where a tall majolica vase stood on a corner pedestal. He pushed open the door of the bedroom which cost the clients an extra guinea. Ellen Jacoby, regal in her black silk and feathers,

71

was standing proudly with her hands on her hips. She was
looking down at Jolie who knelt before her in the absurd but
yet intriguing jockey costume. The dark-haired girl was
kneeling with head lowered and haunches in the air as she
renewed the stitching at the hem of a pleat in Ellen's dress.
The white tights displayed the outlines of her slender thighs
and rounded hips as starkly as if she had been naked.

Dacre lounged in the open doorway, critically examining
the girl as she unwittingly presented herself to him. He
moved slightly, to view her from a different angle, his eyes
running dispassionately over her body. He looked at the tall
blonde, and then back to her companion again. Ellen
glanced up and saw him surveying her willing seamstress.
She muttered something to Jolie and the girl sat back on her
heels, waiting defiantly. Dacre waited a while longer. She
glanced back at him with a glitter of her dark little eyes with
their rather Turkoman slant. He withdrew to the landing
and spoke to Roper.

"The tall one in the black dress. I'll make the arrangements about her. She shall come with me now, and Verity
will never find her."

"No, Mr Dacre," said Roper softly, "that you will not.
Whatever else you want, you shall have. But Ellen Jacoby
must stay with me. She'll be safe, I promise you. They won't
find her."

Dacre laughed.

"You ain't married her, old fellow?"

"No," said Roper uncertainly.

"Dammit man! Then you've fathered a child on her! Why
not say so?"

"Eight months since," said Roper quietly, "a boy."

"Say no more, old fellow. I'll put the other one out of
harm's way. Your woman will be safer with you. What's the
other little minx like?"

"Jolie?" said Roper. "Bit of temperament. Ain't been
properly broken to the saddle yet!"

The two men laughed.

"All right," said Dacre, "let's see what the cavalry can do!"

"She's hot enough," said Roper. "Handle her right, and she'll be at you like a monkey up a stick."

Then Roper went and spoke to the two girls. Dacre watched from the doorway, while Jolie received her orders without any reaction beyond an enigmatic glance, and this time she submitted while Dacre's eyes ran over her, as they might have done over a filly at Tattersall's. It was little more than an hour later, when the girl and her box were accompanied by Verney Dacre to the opulent seclusion of his apartments in Albemarle Street.

7

"It isn't right, Mr Verity, and you know it," said Sergeant Samson.

He walked the next three hundred yards in great thought and then added,

"It's more than not right. It isn't natural."

"Yes," said Verity absent-mindedly, "it isn't."

They strode in perfect step towards the vaulted glass roof of the Great Western terminus at Paddington, there to await the unlikely arrival of Albert Groat, the mad rapist of Gloucester, reported to be making for the anonymity of the great metropolitan wen.

"Look," said Samson, "Sealskin Kite was burgled. Crabstick of "T" division swears he got it from one of his men who's been pleasuring the cook. Went through the house like the charge of the Light Cavalry at Balaclava. Broke the ornaments. Smashed up the desk. Stole some little things."

"What for?" asked Verity.

"Exactly." Samson adjusted his tall hat a little and strode onwards, Verity breathing heavily beside him. "An amateur. It ain't anyone who knows Kite, or knows the things he'll do to a man who's caught at that game."

"That's a fact," said Verity, gasping a little at the pace.

"And Kite, of course, ain't come to the police office, as he means to take his man himself."

"So he does," said Verity abruptly.

"Obliging of him, no doubt," said Samson. "And then there's Ned Roper, who everyone would like to see working the treadmill and eating oats. And what does he do? Comes to Inspector Croaker, to tell him of the state he found you in, along the Haymarket that night, and begs Mr Croaker to call upon his services as a witness at any time that your assailant may be apprehended."

"I told Mr Croaker," said Verity coldly, "I fell up the stairs."

"Down the stairs," said Samson reproachfully. "It was down the stairs last time."

They reached the great glass and iron canopy, under which the steam and smoke gathered in a cloudy atmosphere of its own, and there they stood, conspicuous as if they had been wearing uniform, among the clatter of wagons and the snort of engines.

"But you can't deny there is something very peculiar about the behaviour of the criminal element just at present," said Samson gravely. "Unnatural. Like fearful prodigies foretelling some dire event." It was a phrase he had gathered from a Hoxton melodrama at the Britannia and had now made his own.

"I'll tell you what, though, Mr Samson," said Verity softly, "there are men in this city who believe themselves secure in their wickedness. But I will have them yet in a sure and inescapable snare."

Samson looked at him with respect, thinking that the fiery preaching of Verity's Wesleyan boyhood in Cornwall might have taught the Hoxton melodramas a trick or two. And then Samson and Verity waited dutifully until relieved from their watch. By which time, Albert Groat, who had never contemplated leaving his native haunts, had "coopered" a girl on a field-path near the Badminton estate.

8

Union Bank,
4, Pall Mall East,
London.
5th June 1857

Sir,
In accordance with your instructions to us of the 2d.
instant, we have today despatched 300l. in specie per South
Eastern Railway Company to await your collection from the
Railway Office at Folkestone Harbour Pier. An early
acknowledgement of receipt will oblige.

I have the honour to remain, sir,
Your obedient servant,
Charles Landon Estcourt,
Secretary, Union Bank.

To
Lieutenant Verney Dacre,
19th Dragoon Guards,
The Grand Pavilion Hotel,
Folkestone.

Verney Dacre folded the sheet of paper into his notecase and smiled almost imperceptibly. It was, of course, entirely safe to use his rank and former regiment for several years to come. The previous September, the 19th Dragoons had been marched on board two superannuated East India sailing vessels at Gravesend for the slow route round the Cape to Calcutta. The latest news of the native rebellion in India suggested that one troop had been cut to bits when the mutineers sacked Lucknow, while most of another squadron was annihilated as the Sepoys overran Cawnpore. If Dacre laid claim to a continuing and honourable connection with the regiment, he was unlikely to find anyone still in England to contradict him.

He turned his eyes upon the girl beside him, watching the glimmer of cheap stones in her ear-rings and the energy of her brown, fine-boned hands as she clenched the reins in her little fists. Her cheeks were flushed with exertion and exhilaration as she chopped with her slender switch at the quarters of the off-horse of the carriage pair.

"There ain't no call to destroy them," said Dacre peevishly. "They may be only dumb brutes, but the livery stables charge the devil for them in season. Let the reins go a bit, and they'll pull easier."

The harness brass and the glossy backs of the yearlings flashed in the bright marine sunlight to the accompanying rumble of wheels and clinking of bridles. On its indiarubber bearings the fairy shape of the swan's-neck Pilentum seemed to roll in air above the glittering spokes of its wheels. Top-hatted or crinolined, the strollers on the parade turned to admire the elegant little carriage with its ultramarine lines and hood, its panels an airy imitation of canework in white and amber paint. A few noticed the languid hussar-like figure of Verney Dacre, with his faded fairness, and his long, narrow blue eyes expressing total indifference to all around him. He wore his right arm in a black silk sling, as though it had been broken. It was not, but a small part of his scheme required that it should seem so. He judged it best, therefore, to be seen being driven on the parade by Jolie, the golden tan of her skin shaded by the blue hood of the carriage and by the pink straw bonnet, which matched the skirts she had gathered tightly round her legs.

"This is a great bore," he said at length. "There is nothing else to be seen here."

"I should like to go on, though," said the girl.

"I daresay you should. Nevertheless, have the goodness to turn back to the hotel."

The water had ebbed from the tidal harbour where the railway ran out along the pier. Several men in high boots scooped and shovelled their way along an empty channel between shining grey flanks of mud, a runnel dug out twice a day so that the keel of the Boulogne steamer might clear the sea bed before full tide. A group of stranded fishing-smacks and several colliers, their tall stacks and red paddle-wheels idle, lay like dead sea-monsters among the green slime and weed of the harbour stones. The halyard of the harbour flag-staff hung limp and the little wooden lighthouse seemed to dwindle to a toy in the morning heat. Away from the sea, the laughter of a wedding party at an open window of the Royal George overlaid the prolonged dirge of a minstrel band. An infinite perspective of posters announcing Cooke's Imperial Circus, with ventriloquist, Indian jugglers, and infant phenomenon, faded in a bright shimmering distance.

Jolie still brooded on Dacre's order to turn the carriage back. Her eyes flicked to one side, as though she was half looking at him.

"I'm not your bloody slave girl," she said, blinking fiercely, "though you may think so."

"Ain't you, though?" said Dacre, half-amused.

"Not yours, nor Ned Roper's. I know McCaffery was up to some dodge of Roper's. Half of what I know could put Ned Roper in quod."

Dacre laughed, and dropped his half-smoked cigar carefully on to the road.

"If you suppose I care a damn for that," he said softly, "you are most stupendously mistaken."

"Am I?" There was a rising slyness in her voice, but this only reassured him. He shifted against the cushions a little, in order to watch her as he spoke.

"Swearing a fellow's life away, even a simpleton like McCaffery, is an uncommonly serious business, my love. It's quite the best thing that one of us should protect you."

She blew a derisive, farting sound with her tongue.

"That for your protection!" she said bravely.

Dacre appeared to look sad.

"I don't care to see a girl hang," he said, "that's all. I dare-say they'd put Ned Roper to tread the cock-chafer for a year

77

or two, but they'd fly a black flag for you at Newgate. Over the water to Charley you'd dance, my girl, at eight sharp. It's a long polka, too. None of the poor doxies ever has the tin left to bribe Jack Ketch to pull on their legs and end it smartly."

He watched her body grow tense and felt, for the first time in their four days' acquaintance, a desire for her, a bizarre lust to enjoy her while she was still trembling with the fear of what he had described.

"I only did what Ned Roper made me," she said, half indignant and half pleading.

Dacre yawned with monumental indifference.

"Did y' now? Oblige me by not grippin' those reins like a madwoman. These two nags may be only park hacks in summer and cover hacks in winter, but they don't need their heads pulled clean off."

In their first hours together, he had concluded that fright was beneficial to her. Indeed, she herself had almost seemed to invite it by several half-hearted little threats of rebellion. Dacre had, of course, known girls who appeared to find a strange reassurance in the threats or the blows which their protectors used upon them. Why that should be so, he could not tell, and cared even less. This doxy, according to Roper, had been an undertaker's mute as a child, sleeping on coffin lids in the carpenter's shed, and eating such scraps as might have been given to the shop cat. Even if fear failed to subdue her, her greed for possessions after a childhood of such poverty made her an absurdly easy mark for a man as rich as Dacre.

Before they left Albemarle Street for Folkestone, he had taken her to Howell and Jones's, and to Sawyer's in Bond Street, to buy such costumes for her as his plan might require. In one of the warm, mirrored *salons*, heavy with the scent of camelias, she had watched, lynx-eyed, as the *demoiselles* paraded in *toilettes de jours* and *toilettes de soirée* for her choice. At first she had chosen quickly and indiscriminately, as if frightened that she might otherwise lose the beautiful clothes for ever. Then, confronted by courteous shop-walkers and lady assistants, she had grown confused and in her confusion had actually begun to weep. Dacre was intrigued, but not for long. Women, like men, had their uses for him. When they were not being useful they might, for all Dacre cared, laugh or cry as the mood took them. It was nothing to him.

Back at the hotel, Jolie went ahead of him, moving with bustling little steps up the broad staircase. From the pillared entrance hall, several sets of imposing double doors led to the public dining-room, reading-room, billiard-room, smoking-room, and all the other amenities necessary to a grand hotel. At every door was an elaborate wrought-iron gas pillar with a frosted glass globe that shone like a brilliant moon by dinner time. The centrepiece of the hall was a round ottoman in maroon velvet and gilt wood, which might have sat a circle of a dozen guests. Its tall central back formed a pedestal on which stood the gilded figure of a Grecian girl with a harp, her simple robe having slipped almost to her navel and parted conveniently about her thighs.

As it happened, there were no guests sitting on the ottoman, but Dacre's attention was caught by a copy of a handbill, which he had seen placarded while the girl drove the Pilentum along the Marine Parade.

Every Man Has His Fancy,
"Ratting Sports In Reality!"
A very handsome silver collar will be given by a
sporting gentleman
to be killed for by dogs under 13¾ pounds weight
on Wednesday next at 9 p.m. sharp
at the Hope and Anchor, Dover
Mr Jack Black, Umpire.
Competitors to go to scale at half-past 7.
Rats always on hand for the Accommodation of
Gentlemen to try their dogs.

Dacre folded the bill into quarters and walked into the hush of the deserted and thickly-carpeted reading-room. He chose an envelope from a rack at one of the little tables and

slid the bill inside. When it was sealed, he shot back the
sling on his arm and addressed the cover to Ned Roper at the
house in Langham Place. There was no need to add a word
to the handbill. Roper had his instructions and would know
precisely what to do.

Two days being the time allowed, Dacre walked quickly
to the post office and sent the letter by express mail. Then he
returned, just as quickly, to the Grand Pavilion Hotel. Too
much had been invested in the scheme by this time to allow
the girl out of his sight for long. He had taken the most
handsome apartments that the hotel could offer, including a
day-room which served as a private dining-room, so that
neither of them should be on public view except when it
suited his purpose. The suite included separate bedrooms
and a view of the summer sands, where heavily clad men and
women sat close together on small wooden chairs, reading
the *Morning Post* or holding tasselled parasols to keep off
the sun. Children, like overdressed dolls, trained their penny
telescopes on the sailing barges with rust-coloured sails which
drifted sluggishly down the Channel in the stillness and the
heat.

At the first landing of the stairway, Dacre slipped a key
into the door and let himself into the brightly sunlit day-
room. Jolie was standing before the broad ebony-framed
mirror of a console chiffonier. She had stripped off the candy-
pink dress and bonnet, which lay discarded with her other
clothes upon the sofa-table, and she was dressed in the latest
Parisian *maillot,* an absurd creation which she had insisted
on having as part of her trousseau for the seaside excursion.
It was hardly to be imagined that so fragile a costume would
survive a single immersion in sea-water. The little white silk
tunic, with its short sleeves and crimson edging, ended in a
tight gathering at her narrow waist, subtly emphasising the
almost childish slightness of her body there by comparison
with the swelling femininity of her haunches which filled out
the knee-length pants of the costume. To complete the
picture, she wore a pert little cap, and a crimson sash tied

with a broad bow, whose ends fell in a tail to the back of her knees.

Dacre regarded her coldly.

"I suppose you like to consider yourself a self-possessed beauty in high condition for flirtin'," he said disapprovingly.

"Something of that," she said confidently. "I had three seasons of hard training from Ned Roper, didn't I?"

"Dress yourself properly," he said disdainfully, his voice subsiding again into its broken drawl. "You look like a half-stripped parlourmaid whose soldier's given her the chuck. If you choose to make yourself a freak for every hotel servant to gape at, have the goodness not to do it in my company."

She turned from the glass and straightened up.

"I don't dress to your bloody orders," she said, adding with careful emphasis, "nor undress neither."

Of his own choice, Dacre had made her sleep in a separate room, calculating that by such an arrangement he might still enjoy her when he chose without having to endure more than was necessary of her company at other times. However, this present defiance had to be put down.

"All this coquetting is a damned bore," he said softly, lifting his hand level with his shoulder and apparently searching out the area where he would strike her across the face. "The next time I beckon you, you shall oblige me. If Ned Roper didn't teach you to come when he called, then, by George, I will. Don't play your va-tue with me, miss. It won't answer."

He was gratified to see that she had fleetingly hunched her head down between her shoulders, as though expecting the back-hand blow across the mouth which had been familiar enough in her childhood. Then, snatching up her other clothes from the sofa table, she gave him a dark glance from her narrow odalisque eyes, hurried into the bedroom, and closed the door on him. She did not lock the door, since there was only one key, which Verney Dacre had taken possession of as soon as they arrived.

The elegant brass carriage-lamps of the Pilentum threw tawny pools of oil-light, faintly high-lighting the almost cat-like mask of Jolie's profile. Dacre slid out his gold hunter and tilted its dial towards the steady flame. He touched the girl's arm, helping her to dismount, and speaking briefly to the boy who, for a few pence a day, held the horses of the "quality" at the gates of the Harbour Pier. Before them, along the curve of the Marine Parade, the gas jets flickered and flared in the breeze which had risen with the night tide.

He gave the girl his left arm, and felt her fingers resting there with the lightness of practised poise. It amused him to think that when it came to self-improvement, no vicarage bluestocking could match a Haymarket doxy with an empty belly. From time to time, she was obliged to ease the gloved fingers a little in movements which had all the furtive intimacy of a caress between strangers.

Alongside the Harbour Pier, a constant funnelling of smoke from the thin stacks of the *Lord Warden* rose in a black cloud against the paler night sky. Gusts of steam from the paddle-boxes accompanied the rumbling of the finned wheels as they thrashed the harbour waves to a calm, whispering froth. Dacre led the girl close to the railway office, and waited. Somewhere close by, a bell rang to telegraph the down tidal train from London Bridge. Soon, with the screech of a whistle and a gong-like sound, the two red eyes of the brass-domed engine grew steadily larger in a slow and even glide. Then it slid past them, steam snorting from the pistons and sparks breaking in clusters from the tall copper funnel, until it had drawn the first carriages level with the steamer. Bright patches of light broke out as the doors of the post office vans opened and the guards, stooping under the weight of their sacks, moved like a procession of monks, down the harbour steps to the pier's lower level. There the mail was carried directly over the steamer's paddle-box sponsons to the strong room below the main deck. As the first huddle of passengers, and porters bearing hatboxes and portmanteaus, shuffled down the gangway to the shifting deck, Dacre turned to the girl and spoke peremptorily.

"I shall want a few minutes to collect what belongs to me. I don't choose that you should be seen standing around on your own. It's best you should go back to the carriage."

Without waiting to see his instuctions obeyed, he opened the door of the railway office and stepped inside. At the far end of the heavy wooden counter with its chipped black varnish, the clerk sat on his high stool, gazing absent-mindedly at a ledger open on the desk before him. A boy in waistcoat and baize apron watched at his elbow. Dacre rapped the wooden counter with his stick.

"I have a box addressed to me from the Union Bank in Pall Mall. Oblige me by havin' it fetched at once."

"If it's just come down, sir," said the boy in the green apron, "it'll be with the bank boxes at the steamer. They'll fetch it here presently."

Dacre fingered a receipt and his card from his waistcoat pocket. Ignoring the boy, he tossed them on the counter by the clerk.

"It's of no consequence to me where anything may or may not be," he said languidly; "oblige me by havin' my property brought to me at once. I don't care to be kept standin' here like a fool."

The clerk summed up Dacre's silk hat, lined cloak, and silver topped stick. Without even bothering to read the card, he slid from his stool, ducking his head in obsequious acknowledgement, and handed a key to the boy.

"Ain't no cause to keep the gemmen waiting, Chaffey. Look slippy and find the gemmen's box and fetch it here."

The boy took the key and opened a drawer on the far side of the counter. From it, he produced two heavy iron keys on separate rings, then locked the drawer with the original key and returned it to the clerk. The clerk looked at the twin keys on their separate rings, as though he had never seen them before. With great deliberation, he scratched two entries in the ledger with his quill and offered each to the boy for his signature.

"I could take them keys for the postal packets too," said the boy thoughtfully, nodding at the drawer.

The clerk looked at Dacre, as though for sympathy.

"You get the gemmen's box first, my son," he said to the boy, "unless you want a leathering."

Dacre, having affected extreme annoyance at this elaborate pantomime, waited while a constable was fetched as escort and then followed the policeman and the boy through the maze of apparently abandoned luggage which stretched the length of the Harbour Pier. Beyond the wooden trough, down which trunks and boxes were shot on to the steamer's deck, heavy wagons were loading to capacity from the miniature mountain of coal deposited by the colliers at high tide. Overhead, several horses in canvas slings, and two travelling carriages with gold crests on their doors were being swung aboard the *Lord Warden*. Then, near the harbour steps, down which the mail was carried to the paddle-box opening, Dacre saw a white rectangular shape.

A professional in all things, Dacre took his pleasures coldly, yet the very sight of the iron safe made his heart beat rapidly and violently in his throat, so that for a moment it almost stopped his breath. As the finest rider of the Cottesmore or the Quorn might feel on facing a murderous double jump of thirty or forty feet, so Verney Dacre felt at the sight of the bullion safe. It might destroy him, but if any man alive could beat it, he was the one. It had been heralded by John Chubb himself as the locksmith's masterpiece and the cracksman's despair.

It seemed the most beautiful and the most sinister artefact in the whole world. Within its iron walls, on certain nights, there lay more gold than in any other safe outside the Bank of England. It stood about two feet square and three feet high, painted white with a black rim at the top and bottom. On the side, in a prosaic inscription, was the black-lettered identification.

S.E. RLY.
LONDON
TO
FOLKESTONE

The two locks were set immediately under the upper rim, so that when they were released the entire lid of the safe opened backwards on a safety chain. Three uniformed constables in their long coats and tall hats stood guard over it, accompanied by the inspector of railway police in plain clothes and the top-hatted superintendent of traffic at the Harbour Pier.

Dacre stood well back in the shadows. He did not need to inspect the double lock in order to discover the dangers that lay in wait. He knew that the old game of holding a light to the keyhole and angling a reflector to survey the position of the tumblers would never work here. If they bothered to fit a lock to this, it was one with a metal barrel and curtain, so that the tumblers were proof against all inspection. Dacre knew a way of dealing with metal barrels and curtains but it would hardly do on this occasion. What was worse, the steel curtain inside the lock made it impossible to use more than one pick effectively at a time in the confined space. With such a lock as this, a man might just as soon not bother unless he could use one pick to move the bolt while another loosened the tumblers. Even then, this was a lock that had been fitted with the latest detectors, as sensitive as a hair-trigger on a duelling pistol. A fraction too much pressure on any tumbler and the spring of the lock leapt across, jamming the mechanism and setting off a clockwork alarm. The delicacy of touch required to move these tumblers, even if a man could get at them, was such as to make the touch of Paganini or the Abbé Liszt as crude as a blacksmith's fist by comparison. Yes, thought Dacre, they must really believe it to be the cracksman's despair. It would have been enough, under the circumstances, simply to make the gold vanish, as if at the touch of a magician's wand. To leave the police bewildered and the press goggling. But Verney Dacre had sworn to do something more than that. In a hundred years' time his theft should be thought a greater work of art than Chubb's masterpiece, a public performance of such virtuosity that even Paganini, the devil's fiddler, had never matched its skill.

He watched the keys turned by the superintendent of traffic and the inspector of police. Then, when the handle was turned and the lid opened, he saw that there was a second thickness of iron on the underside of the lid, shaped to block any attempt to drive wooden or iron wedges between the door and the frame of the safe. The same mind that had protected it against subtlety had made it proof against force as well.

The superintendent of traffic shone his bull's-eye into the cavernous iron safe and lifted out a small package the size and shape of a cigar box. He handed both the package and Dacre's receipt to the inspector of railway police, who signed the receipt as witness. The two men locked the safe again, handed the keys to the boy and the package and receipt to the escorting constable. Then, with the policeman leading the way and Dacre bringing up the rear, the little procession marched back down the planking of the Harbour Pier towards the railway office.

Inside the office, as the boy offered the receipt for his signature, Dacre called to the clerk.

"Have the goodness to open the box for me first, will you! I don't feel called upon to put my name to something I haven't seen. And I can hardly open it myself with one arm bound up like this."

The clerk bobbed his head and took the tiny key, which Dacre laid on the counter. Then, under the gaze of the boy and the constable, he unlocked the little box and eased back the lid to display thirty neat pillars of gold sovereigns in paper tubes. There was an intent silence. Dacre was prepared to bet that for all their dealings with the safe and its bullion boxes they had never seen so much gold in their lives before. Each of them looked on more money than he might hope to earn in the whole of the next ten years.

"Very well," said Dacre softly, "you may close it again."

He signed the receipt clumsily with his left hand. Then, refusing all offers of help, he managed to hold both the little box and his stick in one set of fingers. He stepped past the door, which the wondering clerk held open for him, and smiled in the darkness. Best of all, he thought, the constable who acted as escort for the keys had seen the gold coins and the Union Bank receipt. Whoever should subsequently be suspected of the bullion robbery, it would certainly not be a well-dressed cavalry subaltern with a carriage and pair, a handsome young woman, and a ready supply of money from a bank in Pall Mall. What need had such a man to rob anyone? As the liberal-minded readers of the *Morning Chronicle* and the landed supporters of the *Morning Post* knew equally well, criminals were the poor who robbed the rich. "The poor who fought back," someone had called them. A railway constable and a traffic clerk were unlikely to notice the slight flush of exultation that betrayed the rising excitement in Dacre's breast. By the time that he reached the carriage, his heart was almost bursting with jubilation.

"By George, old girl, it's a real starter," he murmured to Jolie. She looked vacantly at him, since he had thought it best to keep all details of the scheme from her. However, in his temporary good humour he so far forgot himself as to give her a playful pat on the face.

9

Above tne long bar of the Hope and Anchor, the tubs of spirits were scorched by the flaring gas brackets, the gilt of their hoops and lettering blistered by the heat. Blond-whiskered subalterns of the Royal Horse Artillery, in camp on Dover's Western Heights, shouldered their way in the crowd against tradesmen's apprentices and coach boys. There was an impatient and frustrated surging towards the up-stairs parlour, where the "Grand Sporting Trial" was to be held. Men with small albino-white bulldogs under their arms, and others who nursed Skye terriers curled like balls of hair, elbowed their way forward with expressions of business-like priority. Around the feet of the crowd, the little brown

English terriers strained at their leather collars, as if tried beyond endurance by the faint, sour smells from the room above. Well apart from the general scrimmage, a great white bulldog with a head as round and smooth as a clenched boxing-glove slept and snorted on an old hall chair in total indifference.

The aproned proprietor of the Hope and Anchor bawled himself red in the face above the shouted conversations of the fanciers.

"Orders upstairs, gemmen, if you please. Leave the bar clear, gents, if you please."

Verney Dacre, tall and sharp, settled his steep silk hat more firmly on his head and folded his white gloves into his left hand. Fortified by brown sherry and game pie, he surveyed the heads of the crowd with eyes devoid of anxiety or self-consciousness. There was no sign of Ned Roper or Ellen.

"I'll be shot if I can see our friends, old girl," he said, as though hardly bothering to address the words to Jolie. "I shall be in the very deuce of a way with 'em if they ain't shown up."

Her almond eyes flickered in brief understanding, and then she pressed her slender, straight-boned young figure closer to his coat-tails as he pushed his way through the slow-moving press of men. At the foot of the stairs, he dropped their shillings into the hand of the boy stationed there to take the money. Then, as he began to climb, he reached behind him and took the girl's hand, so that she was literally in tow.

The dingy yellow paper of the upstairs room was hung with discoloured prints of prize fighters from Corinthian Tom to Bendigo, and every hero of the turf from Eclipse to Running Rein. Several heads of dogs, grotesquely distorted by the taxidermist's art, were mounted in square glass boxes above the fireplace. But the great attraction was in the centre of the room, where the first spectators were pressing against the waist-high wooden walls of a white-painted oval arena. This was the pit, about six feet in length and garishly lit by a

88

branched gas-lamp, which hissed and sputtered in a harsh brilliance immediately above it.

"You don't see them?" said Dacre peevishly, half turning to the girl.

"See them?" she whined irritably. "You might as soon see your grandmother!"

They could hardly hear one another for the squalling and barking of the dogs. The fierce heat of the gas in the shuttered room intensified the sweet scent of hot gin, and the earthy vapour of the sewer which rose from the wooden pit. At Dacre's elbow, a butcher's boy was forcing a peppermint rinse into the mouth of a reluctant puppy to prevent infection if the animal should be bitten on the lips or gums.

Then Dacre saw Ned Roper standing in earnest conversation with Ellen on the far side of the pit. At that moment Roper looked up and stared straight at him without giving the least sign of recognition. Dacre brushed perspiration from his forehead with the edge of his hand and moved cautiously through the crowd, approaching Roper from the back. He was not ten feet away, when Roper swung round suddenly, with the smile of a ferret, and spoke in a loud and swaggering greeting. His words were not addressed to Verney Dacre but to a shorter, fatter man whose shoulder was so close that Dacre could have touched him, but who had appeared to be positioned so that Ned Roper would not have seen him.

"Why, Mr Verity!" said Roper with his sharp neat smile, "you a ratting man? My dear Mr Verity!"

Verney Dacre knew that on the brink of disaster sudden stillness can be as dangerous as sudden movement. He moved with casual ease, turning so that his body was positioned between the plump, dark-haired man and Jolie. Only much later did he feel the cold shock of realising how, by never having seen Verity before, he would have betrayed himself but for Roper's well-timed outburst. For the moment, he fixed his eyes on Jolie and nodded at the doorway, willing her not to raise her voice in a shrill, familiar whine. With his hands on her shoulders, he drove her roughly before him, against the pressure of the crowd coming up the stairs. At the bottom of the flight she turned to face him, a faint flush under the gold tan of her cheeks at being handled in this manner.

"What's this bloody game?"

"It's no game, my girl," said Dacre softly, "there's a screw loose. Ned Roper's got that bastard Verity with him. If Verity sees you with me, then he knows the score and the whole scheme is no bono."

"You been hit a bit heavy, ain't you?" she said with pert satisfaction. "That fool Verity got one over on you!"

Verney Dacre denied himself the inexpressible luxury of feeling the back of his hand smacking her lips against her teeth.

"You stupid little whore," he said softly, "it's your face and Roper's they know at the police office, not mine. Go back to the cab and wait until I come."

"I ain't come here for that," she wailed, "not to sit all night in the cab."

"Then by God you'll sit in a lock-up until they take you before the justices," said Dacre, "you poor fool! It's your neck that's got a rope round it for McCaffery."

She was lost, the fine-boned mask of her oriental beauty stunned with dismay. Behind her, the proprietor of the Hope and Anchor was bawling up the stairway.

"Put up the shutters and light up the pit!"

"Wait in the cab!" said Dacre savagely, and the girl scuttled away like a frightened mouse.

In the upstairs parlour, the "Captain" had taken his chair and the first swarm of dark brown sewer rats slithered from the upturned wire cages into the arena, like a shoal of leaves tipped from a bag. With wet noses twitching, the creatures settled down to wash themselves, pausing from time to time to sniff at their unfamiliar surroundings. Roper, his hat tilted knowingly and his thumbs hooked in his lapels, acted with all the self-confidence of an *habitué* of the place.

"Now, Cap'an," he shouted to the man in the raised chair, "when is this 'ere match a-coming off?"

"Be easy, gentlemen," said the frock-coated umpire, "the boy's on the stairs with the dog."

A butcher's lad pushed his way round the pit, holding a bull terrier in his arms. The animal wrestled against his grip, maddened by the scent of rats in the arena.

"Lay 'old a little closer up to the 'ead," said a stout, florid woman, "else 'e'll turn and nip yer." She and her shopman stood with several other couples on two or three table-tops for a better view of the killing.

Verney Dacre moved slowly towards Ellen's back, past the troopers of the Horse Artillery in their unbuttoned tunics, and the barrack prostitutes whispering their familiar terms of business to a pair of pock-marked tradesmen's apprentices. He positioned himself where he might view Sergeant Verity, whom Ellen confronted like a familiar acquaintance.

"Me 'n Roper goes a lot to the Queen's Head in the Haymarket," she remarked confidentially. "It's the house as Jemmy Shaw keeps. He has some prime dogs there! Oh, my eye, ain't they handsome, though! Gentlemen meets there to show off their dogs. You mean to say you never been?"

"No, miss," said Verity in an ominous tone, "never been."

Dacre watched the tall girl admiringly. The pale oval of her face with its wide blue eyes, high cheekbones, straight nose and chin, was marred only by her wilful little mouth. With her blonde hair worn loose to make her appear younger, she looked like a delinquent child with a woman's body. She cooed derisively at the perspiring and scarlet-cheeked sergeant.

"Oh! You should go to Jemmy Shaw's Mr Verity! Shouldn't he, Roper? I mean, Mr Verity being so interested in dogs and ratting."

Roper half turned from the wooden pit, the quick ferret-smile flickering again under pale ginger moustaches.

"I fancy Sergeant Verity knows the Haymarket quite as well as you, Miss Ellen. Why, I expect he's had one or two scrapes that way as he never expected."

Ellen smoothed her dress with one hand and then began to

stroke her long fair hair, as though this self-caressing gave her physical satisfaction.

"I don't think Mr Verity was quite himself that night," she said softly. "Why, he even wanted to send me to Mr Miles's house of sorrow.

Verity regarded the pair of them, goggle-eyed. His cheeks were flushed the colour of ripe plums, and his jowls trembled with the outrage of it all.

"Be damned to you Roper," he said, barking out the words as though they might otherwise choke him. "Be damned to you for a brawling, boasting, ill-conditioned little reptile!"

"Save it all," said Roper coldly, turning to watch the ratting again. "Take your licking and don't squeal. You ain't the first jack that's been taught a trick, nor you won't be the last!"

Sergeant Verity's blunt, heavy head with its black hair plastered flat over the scalp for neatness, thrust itself forward in the manner of a game cock. Dacre thought at first that he was about to hit Roper with his clenched fist, but when Verity spoke he seemed to have regained his restraint a little.

"The treadmill in the house of correction ain't called a cockchafer without reason, Ned Roper. The way it makes a man run, he gets the skin took off his privates the first day. And it don't grow there again while the turnkeys have charge of him. And once you're put away there, crows shall sing like Jenny Lind before you see the light of day again! You'll have little enough left to pleasure your whore with after that."

Ellen elbowed her way between them and turned her blue eyes, in their doll-like innocence, on Verity.

"Don't be such a rummy cove," she said reprovingly, "Roper ain't done you no harm."

"Cross me, miss," whispered Verity, "and you have a reckoning to pay."

"But me 'n Roper's pleased to see you any time at Jem Shaw's," she said, taunting him with her eyes still, and nudging her hips towards him.

"Catching rats being a partiality of ours," added Roper, with no attempt to veil the insult in ambiguity. He turned his back disdainfully and made for the door.

"Roper!" bellowed Verity, lunging after him with all the sounds of a goaded drayhorse. "Roper!"

" 'Ere!" squealed Ellen, "don't go, Mr Verity! Ain't you partial to a serving of greens then, when you sniffed a girl's tail all the way down from town?" Then she laughed until a coughing fit seized her.

Verney Dacre had grudgingly to acknowledge to himself that Roper and his doxy had driven Verity almost hysterical with pent-up rage. As the black-suited sergeant lumbered towards the stairs, like an ill-tempered Pickwick in pursuit of his quarry, Dacre lodged his elbows on the rim of the pit, next to Ellen. A few feet away, an obese and snorting bull-terrier was lowered struggling into the arena. The rats huddled together against the wooden wall, while derisive shouts from the spectators greeted the overweight dog.

"Why don't you feed you dog, then? Bleeding shame to let the poor, suffering beast fade away!"

Ellen turned aside to Dacre, her forearm laid along the pit's rim.

"You seen Verity? Bugger followed us every inch from London Bridge. Ned Roper's getting windy."

"No one but Verity?"

"Not that we saw."

Dacre brushed his moustaches softly with the back of his hand.

"Then it's personal," he murmured, "not police duty. He's going to see you broken for pure love of the thing."

"We flushed him out, though," she said, letting her tongue peep confidentially between her lips, "didn't we?"

"Where's Ned Roper gone?"

"He's taking our friend round the town. We bet he'd follow Roper and not me."

Dacre looked carefully round the room.

"Then here's the news for Roper," he said: "the railway office at Folkestone Harbour pier. The night after tomorrow at eight. There's another message for Cazamian. When he sees the boy from the luggage office walking down to the steamer with a policeman he's to go to the clerk in the office and query a bill of lading. It don't signify what, but he must make the clerk walk as far down as the train while the boy's away at the steamer."

"What if the boy ain't got occasion to go to the steamer?"

"He will," said Dacre, looking down at his hat brim as he polished it on his sleeve. "And tell Ned Roper to come tooled up."

There was a rising murmur of excitement as the terrier worried its twentieth rat. The chairman kept the time, holding out his watch at arm's length and looking at it as though it might explode. Still jerking spasmodically, the rat lay with its neck broken. Dacre ignored the girl, turning from her and giving his full attention to the sport as he joined in the cries of the terrier's backers.

"Dead 'un! Drop it! Good dog!"

A boy in high boots stood in the pit, sweeping the dead and dying rats into a central pile with a long broom. Then the dog seized another furry neck and smashed the creature against the wooden wall, leaving a strawberry blotch on the white paint. A spot of blood flicked upwards and landed in a crimson star on Ellen's white cuff. She gave a squeal of disgust and anger, while Dacre drew back, carefully disengaging himself from the incident. It was a portly tradesman, several inches shorter than Ellen herself, who edged forward with a quick tip of his hat as he offered her his cambric handkerchief.

"Can't have a little lady being upset," he said hopefully, as his arm went round her in a proprietorial manner. When this was not resisted, his hand sloped downwards a little across her hip, as though to satisfy him that such shape required no artificial moulding.

Verney Dacre walked casually to the door. Just before he reached it, Ned Roper, still immaculate in his fawn-coloured suit and blue stock, strolled in from the stairway. He looked the very pattern of a successful master of the *rouge-et-noir* tent on a large racecourse. He passed Dacre without a glance. At the top of the stairs, Dacre paused for a moment to view the bulky figure of Sergeant Verity, who gasped as if his heart must burst as he almost threw himself up the last few steps in order to keep Ned Roper in his sight.

Then Verney Dacre pulled on his gloves. He recognised in Verity the stubborn qualities of the men who had endured the savage winter of the Crimea and beaten the Russians into the bargain. He also sensed the stupidity that went with uncomplaining obedience. Verity was not astute, and that was no doubt a failing. But he was brave, loyal, and determined in a predictably plodding manner. Dacre smiled to himself as he thought how the very qualities on which the sergeant doubtless prided himself should be made the means of his destruction. Indeed, as he went down the stairs it occurred to him that for all their antagonism, Verity and Roper matched one another's mediocre abilities.

Outside in the cab, Jolie sat silent and a little frightened beside him, while Dacre thought of what was going to happen to Sergeant Verity. It was no longer the luxury of revenge; Verity had unwittingly made himself part of Verney Dacre's scheme.

In the day-room of their hotel suite, Dacre rang for brandy and hot water. He sat well back in a Coburg chair, his long legs crossed and his feet resting on the sofa-table. Even in June, the fire was lit, glowing and fading alternately in the draught from the chimney. He lit a spill at the grate and set it to his cigar. The light glinted in Jolie's dark, vigilant eyes as she sat in a nursing chair and stitched at a button. In the Pavilion gardens, the band of the 9th Lancers was playing "The Bird in Yonder Cage Confined" for the entertainment of the summer evening crowds. Dacre smoked with his eyelids half lowered, as though thinking.

"Why shouldn't we go out to the band?" said the girl, apparently resuming an earlier argument. "Where's the harm?"

Dacre half-turned his head to her, across his shoulder.

"I don't see the necessity." Then he turned full round. "Oblige me by goin' into your room and taking off your things for me. It's absurd to sit indoors in your cloak, when you ain't goin' out."

"Why take them off?" she asked, with the faintest tremor in her voice.

"Because I should like to see you without them."

In the eastern stillness of her beauty only her eyes betrayed hostility.

"Oh, should you?" she said, looking down at her needle, but not working it. "And what if I shouldn't like to show myself to you?"

"Pardon me, miss," said Dacre, swinging round from his chair, "but when a girl's paid for, her liking don't come into it. It ain't inconvenient to me to pay for what I take."

She raised her forehead a little, but not enough to meet his gaze.

"I'm not bought!" she said fiercely.

"That may be," he said with a yawn, "but y' may be driven, for all that. I take no pleasure in knockin' a young woman about, but if it should come to that, you'll have cause to remember it."

She stood up and went into the other room, her face a diminutive reflection of the classic pride of the sphinx. Verney Dacre gave her a moment, yawned again, and set the bedroom door wide open. Jolie stood with her back to him, staring into the reflection of her own eyes in the mahogany-framed mirror of the dressing-table. Neither of them spoke. Then Dacre began to draw off his belt and the girl bowed her head a little, as though acknowledging defeat.

"You couldn't name the favour that can't be had for money!" she said bitterly, and untied the blue cloak at her neck to lay it on the dark mirror-gloss of the polished wood beside her gloves. Dacre felt an exultation greater than any lechery as she dropped her head forward, loosened the fastenings at her waist, and rapidly shed the turquoise skirt and underskirts like successive layers of skin. Without a word or a glance at him, she unbuttoned the tight-waisted jacket and dropped it carelessly on the other clothes.

Despite his first reluctance to use her as a mistress, Dacre felt a natural eagerness at the sight of her slim strong back, the pale gold of her skin, and the black gloss of her hair as it brushed loose against her bare shoulders. The whiteness of her tight bodice and pants seemed to make her thighs and arms glow a warmer tan by contrast. With her hands inverted behind her, she unlaced the bodice, and then stooped to unhook the buttons of her boots. Dacre ran his fingers across her brown, lightly muscular shoulders, as if testing the smoothness of the cool skin. His other hand moulded her hips, feeling the warmth of her body through her white cotton drawers. She pulled herself away at once and shed the knickers quickly, as if determined to give him no extra pretext for handling her.

At last she stood with her back to him, entirely naked as she faced the mirror with her slender arms crossed over her small tight breasts. Dacre surveyed the girl's trim calves and firm thighs, the curve of her narrow back, the slight heaviness of her whitey-brown buttocks. He lifted up the glossy black hair from her neck, touching the dainty nape with his lips and kissing the neat whorls of her ears. In the glass he saw the cat-like beauty of her eyes suffused with silent hostility. That was nothing to him, since his actions were dictated by his own pleasure, not hers. However, he held her gaze in the mirror and moved his hand down slowly, brushing the velveteen lustre of pale copper skin in the small of her back. Then the smooth ovals of her bottom came under his hand, his fingers slipping between the cheeks, probing the intense and intimate heat of her body. Finally, between her warm thighs, he touched the most sensitive spot of all. She checked the involuntary shudder that ran through her by tensing the muscles of her legs and thighs.

Dacre fingered her skilfully until, despite herself, the girl began instinctively to hold her breath as the tension of pleasure increased, which obliged her to release it in a long sigh. Her muscles started to relax, her thighs softened and yielded more easily. She turned her face from Dacre's gaze and dropped her head a little, so that he should not see her expression in the mirror. With his free hand he took her dark, soft mane, and firmly pulled her head back again, watching with calm satisfaction as her eyes turned this way and that, while her teeth tightened on her lower lip. In a few minutes more she ceased to resist him. Supporting herself with her hands on the dressing-table, she bent more fully to his caresses, her eyes closed, her teeth set, and the warm smoothness of her legs squirming restlessly against his hand. Then Dacre drew back from her.

"Arrange yourself on the bed," he said quietly.

She obeyed, without looking at him, walking neatly with her hips held in check like some demure temple-maiden of the Nile. Dacre shrugged off his clothes and approached her, erect. She watched with the frank curiosity of a girl examining her lover for the first time. As soon as he was crouched over her, she adjusted her body to him, so that he entered her with ease. Her raised legs crossed lightly over his back, her hands clenched into fists and bent upwards against the pillow. Quickly but erratically, her heavy-lidded eyes scanned his face, though she still struggled to preserve her silence. Dacre moved rapidly, intent on taking his pleasure with the least delay. Had it only been Ellen Jacoby, he might have prolonged it more fastidiously. Throughout his labours, Jolie kept her hands clenched and her face turned aside on the pillow. As she felt his movements quicken, she turned to watch him with the contemptuous curiosity of a street-girl. He tried to kiss her, and she stuck her tongue out defensively, as though it were a childhood trick to ward off the coster boys' kisses. But then she lifted her head, wound her arms round his neck, and touched him with the flickering of her tongue. It was not done passionately, nor out of love for Verney Dacre, but in a manner which suggested that she might have been taught it by another girl as a well-rewarded trick of the trade. Then her body quivered, her heels beat impatiently on the small of his back, and in that moment the tension of Dacre's own pleasure burst at last.

Lying beside her in the warm room, he was disagreeably aware that the girl's thoughts had been elsewhere, and that such excitement as she enjoyed was by memorising the love-making of some absent partner. Though he knew it to be the common practice of her kind, it was not to be borne without a reprimand. As if to confirm his misgivings, she said sharply,

"You ain't going to forget, I hope, that such favours have a price?"

Dacre laughed.

"Fetch me the purse that's on the dressin' table."

She was on her feet in an instant, half running to bring him the little wash-leather pouch with its heavy metallic weight. He took out a sovereign, and the girl's eyes followed it, unblinking and expressionless. He crooked his forefinger round the little coin and threw it hard against the furthest wall. It spun and rang against the plaster and on the floor, running away under the washstand of grey marble and inset basin. She flew naked after the tiny gold disc, as it glinted in gaslight and shadow, her movements suggesting the alertness of a puppy fetching sticks. But before she could find the first coin, Dacre threw a second one in the opposite direction, so that she twisted round and temporarily abandoned her search for the first. In her eagerness to lay hold of this second golden prize, she threw herself into every variety of out-landish posture, her head twisted against the carpet as she squinted under tallboy or chiffonier, her haunches absurdly elevated and spread to show a dark straggle of hair between her thighs.

Dacre gave a short, barking laugh of derision. Looking at her, as she crouched on the floor waiting for the next coin to be thrown, it seemed to him that she now knew who her master was. Pulling himself up a little, he took a half-sovereign and lobbed it expertly, so that it fell into the con-cave bowl of the gasolier.

"There's a half Victoria up there," he said with another snort of laughter, "supposing you can get it out before it melts."

She wriggled up the tall brass corner-post at the foot of the bed, "like a monkey up a stick," as Roper had phrased it, reaching perilously close to the white gas mantles and giving a sharp squeal when she once burnt her fingers. Watching the light made Dacre's eyes water badly, so he looked aside at the reflection of her coppery nakedness, as she perched with knees tightly locked round the brass pole.

"You'll do well to remember," he said in his most precise manner, "that goold has to be earned. When a woman is awkward in giving her favours, I can be deucedly tiresome in paying the account."

With that, he took a button from the purse and tossed it to the far end of the room. She could not see it from her perch, though she heard it land.

"And that's the last you'll get," he added, wearying of the sport. He gathered up his clothes and went into the day-room, locking the door of the bedroom to keep her in. When he had dressed again, he rang for more hot water, added it to his brandy, and lit another cigar. Later on, when he went to his own room for the night, he could still hear the girl scrabbling determinedly for the final, non-existent coin. As he closed his eyes, Verney Dacre smiled.

"Why," he said softly but audibly, "the last part, of itself, was worth two and a half sovs of any fellow's money."

Stringfellow stood with his back to the horse and cab, which he had brought round from the mews so that the animal might have its nosebag outside the house.

"Dover?" he said incredulously. "On your own hook?"

"Own hook," said Verity solemnly. "And there's no denying the consequence. I went in for the running and got distanced."

"Superior numbers," Stringfellow shook his head. "What's a man to do against superior numbers, Verity? 'oo was they?"

Sternly, Verity avoided the injudicious question.

"You want to keep the leavings from the last nosebag," he said, with a nod at the horse's bony flanks. "Always scatter them on top of the next feed. Somehow, it gets a 'orse eating. We learnt that in camp before Sebastopol. That creature of yours hardly eats enough to keep the parish cat alive."

Stringfellow hoisted himself to the seat of the hansom with his hands and his one good leg. He set his hat right and looked at Verity with gruff disapproval.

"If it was on your own hook, and not for Mr Croaker, you might as well tell a friend," he said, delivering the words as a statement rather than a request.

"It was Roper," said Verity, "and his dollymop."

"Was it?" said Stringfellow thoughtfully. "And what did they do at Dover, this Roper and his woman?"

"Went ratting at the Hope and Anchor," said Verity with irritation.

Stringfellow shook his head, as though Verity should have known better than to offer such an explanation.

"Now you ain't trying to persuade me, Mr Verity, that you went to Dover last night and come back here at six in the morning, all to watch a magsman and his whore catching rats?"

Even in the cool early sunlight, Verity's cheeks glowed the colour of port wine.

"It ain't that," he said: "there's something afoot, and Dover's the place for it."

"I don't see what you can do at Dover as you mayn't do better in London," said Stringfellow doubtfully, "except catch fish and smuggle contraband. Did they look like they was going smuggling?"

"They watched the dogs killing rats," said Verity. He kicked at the ground with the toe of his boot. "I never lost Roper for a blind second. I only missed the girl for two minutes, when he went out of the room to ease nature and I followed him. Even then she couldn't have got out past the door without me seeing her."

"Ah," said Stringfellow, shaking a finger, "they split! Superior numbers, Verity. That was how they had you before. One man can't follow two, however much he may want to."

"I'd follow those two to 'ell and back to see Roper quodded," said Verity with a melodramatic tremor.

"Whereas," Stringfellow persisted, "if I'd been there, splitting wouldn't have helped them. And they wouldn't have twigged me, a-cos they don't know my phiz from the Princess Royal's."

"It ain't exactly work for you," said Verity in a huff.

"Ain't it, though?" said Stringfellow indignantly. "Miss Bella may be good enough to cook, and sew, and nurse, but that's as far as the joint stock company's a-going, eh?"

"No," said Verity wearily, "that's all gammon, as you well know, Stringfellow."

"Then we'll try it together."

Verity looked up with some anxiety.

"Try what?" he inquired.

Stringfellow leant down and patted the bay horse, which responded by lifting its tail and depositing a dozen rounds of dung on the roadway.

"Bella!" roared Stringfellow. "Brush and shovel! Sharp's the word and quick's the motion!"

The girl hurried out of the doorway, swept up the droppings, and scuttled indoors again.

"Let that dry and the air's thick with the dust of it by suppertime," said Stringfellow ruefully. "But seeing as you spent half the night in Dover, travelled by a train at some unholy hour . . . "

"Ferry train," said Verity gruffly, "a very decent sort of train."

" . . . and then walked from London Bridge to Paddington Green at daybreak, I'm a-going to make an exception for you. Today you goes to Whitehall Police Office in the 'ansom."

Verity puffed and grumbled.

"Not a word more," said Stringfellow steadily.

At the Cumberland Arch, he looked down through the little hatch on to his plump passenger.

"Care killed a cat, Mr Verity."

"No doubt," said Verity, and they rumbled without speaking past the houses and gardens of Oxford Street. At Regent Circus, Stringfellow lifted the hatch again.

"I don't suppose," he said half-diffidently, "it ain't possible, I suppose, that this Roper and his blowen went to Dover just to do what you saw them do?"

"What's that?" asked Verity with suspicion.

"Catch rats," said Stringfellow hopefully, flicking the horse.

"No," said Verity in his sourest manner, "it ain't possible."

Stringfellow shrugged, and the elderly horse ambled the rest of the way to Whitehall Place without another word being spoken by either man.

10

The blonde hair that normally hung loose to her shoulders was now put up in an elegant coiffure. Ellen Jacoby was in mourning. Her boldly flared dress and its cape were of black satin, heavily trimmed with crape. Yet with her coquettish little parasol, in black with a white silk lining, and the sweet trail of perfume diffused by the heat of her young body in the warm vestibule, she displayed a perversely intriguing combination of the costume of death veiling an animal eroticism. As she held up her skirts a little, to climb the grand staircase in the wake of the footman, she offered a furtive glimpse of ankle and calf in the patterned silk of black stockings. But the gesture betrayed her. A born lady would have sailed confidently up the broad stairs, not clutching at her skirts like a housemaid.

It seemed that the gaze of every man and woman in the vestibule of the Grand Pavilion Hotel was drawn by the tall girl in her narrow-waisted funeral dress, her broad hips swelling more fully as she laboured in her climb. Even the long veil, anchored by the back bonnet with its silk bands, marked her out as a young woman of intrigue rather than a cast-off widow. It was just as Verney Dacre intended. The witnesses, if they were ever asked, would remember his charming visitor as a tall girl in fashionable mourning. Whether she was Ellen Jacoby, or Laura Bell, or the Princess Louise, they would have no idea.

The men, in their black or bottle-green evening coats, glanced wistfully upwards at her retreating shape, and then continued their slow promenade towards the public dining-room. At the first landing, with its Indian carpets in burnt red and its palms in fat-bellied bronze jars, Ellen paused. The bewigged footman tapped at the door of Dacre's rooms and murmured an inquiry. Then the girl was admitted and the flunkey withdrew. As soon as it was safe, she lifted off her bonnet and veil, still breathless from the stairs.

"Roper's on the Parade, by the bandstand. 'e's tooled up and ready. 'e said to tell you that."

Silently, Verney Dacre put out a bony hand and touched her face with the back of it. There was no affection in the gesture, he merely wished to feel her skin, in case there should never be another time. Ellen smiled awkwardly, and rubbed her cheek against his knuckles like a kitten. She was Roper's girl, but where was the harm in obliging the young soldier who was going to make them all rich? So, at least, Ned Roper had hinted.

"What's tonight's game, then?" she asked softly, though not as if she expected to be told.

Dacre almost snorted with derisive laughter.

"It won't be *vingt-et-un* at sixpence a dozen, my girl, you may be sure of that much."

She drew back from his touch. Dacre swung round, looking from her to Jolie, who sat in an elbow chair by the fire, which was lit despite the heat, watching the play of hot coals between the bars of the grate, as though absorbed in some secret drama that was being acted out there.

"And I want it understood," resumed Dacre, fastening his cape and adjusting his hat, "that neither of you is to leave these rooms, nor ring for the servants, until Ned Roper or I shall come back."

He picked up his white kid gloves in one hand and a small sealed package in the other, addressed to the Crédit Étranger in the Rue Royale, Paris. Then he gave a final glance at the two girls, who seemed anxious to look anywhere but at him, and went out. Once on the landing, however, he turned a key softly in the lock of the door. With Jolie's continual fidgeting to show off her new clothes, and with Ellen whimpering like a filly for a stallion, it seemed wise to him to take such a precaution.

The Marine Parade lay in a forlorn and sunless gloaming. Unkempt horses were rattling the last of the bathing machines over the shingle and away from the glimmer of the flooding tide. Ned Roper saw Dacre coming and took the lead, easily recognisable in his brown sportsman's suit and tall, pale grey hat. Dacre walked carefully a dozen paces or so behind him. At the approach to the Harbour Pier, Roper dropped back, and when the two men drew level, he emitted a loud, barking belch.

"Ease afore convenience," he remarked unapologetically.

Dacre's thin dry lips twisted briefly with anger. Though he had the taste of East Indian sherry on his own tongue, always preferring a warm belly for a job like this, it was clear that Roper had been drinking steadily for most of the day.

"I'll be fucking smothered if our ferry train ain't in already," said Roper foolishly.

"It's of no consequence," said Dacre, not trusting himself to look at his companion. "Follow me at a distance, and do exactly as I order, unless you want to ride back to London between a pair of private clothes constables."

Ned Roper seemed to steady himself a little. Dacre, striding ahead down the platform, recalled with dismay that he had once thought of letting Roper play the part of cracksman on this preliminary job. He opened the door of the luggage office, leaving Roper to wait in the shadows. The same traffic clerk and the same boy were on duty behind the broad wooden counter. The boy, with pop-eyes and full-blown cheeks, looked at the little parcel in Dacre's hand.

"All them packets is gone down to the steamer, sir," he said earnestly, "you'd have to catch the carriers down there."

Dacre ignored him and turned to the thin, balding clerk.

He held a sovereign between his finger and thumb, the little coin glowing a deeper and richer gold in the light of the oil lamp.

"It's a matter of some importance that this packet should be in Paris tomorrow night," he said languidly. "Oblige me by seein' to it at once."

The clerk's expression hardly altered. Dacre gave him credit for that. A whole sovereign was as much as the man could expect in six months of normal bonuses and gratuities. He entered the details of the packet in his ledger and held the page for Dacre's signature.

"Ain't no bother, sir," he said softly. "She don't sail for more 'n half an hour yet. Chaffey! Down to the post-van with you, and see the gentleman's packet goes in with the mail."

Dacre waited until the boy had gone out before putting the sovereign on the counter.

"That boy'd eat 'isself silly, if he wasn't found something to do," said the clerk self-consciously, pocketing the coin. With the pride of one who was not entirely a menial, he could not quite bring himself to acknowledge the gift directly. Dacre nodded to him and went out, elbowing his way across the platform through the straggling groups of passengers, and the evening strollers with nothing better to do than to watch the Boulogne steamer come in. Among the tall hats and parasols, he watched the *Lord Warden* blowing off gusts of steam from her paddle-boxes. Now it was up to Cazamian and Roper to give him time for the job. Roper stood a few yards from the door of the luggage office. He looked so obviously furtive, with his quick eyes and rodent smile, that Dacre regretted bringing him. Of Cazamian there was no sign. Dacre turned his gaze on the guard's van in the distance; his habit of running the safety chain of his watch between fingers and thumb was the sole betrayal of his nervousness.

At last he saw a cropped, grizzled head, and Cazamian shouldered his way through the crowd towards the luggage office, a sheet of paper in his hand. Within a few minutes he reappeared with the clerk, Cazamian talking insistently and the other man looking puzzled. The clerk locked the office door, tested it, and then they both set off towards the end of the train, their heads bent in argument.

A single railway policeman, easily distinguishable by his stovepipe hat and long, belted tunic, stood about forty feet away. That at least was no problem, and in any case the man was looking in the opposite direction. Dacre reached the door and faced it, his exact movement covered by his cloak. Yet this was the easiest part, so long as his silk hat, his cloak with its deep blue lining, and his clothes immaculately cut by Mr Sporrer of Bond Street, afforded their necessary protection. Even a railway constable might hesitate to challenge a man who looked and acted so obviously like a director of the railway company. Each director, in return for his investment, had the personal power to appoint, promote, and even to dismiss, such individual employees as he chose. The servants of the company were not over-anxious to quarrel with their directors.

From his pocket, Dacre had slid a key, an exact imitation of the one brought him by Cazamian, except that the metal of this one shone bright and raw, where he had filed the last indentations to make a precise copy. But no key that was made "blind," without the chance of testing it on the lock, was ever perfect. The perfection lay in the bony, agile fingers of a man like Dacre. His key entered the door-lock easily enough, but jarred against a tumbler as he tried to turn it. If the lock were found damaged the whole scheme would be ruined. There must be no force. He drew the key back a little and turned slowly, feeling the tumblers move. It scraped lightly against the barrel of the lock, but there was no harm in that. He opened the door, stepped inside, and then carefully locked himself in. A single oil lamp by the clerk's stool still lit the bare wooden room. The windows were uncurtained, but being of frosted glass there was no danger of his being spied on. He opened the little wicket and let himself through to the clerk's side of the counter, setting

eyes for the first time on the cupboard in which the keys of
the bullion safe were kept.

It was built into the counter, close to the clerk's stool, and
its door was of sheet iron. Dacre folded his cloak into a
rough cushion and knelt upon it, taking two small tins from
his pocket and a notecase, which unfolded as a wallet of
slender metal probes. Pulling off his white kid gloves by the
fingertips, he examined the lock, and his heart beat faster
with the knowledge that it was a difficult one, but possible
for Verney Dacre.

It was not a Chubb, but a Bramah. A few years before, at
the Great Exhibition, he had watched with professional
sympathy the humiliation of Mr Hobbs, an honest but
nimble-fingered American locksmith. Hobbs had accepted
a public challenge from Joseph Bramah to open such a lock
before an audience. He had toiled for nineteen hours and
merely succeeded in breaking the lock, which a common
sneak-thief with a drayman's muscles could have done. But
Verney Dacre must succeed where Hobbs had failed, and
must succeed quickly. If he took nineteen minutes, let alone
nineteen hours, he could expect to spend the rest of his life
in a prison settlement.

The Bramah offered him nothing but the tiniest mouth
with an even tinier tongue of metal inside, over which the
key would fit, if he had had a key. And that was all. A solid
curtain of iron masked the rest of the mechanism. Dacre felt
a physical tightening round his throat, the dry pressure of
controlled fear, like a coarse velvet noose. The Bramah used
no tumblers and was proof against any single probe or pick
known to the criminal world. It worked on a simple and
almost perfect principle.

Round the central tongue, which he could see, and lying
paralled to it, were eight iron "sliders." When the lock was
closed, a powerful spring kept them pressed forward towards
its mouth. Each slider had a tiny knob upon it. Within the
cylindrical iron barrel of the lock were eight notches, cut at
varying depths from the mouth. In order to open the
Bramah, the eight sliders had to be pushed back simul-

taneously by varying distances, until each engaged in its secret and individual notch. Once that had happened, the powerful spring was no longer able to force them forwards. The twist of the key would then turn the barrel of the lock, releasing the bolt. It was easily done with a key which had been cut to push each slider back by the required distance. But the movements were calculated within fractions of a millimetre. The cracksman who could not see the inside of the lock (and the iron shield with its tiny keyhole made certain that he should see virtually nothing) might just as well give up the job.

All this and much more went through Verney Dacre's mind, as he wiped his moist palms on his trousers. The heat of the summer day had left the little building intolerably warm under its tin roof, but he felt the exultation that came from the challenge. To enter such a lock and make it move at his command gave him an intensity of pleasure which some of his brother subalterns had claimed to find in the entry and possession of a woman's body.

From the open wallet beside him, he took two slender half-cylinders of metal, each smaller than a hollowed half of the tiniest pencil split lengthwise. Moving cautiously towards the oil-lamp, he held each of them in turn above the flame, twisting them to and fro until they were coated with an oily black carbon from the smoke. There was no time to "smoke" the lock itself, but this was the next best thing. He drew back, mopping the water which started in his pale blue eyes at the heat and smoke of the lamp. Kneeling down again, he slid the first tiny half-cylinder into the hole of the lock, keeping it over the central tongue of metal and away from the wall of the lock barrel. When it would slide in no further, he moved it slowly but firmly into contact with the barrel wall, twisting it gently half an inch or so in either direction, in the motion of a key. Though his eyes were a little blurred once more by the nervous watering which the oil-lamp had started, his white, skeletal hands moved with the smooth sensitivity of a watch-maker's or a surgeon's. Then he withdrew the first half-cylinder and repeated the operation with its twin on the other side of the keyhole. When the two halves were placed together, they formed something like the shaft of a key.

More important, when they had been brought briefly into contact with the barrel of the lock, it had left its markings on the oily carbon with which they were covered. To the unpractised eye, the scrapes and smears were indecipherable, but Verney Dacre read them as though they were plain as italic script. On each of the half-cylinders there were four tiny patches where the black coating had hardly been disturbed. They told him at a glance the position of the eight notches in to which the eight sliders must go.

He took another probe from his wallet, far too thick even to enter the little keyhole, but it was merely the handle of a device, known as a "Hair Trigger" because of the delicacy and practice needed to operate it. Into this handle could be screwed a number of iron needles, adjusted at varying depths. When they were in place, the hair trigger appeared like a rough key whose shaft was split into long, uneven segments. To Dacre, this was the key to all the Bramah locks in existence.

He checked again to ensure that the length of the iron segments corresponded to the varying depths of the marks left by the lock barrel on the carbon-coated probes. Then he eased the makeshift and fragile-looking key over the metal tongue of the lock, sliding it deeper into the barrel, until he felt it touch the metal sliders and the powerful pressure of the spring which held them forward. He pressed the hair trigger forward by no more than another eighth of an inch and gently twisted it sideways, still pressing forward, feeling the contours of the lock as they were transmitted through the pressures on his fingertips. He felt the sliders yield and there was a tiny, well-oiled click as they fell into the notches of the barrel. But for all the pressure he could put on the hair trigger, the barrel of the lock would make only a three-quarter turn, and the iron bolt remained closed.

He took a deep gasp of air, realising that for the last half minute he had been holding his breath in anticipation. He withdrew the hair trigger, leaving the lock in its three-quarters position, and inserted the slenderest of probes. One slider had failed to reach its notch, by a millimetre or less. He coaxed it backwards, the whole pressure of the lock-spring driving the probe like a needle into the palm of his hand. The pain was nothing, what mattered more was that the diminutive probe should not snap under the stress. He held his breath again, angling the instrument to take all the pressure along its central axis. A single bead of blood trickled down the lifeline crease of his palm. But the probe held. He felt the slider give way and then engage the notch on the barrel. When he used the hair trigger again, the barrel of the lock completed its circle, and the bolt was drawn back with a soft thud.

As he swung the iron-plated door open, he saw that a variety of keys hung in the cupboard. Indeed, it struck him as quaint that, after the imposing iron door, the other surfaces of the cupboard were made of wood. However, one did not discover that until the door was open. He recognised the keys of the bullion safe at once. It was a moment's work to open his two tins, each packed with soft, bile-coloured wax which smelt of cobblers' shops, and to press each key twice, keeping their impressions in separate boxes. Some men were happy with one impression of a key, but they were the men who bungled their trade. Dacre knew too well that a key which appears plain enough on one side may be bedevilled by irregularities on the other. When he had finished, he wiped the keys carefully on his silk handkerchief. In a few more weeks, the South Eastern Railway Company, and Scotland Yard, would have cause to examine them with microscopic care. When that happened, there must be no specks of soft wax there. It was such trifles which led to an examination of the cupboard lock, a strict interrogation of the traffic clerk, and a perusal of all those whose names appeared in the clerk's ledger. One of the names was Verney Dacre's, and the clerk would remember him.

As he was putting the keys back, the wooden building vibrated with a heavy blow against the door, which froze

Dacre's movements and made his heart jump to his throat. There was no more. He knew it was Ned Roper's signal that the traffic clerk had started to make his way back from the train. Two such blows meant that the man had reached the end of the platform, and that Dacre must leave then or never. After that, Ned Roper could be counted upon to scamper for the darkest alleys of Shadwell or Wapping, until his accomplice was safely chained aboard a convict hulk, with his head shaved, and a diet of oatmeal to graze and make callous his intestines, so that he might not be a burden on his captors for too long.

Dacre replaced the bullion keys and closed the iron door of the cupboard. When he inserted the hair trigger, the barrel of the lock refused to budge. It was impossible to leave the door unfastened without having to abandon his entire scheme. He took a chance on the same obstinate slider. With a hooked probe, he lifted it clear of its notch and it sprang forward with all the power of the lock behind it, in a blow that might have broken the finger of an inexpert cracksman. Then he tried the hair trigger again and the bolt closed softly. As he was measuring with his probe to ensure that all was as it should be, Roper's heel crashed twice against the door. But Verney Dacre could no more have left his masterpiece at this moment than he could have left a woman's body at the moment of a most intense explosion of pleasure. Let them take him, if necessary, he would not abandon it all now.

When he was satisfied that nothing would be noticed, he folded away his tools, pocketed the tins of wax, gathered up his hat and stick, and then vaulted the counter with his cloak over one arm, fixing it round his neck as he made for the door.

The copy of Cazamian's key jammed in the door-lock, and he remembered as though from a very long time ago that one had to draw it back a little to release the catch. He opened the door a fraction. Roper still hovered a yard away, with every sign of self-conscious guilt upon his puckered face. Twenty yards away, the traffic clerk was approaching slowly, in conversation with a driver in canvas suit and oilskin cap. His head was lowered towards the other man's and he was not looking directly at the door.

"Cut and shuffle, Mr Dacre!" Roper's mouth twisted in a backward whisper, as he almost danced heel over toe in his anxiety to be off.

"Block their view!" said Dacre savagely, before his accomplice could begin to move away.

Ned Roper paused, and then turned reluctantly to face the oncoming men. Dacre slipped out of the door, opening it as little as possible, and locking it under cover of his cloak and the knot of waiting passengers. As he moved away, the traffic clerk saw him, the first sign of recognition kindling in his eyes. It crossed Dacre's mind to inquire after the safety of his package, but he checked himself. That would have been Ned Roper's way of doing things. A gentleman of the Hussars did not attempt to explain his presence to a menial. He turned and strode away towards the glimmer of gaslights that now mapped the shore-line of the Marine Parade. His hat was perched at a slight angle and his malacca cane swung confidently from his gloved hand. Roper followed at a little distance. Verney Dacre could almost have dropped back and shared his good humour with the man. But then, with his brown suit and thin, whiskery smile, the damn fellow did look uncommonly like a rat-catcher gone racing.

Verney Dacre had done it, he told himself, swinging the cane in a wider arc, and had done it almost alone. It had taken a little time and more than a little money, but the two tins in his pocket contained the secret which would enable him to open the South Eastern Railway Company's bullion safe at any time of his choosing. He thought of the Secretary of the Company, Mr Samuel Smiles and his constant harping on thrift, and self-help, and economy. Mr Smiles was about to witness self-help on a scale he had never dreamt of.

Dacre thought with satisfaction of the busy minds in the police office, all of them working unwittingly in his favour. The detective police knew a dishonest mechanic because he could never pass as a gentleman. And they knew a dishonest gentleman because he lacked the practical abilities of a craftsman. But what if a man should be both gentleman and craftsman, and dishonest into the bargain? Might he not conquer the riches of the world? Verney Dacre thought he very probably might.

At the door of the hotel suite, Dacre turned the key soundlessly in the lock. But even as he stood on the open threshold, he sensed something amiss. The day-room was in darkness and there was no sound of the two girls. For a few seconds he half-believed that they might have gone to sell their evidence for the highest price. But Verney Dacre's nerve was not to be shaken easily. They knew too little to be of value, and Jolie at least lived in terror of the noose for her part in McCaffery's death. No, it was nothing worse than he and Roper returning before their time to find that the witless little sluts had gone flirting their way among the sergeants of the 17th Lancers at the band concert. But how had they passed the locked door? As he grew accustomed to the dying twilight, he saw that there was not a cape nor a parasol in the room. Dacre wiped the back of his hand across pale eyes that watered with anger.

He had almost turned and gone straight down again to the Parade Gardens, where Roper waited for Ellen. But he was detained by a sense, in the hot airless room, of the intimate animal warmth of the two young women and the overlying sweetness of perfume. He stepped further over the dark threshold and saw a long triangle of light falling on the carpet from Jolie's partly open door. By moving softly forward, he could see a whole segment of her bedroom reflected in the ornate chiffonier mirror.

The golden-skinned girl lay on her back upon the bed, and though the lower part of her body was hidden from him, her little breasts with their pert upward tilt were quite bare. Ellen Jacoby, her back to the door, stood over her companion. Ellen still wore the patterned black stockings of her mourning costume and the short bodice in black satin, which ended in a crape trimming round the tops of her hips. Even in his anger, Dacre's blood quickened at the sight of her long firm legs, and the brilliant pallor of her smooth flesh from her waist down to her knees. The tightness of the bodice at her waist made the tall girl's hips swell in an apparently fuller, whiter nudity, her broad rear cheeks curving firmly with all the elasticity of her youthful body.

As Dacre watched, Ellen stooped down, her face lowered to her partner's her mouth moving restlessly over the other girl. Jolie's fingers, slender and agile as a milliner's, moved down the white smoothness of Ellen's curved back, starting between the shoulder-blades and following the indentations of the vertebrae. The fingertips played tauntingly at the base of the spine before moving with a brusque insolence between the arched buttocks and towards the blonde girl's legs.

Dacre watched with his anger and desire rising in conflict. Then he turned abruptly and walked from the day-room, down the grand staircase, and out into the lamplight of the Parade Gardens. Roper was standing near the rostrum, where the band of the Lancers played.

"Where's Miss Ellen?" he asked, tucking a toothpick away.

"Where you left her," said Dacre vindictively, "except that you've been cuckolded by that other bitch of yours."

"Cuckolded?" said Roper, straightening up warily. "Cuckolded? By a girl? There ain't such a thing."

"I shan't make it any plainer, Ned Roper."

"You don't 'ave to make it plainer, Mr Dacre. I'm obliged for the hint, all the same."

Dacre, in his narrow fury, turned away and wiped at his eyes once more, which made Roper suppose at first that his companion might be weeping. Then Dacre turned back and said levelly, "As I don't choose to be made a fool of, I leave it to you to see that your blowen gets her desserts."

Later that night, in their weekly lodgings at Dover, Ned Roper watched Ellen strip off the cloak, veil, and bonnet of her widow's weeds. As he moved towards her, he chuckled to see that she had taken the role of bereavement so carefully that even her drawers were black with a crape bow. When he drew her down on the cheap brass bed, it seemed that the cuckolding of which Dacre had spoken had merely given her an extra erotic eagerness. She responded almost violently to Roper's handling. At length he said reproachfully,

"You been letting a woman do man's work with you, Nell."

She turned over on her side, facing him.

"It ain't no harm, Ned," she said softly, "it was only in fun."

"That ain't how Mr Dacre put it."

"No," she said sharply, "he wouldn't. Mr Dacre wants me given a hiding. He'd fancy me himself, I can tell by his looks. But he knows he can't have that, so the next best thing in his book is to get me a broken jaw out of spite."

"May be," said Roper sceptically. "What you do with a girl don't signify. It might be a game, and even if it weren't, a girl ain't got nothing that needs cod-buttons. But cross me with a man, Nell, and I'll break your jaw and 'is."

Then she kissed him and settled her body to his. Her long legs moved with such energy that Ned Roper swore to himself that perhaps it wasn't such a bad thing to have been "cuckolded" by a woman first. But while Roper lay drained of tension and at peace with his companion, Verney Dacre stared at Jolie's vacant bed with a hate that ran like acid in his veins. Now he knew why the girl had been so cold with him, as she might be to all men. The sheet bore the imprint of two bodies upon it, and a black garter lay in one of the folds. He glanced towards the day-room of the apartment, where she awaited judgment, furtive but unrepentant. To put all his schemes in peril by dealing with her as she deserved was out of the question just then. With his hatred pent up in the narrow coffin of his breast, Dacre turned away from the bed. Swift vengeance and hurried sensuality were to the taste of men like Ned Roper. Verney Dacre had taught himself to taste satisfaction fully, and after a proper delay. When the proper moment came, Jolie should pay her debt with interest.

"There ain't nothing in the world," said Roper jovially, "as don't look better when seen through a glass of Coke-upon-Littleton."

He set the steaming pewter before Cazamian, and then sat down at the bare wooden table with another pot of his own. The grime on the tiny window panes of the Green Man was sulphur yellow, so that the far side of Tooley Street, where the great brick arches reared seventy feet upwards to bear London Bridge station and all its metal roads above the chimney pots of Bermondsey, seemed half lost in a fog.

Roper drank, wiped his mouth, and glanced round the little room. Two girls, in shabby cloaks and feathered bonnets, sat at a table with a pair of clerks in tall hats, who had picked them up for a "spree." Along a black oak bench by the open hearth were several foreign seamen from Stanton's timber wharf, beyond Mill Lane and the bonded warehouses.

Cazamian, his face pale and perspiring under the cropped, grizzled hair, had removed his cap, but the long coat would have betrayed his profession quite as easily.

"I daren't stop more," he said anxiously. "If I'm found 'ere, Mr Roper, I'm done for, and so's your caper."

"Ten minutes," said Roper easily, baring his teeth with hardly a smile, "ten minutes is all that is required."

"You don't know how easy they sack a man," Cazamian grumbled, between sips of the toddy. "That was my trouble the first time. You imagine it, Mr Roper. Derby to Leeds and back, six days one week and seven the next. Then some of us goes to ask Mr George Hudson if perhaps we mayn't spend our Sundays like God-fearing men. Next thing is, Mr Hudson gives us all notice. I'd pawned my very boots, Mr Roper, to get the fifty pounds security I had to put down before they'd let me 'ave that job. And my family pledged as much again. I never saw much of that again, Mr Roper. Bloody 'udson took it with him when he went smash. So 'ere I start again on the South Eastern. But Mr Smiles and the directors don't believe in making a man soft by putting his money up. They hardens him like, by putting his wages down. Twenty-seven bob a week I started at. Twenty-four and a tanner it went down to seven years ago. Twenty-five and twopence it is now.

As God's my judge, Mr Roper, those bastards owe me every-thing I can take. And I ain't anxious to get sacked before I've took it."

Roper's eyes missed Cazamian's gaze, and peered through the murky window towards a hansom cab that stood idly in the street. The seamen on the bench talked in some unrecognisable *argot*, while one of the whores broke tunelessly into song for the amusement of her hirers.

> *"The first I met a cornet was*
> *In a regiment of dragoons.*
> *I gave him what he didn't like,*
> *And stole his silver spoons . . . "*

An elderly woman in drab cap and dirtier shawl appeared at the hatch which served the bar.

"Less of that, miss!" she called, "or I'll turn the lot of you out!"

Cazamian said softly,

"I daren't stay longer, Mr Roper. Not in the afternoon. I'll be missed for certain."

"So long as you're of our party," said Roper smiling, "you'll stay where we need you. Of course, if you ain't of our party, old fellow, you have only to say the word."

The foxy moustache lifted a little more as the smile broadened, and Cazamian read the promise of unspeakable forms of suffering in the sharp blue eyes.

"However," remarked Roper almost at once, as he glanced through the window panes again, "it seems I don't have to keep you no longer. Cut along, old fellow and leave the reckoning with me. We always likes to treat a friend."

The first seconds of Cazamian's ten-minute absence had hardly passed when Verney Dacre stepped from the buttoned-plush interior of the hansom. He crooked a finger round a half-sovereign and held it up, as if for the cabman's admiration.

"I don't care to be kept standin' about while they fetch a cab off the station rank," he said coolly. "Have the goodness to wait here. I shall want you again in quarter of an hour or less."

The man watched the elusive little coin.

"No," said Dacre decisively, "you don't drink any part of it till you complete the journey."

The station forecourt had been designed to appear more like a Venetian piazza than a railway terminus, complete with a smoke-blackened campanile. Dacre kept to the left and approached the concourse through the long and elegant arcade of shops, where women's trinkets, boots and gloves were set out behind bow windows which would not have disgraced Regent Circus or the Burlington Arcade. Under the arched glass canopy of the station itself, the hot stagnant air of the summer afternoon was thick with the taste of soot. A few City men, distinguishable by the silk sheen of their black hats and the heavy gold of their waistcoat chains, strode slowly to and fro, perspiring discreetly. Here and there a mother or a governess, absurdly overdressed for the heat in cloak and bonnet, waited with a little group of children for the summer train to Folkestone or Margate. But on the far side of the platforms, the tidal ferry train stood unattended at the place where it had been left since its arrival that morning. It was a long cortège of individual carriages, each strongly resembling the outline of the stage coaches from which they had evolved. The engine, its low line topped by two bell-shaped humps and a tall funnel, was deserted. Only at the near end, where the passenger luggage van stood, was there a solitary porter. Dacre approached the man.

"You!" he said sharply. "Yes, you sir!"

The man came forward slowly, his suspicion tempered by apprehension.

"Name?" said Dacre briskly.

The man stiffened, summing up the well-cut frock-coat and silk stock, and sensing an official inquiry.

"Geddes, sir."

"Geddes," said Dacre, as though with a certain distaste. "Very well, Geddes. The compliments of Mr Samuel Smiles, secretary of the company, to the station master. Two gentlemen of Mr Smiles' acquaintance have had their notecases snatched by urchins in the arcade. The urchins in question were seen to disappear into the campanile tower and may be making their den there. What is the station master and what are his railway constables doing about it? Mr Smiles will be obliged by an answer before four o' clock."

Geddes looked at Dacre uncertainly.

"Cut along!" said Dacre impatiently. "Your train will still be here when you get back, unless the guard should drive it away of his own accord!"

With these final words, Dacre saw the realisation of defeat in the man's eyes. Geddes could hardly admit that Cazamian, with his knowledge, was absent from duty. He ducked his head a little, mumbled an acknowledgement, and shambled off.

Dacre waited until one of the iron pillars supporting the glass vault stood between them. Then he moved purposefully forward towards the unattended guard's van with its low roof. He stepped into its darkness, among the smell of straw and hot wood. When the bullion safe was in use, no precaution seemed too great, but when it stood empty through the summer afternoon, a single porter and the guard himself were regarded as an ample protection. The keys which Dacre had made from the wax impressions were bright and rough from the file. When he inserted the first in its lock, it turned as smoothly as in air. The other caught feebly, and he made a mental reservation about having filed it a little too close. But for all that, he felt the tumblers move, sensing, rather than seeing, that the lid of the bullion safe was now free. Much as he would have liked to explore the mechanism further, it was too great a gamble to be compromised at this stage. He turned the keys back in the locks, carefully withdrew them, and stepped out into the cloudy sunlight which filtered through the station vaulting. No one challenged him as he strode back towards the arcade, a figure of self-evident authority. He took the side steps down into Tooley Street, and beckoned his cab towards him. As the hansom whirled him away towards Albemarle Street, he caught sight of a man

in frock-coat and trousers, accompanied by several constables
in long belted tunics and chimney-pot hats, hurrying towards
the towering campanile.

Next day, several radical evening papers followed the
Morning Chronicle in denouncing the current plague of
hoaxes perpetrated against railway officials by idle and
arrogant young officers of the Hussars or Lancers. "Gentlemen of fashion," said the radical press bitterly, "who are
always ready with a sneer at the decent manners and honest
occupations of their more plebeian contemporaries."

I I

While the readers of the newspaper reports awaited a sequel
to the campanile story, Sergeant Verity squatted in the velvet
blackness of a dwarf-sized tent and fumbled with a thick
glass plate. As a sole concession to the warmth generated by
the heavy black material all round him, he had removed his
hat, but the sweat still gathered in his dark, oiled hair and
on his brow, running downward and soaking his tight collar
where it rubbed most sorely. Beyond his little cone of darkness, in the brilliant light of June, he heard plainly enough
the rattle of carriage wheels, the crash of the iron-rimmed
cartwheels on cobbles, and the loud, hoarse hum of the
street. From the general hubbub, there rose an occasional
boisterous laugh or the jingling of a song, only to be lost
again among the surge of voices and the tramp of footsteps.

Holding the thick square of glass in its black sheath,
Verity watched the world outside through the wide lens of
Sergeant Samson's Ottewill Folding Camera. The polished
sides of the box had been cared for so diligently by its owner
that their gloss suggested the surfaces of a Hepplewhite table
or a Chippendale commode. The rear half of the box slid in
and out of the front, like a drawer in a desk, adjusting the
distance between the lens and the ground-glass viewing

screen at the back. For all Samson's pride in it, the Ottewill Folding Camera was far from new. To Verity, however, the world seen through its lens had an air of intriguing un-reality, as though it were a shadow play or the Chinese shades.

The glass plate in his hands still smelt faintly of alcohol and ether. With Samson as his guide, he had learnt how to dissolve cotton wool in the mixture and then coat the glass with the sticky collodion that it produced. Once the plate was washed over with silver nitrate, dried, and sealed in its black case, it could be used under almost any conditions.

Turning his attention to the lens again, Verity lengthened the focus, until the view on the ground-glass screen was of a fine stone doorway, from lintel to pavement. To one so inexperienced in the matter, the clarity and magnification seemed breath-taking. Secure from observation himself, within the tent of black cloth, he settled down to watch the comings and goings at Ned Roper's bawdy-house. From time to time, he took a glass plate from its sheath, slid it into the slot in front of the viewing screen, removed the cap from the lens and took a "shilling portrait" of the doorway. But he always waited until a man and a girl, or a man alone, stood on the steps while their knock was answered. In the bustling street, the wink of the lens in the bright sun was hardly perceptible, and few of the passers-by stopped to watch an itinerant street-photographer at work. For ten years and more the sight had become too common to stir curiosity.

Verity felt a secret pride in his strategy. Even though his was a private score to be settled with Roper, it seemed to him a system of espionage on which a detective policeman could be professionally congratulated. From a secure distance, he saw the clients come and go: hussar subalterns, swells in silk hats, and country gentlemen who had been caught within half a day of their arrival in the great Metropolis. As they walked from the pavement up the half-dozen steps to the door, they all seemed to turn and face the street while waiting for admission. Standing there quietly, too preoccupied to notice the black cone of cloth among the dark clothes of the crowds, they made a perfect subject for the patient photographer.

"It couldn't be better," said Verity to himself, "if they was all sitting to Mr Archer for their portraits."

He hummed a little tune and slid another glass plate safely back into its black sheath. When half an hour had passed, most of the plates were used, but it was nonetheless an aggravation to find the view from the lens abruptly blocked by an indistinct and immobile blur. With all the belligerence of a bull breaking through a hedge, Verity fought his way out from the black folds of the woollen cloth and stood upright and blinking in the afternoon glare.

Not a dozen feet away, two girls were standing close together by the pavement's edge, their backs to the carriages as they watched the unattached male strollers, hoping for a "catch." The nearer of the two, who was blocking the lens, was a tall, auburn-haired young woman with a grave expression. Her brown cloak and red skirts were too shabby for one of Roper's women, Verity thought, and the sight of a small child clinging to her knees put the matter beyond doubt. Her companion, several inches shorter with broad hips and dark hair cropped to emphasise the urchin quality of her features, was dressed in a pale grey of equal shabbiness.

Verity waited, assuming an air of professional indifference. A glimpse between the moving figures of the crowd showed the door of Roper's establishment open, and Roper himself standing on the steps with a male companion. They stood there in conversation. Verity pulled the cap from the lens and almost danced with impatience as he waited for the tall auburn-haired girl to shift her stance a little. At that moment she handed something to the other girl and stooped to attend to the child which was pulling irritably at her skirts. The view over her head, to where Roper was talking to a swarthy, bald-headed stranger, was clear. With a plate in the camera, Verity took their portrait. Though the girl straightened up again, her attentions to the child were by no means over. When she stooped once more, there was a fresh plate ready in the Ottewill camera. The two men were facing him and the focus was perfect at the second exposure, which promised to be as sharp as the work of any back-yard studio in Holborn or Lambeth. Verity straightened up, aware as he did so of the brunette's curious gaze. She tugged her friend's arm urgently, as if pulling her away.

" 'e's done that again! 'e's took a portrait!" she squealed, and then shouted for Verity's benefit, "Did yer get a good picture of us?"

Half-mocking and half-frightened at what they believed to be a photographic record of themselves, the two amateur whores scurried away, the taller one dragging the child after her, the brunette looking back over her shoulder until they were safely round the next corner. Verity, in his moment of triumph, regarded them with magisterial indifference. Returning to the stagnant heat of his little tent, he watched through the lens as Roper escorted his client down the steps to a waiting brougham with all the professional unctuousness of a dishonest valet. The door closed again, and a long, uneventful ten minutes passed in the sunlit street. Verity ran his hand ruefully over the horizontal creases in his waistcoat, conscious of not having eaten since breakfast.

A little crossing sweeper, not more than ten years old, leant on his broom nearby and watched Verity at work. The grime on the child's face was as dark as coal dust on the features of a collier.

"Here!" said Verity with a peremptory snap of his large fingers, "mind this for a minute or two and there's a copper for you afterwards."

"Wery good, yer worship," said the boy smartly, taking up a sentry-like stance with his broom. Verity left him to his guard duty and strode away towards the little shop near Regent's Circus, where the black lettering on the gas globes above the door proclaimed Signor Flores' Confectionery.

"Lumps of Delight, miss," he said to the little girl who served there: "Quarter. Quick-sharp, if you please." Even before he was out of the doorway, his fingers closed on the first soft Turkish sweetmeat in its thick powder.

At a little distance down the street he thought at first that the child crossing-sweeper had fallen in a dead faint. But all too soon it was apparent that the huddled figure on the pavement was the tent of black cloth fallen upon the remains of Sergeant Samson's camera and its stand. As Verity lumbered forward and snatched away the cloth, his mind was dominated by the appalling and intimidating prospect of his next meeting with Samson. The polished sides of the wooden camera were splintered and its brass hinges warped, as though the whole box had been struck by some tremendous downward blow. He stared at the wreck in utter dismay.

"I was jist a-sweepin' for a lady across the road when it happen," said the boy shamefacedly, "when the two gentlemen with the iron bracket slipped and dropped it. Right across the cloth it went. Wery sorry the gentlemen was, and said they'd be back in two minutes to settle up for any damage. Only they ain't come back," he concluded superfluously.

"It's not even as if it was mine!" said Verity helplessly.

He was still pondering this when the boy touched his sleeve confidentially.

"You was lucky, you was, yer worship," he said gently, "you might 'ave been in there when it happen."

Verity looked at him, still clutching in his hand the packet of plates which he had carried to the shop and back. He felt a sudden chill in the heat of June.

"That's just where they thought I was!" he said, his eyes widening with consternation and anger. "When they didn't see me standing by it, that's where they must have thought I was! They bloody well meant to cooper me! That's what!"

That evening, in the attic room in Great College Street, Westminster, which served for his lodgings, Sergeant Samson said for the third or fourth time,

"It ain't the cost, Verity. Money can't mend it!"

"So soon as I can, I'll pay the account in full," said Verity firmly. "There's better cameras than that can be got for five sovereigns from Gilbert Flemming's in Oxford Street. I'll do it so soon as I can. Only don't go prosing on about it, there's a good fellow. They meant to do for me. They thought I was still in there—and I might've been!"

The room was almost in darkness and he could just make out the black bulk of his colleague as Samson rocked the heavy glass plate in a dish of liquid. On his fingers, Verity felt the wrinkling from the astringent film of pyrogallic acid.

"What beats me," said Samson, watching the dish carefully, "is why you can't just settle with Roper, man to man. There's enough dark corners, ain't there?"

"It won't do," said Verity, growing stern.

"I don't know about that," said Samson beginning to reminisce, "they don't squeal after, not hardly ever. I 'ad trouble once with a great cove in St Giles's. When it came to, he let me knock him down with no more fight than a baby. In the pushing about, I bent his left thumb and finger back so far that they bust right across. I promised him next time it'd be his right hand. Let him try a lock or a pocket with fingers like a bunch of old twigs. You've no idea how useful he was to me ever after."

The glass plate rattled against the dish once more, as Samson drew it out of the pyrogallol solution.

"That's the two of Ned Roper and his friend," he said with exaggerated patience. He set a match to the mantle and held the two squares of glass against the light. Both were uniformly and deeply black.

"I took their portraits!" said Verity with some indignation.

"That's as may be," said Samson, putting the plates down again, "but the art of portraits ain't learnt in one afternoon."

"Keep 'em!" said Verity optimistically. "I've heard they sometimes brighten a bit with keeping."

"Have you?" Samson nodded glumly. "That's what all the sharps tell their poor gulls when they hands them a no bono plate. 'Only keep it, sir, and you'll see it'll soon brighten up!' I'm surprised you ain't tumbled to that trick before. I'm rather afraid you had a bad afternoon of it."

"Oh?" said Verity stubbornly. "I get so close to the secret

of the conspiracy that they think it worth killing me! Close as McCaffery ever got! I don't call that a bad afternoon. If you was half as good a hand at constabulary vigilance as you are at shilling portraits, Mr Samson, you might go a very long way indeed!"

Sergeant William Clarence Verity, of the Private Clothes detail, Whitehall Office, presents his compliments to Inspector Croaker and has the honour to draw Mr Croaker's attention to complaints made by the public to Sergeant Verity in respect of the premises known as 84, Langham Place. These complaints concern misdemeanours and felonies committed by street women and their keepers who frequently resort to this house. It has been brought to Sergeant Verity's notice that the dupes of these women are robbed and physically assaulted on the premises, the proceeds of such robberies being kept in the charge of a woman of low repute, Jacoby, common law wife of the keeper of the house. The victims of such assaults have been left upon the area steps without coats or jackets, and even without trousers, to the great scandal of the public peace. Sergeant Verity appends a statement by Mr Julius Stringfellow, of Paddington Green, to this effect.

Sergeant Verity is also informed that the house is a resort of men of depraved taste and morals for criminal intercourse with female children of tender years. Among further information offered is an allegation that the premises are used to harbour felons who may thus evade the pursuit of police constables, and that a concealed way has been made, opening from the premises into a stable-yard on another street.

Sergeant Verity therefore requests that Mr Croaker may take steps to obtain a justice's warrant, whereby officers of the Division may enter these premises in search of the proceeds of various robberies, and of evidence of other felonies and misdemeanours.

Sergeant Verity has the honour to remain Mr Croaker's obedient humble servant.

W. Verity, Sgt.

19th of June 1857

Inspector Croaker is in receipt of Sergeant Verity's communication of the 19th instant. Mr Croaker must observe at the outset that the memorandum does not appear to have been copied into the letter-book. Sergeant Verity will have the goodness to make such copy at once and not to allow the omission to occur in the future.

Mr Croaker is also bound to observe at once that the evidence submitted to him by Sergeant Verity is in no way substantial enough for any application to be made to a justice. A house of ill-repute is not amenable to search as such. Sergeant Verity should know this, and, if not, he will learn it for the future. There appears to be no corroborated evidence, in this instance, of the robberies of persons as alleged by Sergeant Verity's informants. Mr Croaker is surprised to learn that the other forms of disorderly conduct alluded to have not been suppressed by Sergeant Verity and the other officers of the Division in the proper discharge of their duties.

Mr Croaker regrets to hear that instances may have occurred in which females in early womanhood may have forfeited their virtue in the manner described. He must, however, observe that the duty of the police is to enforce the law as it at present exists. By that law, a young woman is competent to consent to her own seduction at 12 years of age. If Sergeant Verity has corroborated evidence that children of more tender years have been criminally abused, Mr Croaker will expect to hear it. Mr Croaker finds it necessary to remind Sergeant Verity that the cause of virtue is not aided by a feebly based prosecution which ends in the acquittal of those accused.

*Finally, Mr Croaker is aware that the tenant of the
premises referred to is Edward Roper, with whom Sergeant Verity appears to be conducting some personal
feud. If Sergeant Verity's communication is prompted
by any such vendetta, Mr Croaker must reprimand
him •severely. Should Sergeant Verity ever attempt to
incriminate Mr Roper by unsubstantiated assertions,
Sergeant Verity may render himself liable to prosecution for attempting to pervert the course of justice.*
Mr Croaker remains &c.

H. Croaker, Inspector of Constabulary
21st June 1857

"Pervert the course of justice!" The broad nape of Verity's
fleshy neck glowed with indignation. He glowered across the
bare wooden table, on which lay the remains of a supper of
broiled bones, ham and eggs, and bottled stout. Stringfellow,
to whom a dinner-table was only a dinner-table so long as
the meal was in progress, busied himself in poking dust from
the crevices of a harness brass with the corner of a handkerchief. In an old green shooting coat, a billicock hat, and
brown breeches, he looked the perfect image of self-
confidence.

"Not what I should have written at all," he remarked,
clouding the brass with his breath. "First into the Redan
you may have been, Verity, but you ain't got a hand for a
letter."

"You 'ave, though?" said Verity with some scepticism.
Stringfellow hoisted himself up.

"I don't know but what I mightn't 'ave. Getting into a
whorehouse in Langham Place ain't no worse than breaching
the walls of Bhurtpore with a line of Cherry-pickers."

"What about the letter?" Verity insisted.

"Well," said Stringfellow, "I never was at a dame school,
and on my soul I ain't no sort of cove with a pen in my
hand. But I can compose after a fashion when the fit is on."

He lifted the latch on the wooden doorway of the lean-to

and bawled into the interior room of the little mews dwelling.

"Miss Bella! Bring a ink-and-dip! Sharp!"

Bella, brushing back stray blonde curls with one hand, and holding a little wooden writing-tray in the other, flitted into the low-ceilinged scullery. Verity, who was burnishing the pimpled leather of new boots with a hot iron, in preparation for plain clothes duty at the Victoria Cross parade, looked up at the girl. At his gaze, the colour flooded into Bella's plump young cheeks.

"Sit down," said Stringfellow brusquely, "and take 'un all down as I say."

Verity listened. With the leather ironed smooth, he had burnished the toe-caps of the boots to a pair of black mirrors before Stringfellow finished.

"There!" said Stringfellow finally. "Now tell me if you ever heard a letter that was the like of that! A daughter's innocence ruined! The mother demented with grief! The ultimate suicide of both! And all that along o' a 'ouse of abomination in Langham Place, run by a villain called Roper! Now, 'ear the sorrowing father and 'usband plead for the safety of 'is one ewe lamb, lured to that place of sin! See 'im beg the protection of the common law, on bended knee! Behold 'im, spurned by the haughty Croaker of the Whitehall constabulary! Oh, the pity of it, my friends, the pity . . . "

"Your daughter ain't made away with herself," said Verity with some heat, "nor she ain't never been in a 'ouse of sin. And I was given to understand that the late Mrs Stringfellow went off with the cholera."

"Draw it mild, old fellow," said Stringfellow reproachfully. "You ain't ever going to see the inside of Roper's whore shop unless we pitch it strong."

"Pitch it strong as you like," Verity remarked, "you won't shift Mr Croaker. He's hard as a file. Why, he wouldn't turn a hair if you and all the cabmen of the city, and all their wives and daughters, hanged yourselves in a row outside his window."

"But this letter ain't going to Mr Croaker," said String-fellow with a flourish of his stick. "Take your eyes off the lodger, Miss Bella, and write at the bottom, 'To the Right Honourable and Right Reverend Secretary, The Society for the Suppression of Vice, Essex Street'." He turned to Verity again. "Your Mr Inspector may be 'ard as a file, sir, but I once had the honour to drive this right reverend gentleman from Hyde Park Gate to Exeter Hall. Mean as a ferret and sour as vinegar! Shouldn't wonder if he was to make your Mr Croaker feel quite poorly for a day or two."

Anonymous in regulation tunic and tall hat, Verity marched among the other members of the search detail, following Inspector Swift towards the plain black wagon. Two parallel benches accommodated the twelve constables.

"A reverend gentleman it was," said Sergeant Samson furtively, "came calling on Mr Croaker. You wouldn't believe how Mr Croaker took on afterwards."

"That's all gammon!" said Meiklejohn, a youngish, fair-haired sergeant with a Scots brogue. "One of the light-fingered gentry turned evidence as to the whereabouts of Joe the Magsman and a hundredweight of silver plate. That's the lay."

The horses sprang forward at the crack of a whip and the whole conveyance bounced and rattled across the cobbles. Verity sat in silence as the wagon rumbled the length of Nash's elegant quadrant, and then drew into a mews somewhere just beyond Regent Circus. Much as he wanted to see the inside of Ned Roper's establishment, he hoped that Joe the Magsman, rather than Stringfellow's letter, had been the reason for the search. By arrangement with Inspector Swift, the uniformed men were to lead the assault, the plain clothes detail following up as soon as any prisoners had been taken or any suspects cleared out of the way. Swift's strategy on these occasions was to keep the plain clothes detail, even though wearing uniform, out of sight of those whom they might subsequently have to hunt. Verity, knowing that a uniform alone would hardly conceal him from Roper, was duly grateful.

As Swift, two sergeants and four constables, marched up the steps in a phalanx, the remaining officers were drawn up in a line on the pavement below with all the precision of infantry awaiting the order to advance. Swift set up a thunderous knocking at the door which must have alerted all the occupants. Verity and Samson drew back a little to see if there was any attempt at an escape over the roof. After a long minute, the door was opened and the six uniformed men disappeared through it at a run, as if Bill Sikes and all his confederates might even then be swarming out through the skylights. There was an obscure scuffle, somewhere within the lighted vestibule, a scream of agony which was clearly heard in the street, and two heavy blows followed by almost complete silence.

A crowd of spectators from among the passers-by was beginning to gather at the steps when Inspector Swift reappeared and beckoned Samson and Verity.

"Quick as you can, my boys," he said in a jovial whisper, "the woman Jacoby and two bullies are under detention in the little parlour. Make your way through the rest of the house smartly as you can."

As the two men moved through the entrance hall, Verity began to imprint on his memory the plan of the house. One side of the ground floor was taken up by the front parlour and the well of the stairs behind it. On the other side, a long "music room" ran from the tall front windows with their deep velvet curtains and pelmets, to the smaller bow-window, overlooking the mews yard at the rear of the house. A fine Broadwood grand piano, French polished to a deep chestnut gloss, and a dozen little chairs with tapestry seats and fluted legs made up the furnishings. The sheen of the parquet floor confirmed that this was the "introducing room," where officers and gentlemen drank and danced with the girls until they found partners to match their tastes.

Above the black and white tiling of the entrance hall, the wrought-iron balustrade of a graceful staircase ascended in a series of diminishing ovals to the coloured glass of the sky-light, far above. Sunlight falling through the lofty stair-well threw diffused patterns of rose and turquoise on the pale oak panelling. Verity and Samson climbed to the first floor, half of which was occupied by the most expensive of the bed-rooms with its pink-shaded lamps, nude statuary, and large gilt-framed mirrors. The room was unoccupied, as was the first of the two smaller bedrooms on the floor. At the door of the second room a uniformed constable, his tall hat still firmly on his head, stood at ease. He brought his feet together at the two sergeants' approach, without quite standing at attention.

"Three persons detained, Sergeant," he said proudly, "on Mr Inspector Swift's orders. One male person and two female. The male person claims to have been accosted by the women and brought here. Seems the small rooms is let by the hour during the afternoons for any street woman with the money. An accommodation house, you might say. They all refuses to give their names, except that one girl calls herself Adeline and the other Elaine. I'd say they was eliases."

"Aliases," said Sergeant Samson knowledgeably, pushing open the door.

The room was the smallest and shabbiest so far, no doubt let to street girls for that reason. A washstand, two small chairs, and a large iron-framed bed stood as if in a white-washed cell. A silk top-hat, a gold hunter, coins and keys, lay on the washstand. On the chairs were a pile of skirts, a frock-coat, and a pair of trousers. The man lying back in the bed was in his fifties, more than a little drunk, and grinning stupidly through his grey mutton-chop whiskers. Though his shoulders were covered by his shirt, Verity had no doubt that he was naked otherwise under the sheet. Completely revealed on top of the sheet, a naked girl lay either side of him. The elder, who had called herself by the newly fashionable name of Adeline, was a fleshy adolescent of sixteen or seventeen. Her companion, Elaine, was no more than fourteen or fifteen. She seemed a younger version of the elder girl, with the same narrow, insolent eyes, the same snub nose and lank brown hair hanging loosely down her back. At Verity's entrance, neither girl made any effort to conceal herself beyond rolling over on her stomach with a squeal of amusement and grinning back at him over her shoulder. The man too, knowing the powerlessness of the law on private premises, joined in the laughter, placing a well-manicured hand on each of his young mistresses. Verity looked at the two girls with distaste, taking in their blackened feet and mud-spattered calves, the sores at elbows and knees, and the constellations of tiny red spots across their buttocks. For all his experience, it still dismayed him that a man of evident wealth should endure the embraces of two girls whose worst diseases were probably infinitely more horrible than any visible blemishes. He closed the door to a shout of derisive amusement and climbed the stairs again with an involuntary shudder.

The second floor revealed two small bedrooms and the up-stairs drawing-room, with its padded door and its deadness of sound-proofed space. It seemed more like a nursery than a drawing-room, since a painted rocking-horse stood in the centre of the carpet casting a long shadow in the dying sun. There were two Coburg chairs and a heavy sofa in blue velvet, a riding switch of bamboo cased in leather thrown at random on its cushions.

Higher still were two attic rooms, but the final curve of the stairs was blocked by a wrought-iron wicket-gate, extending the full width of the stairway and from the ceiling to the level of the steps.

"Try it," said Samson at Verity's shoulder, "it don't seem to have a lock."

Verity pushed, then pulled, and the gate swung open towards them. But the attic rooms were completely bare and had evidently not been used. The windows were barred, suggesting that they had once served as bedrooms for very young children, which, Verity, supposed, might also explain the wicket-gate on the stairs. With Samson's assistance, he raised a floorboard from its joists and explored underneath with the aid of a lantern. There was nothing to be found.

"Stands to reason," said Samson huffily, as the two men went back down the stairs. "Where would you hide a leaf?"

"In a tree," said Verity glumly.

"Where would you hide a dead body?"

"In a churchyard."

"And where would you hide a pile of money?"

"In a bank."

"There you are," said Samson triumphantly. "They stripped this place clean as the breast of a Christmas goose. You only got to look at the rooms! There ain't nothing now but a paper note of 'ow much money is on deposit to Coutts! Much chance there may be of finding that."

"What about the man with the two young women?" suggested Verity hopefully.

"Well, now," said Samson, "you might break his nose, or his jaw, for satisfaction. But you ain't never going to get a brief swore out against him. A-cos it wouldn't stick."

They went down to the basement of the house, as a matter of routine interest. It consisted of a kitchen and a scullery, whose only occupant was a girl, with the deformed head of imbecility, crying into an apron. Adjoining the scullery, a coal chute ran upwards to the mews yard at the back of the music room.

"You don't need secret ways nor skylights," Verity remarked, "not when you could be up there or through the back window, and get three or four streets away before the first constable was through the door at the front."

Back in the entrance hall, they could hear the voices of Ellen Jacoby and one of the bullies swearing total ignorance of the very existence of Jerome Sant, *alias* Joe the Magsman. From the other bully there was no sound beyond a whimpering that seemed to subside to an intermittent groaning. Verity took a furtive peep and saw Tyler sitting in a chair. His face was the colour of yellow clay, one eye almost closed by an ochre-coloured swelling, and his teeth awash with blood. When one of the constables thoughtlessly touched his right arm, Tyler emitted a sharp, involuntary yelp. Meiklejohn, the Scots sergeant, made his way out to join

Verity and Samson. His large, freckled face was radiant with satisfaction.

"There was no need to look in the basement again," he said. "Nothing there—nor anywhere else. Mr Tyler took me down there."

"Tyler?" said Verity suspiciously.

"Aye," said Meiklejohn, "I fancy he misunderstood the request at first. But then, why, bless you, he was in such a hurry he quite missed his footing on those dark stairs."

Meiklejohn kneaded the knuckles of his large right hand reminiscently, and favoured his two companions with an unambiguous smile.

The Boulle clock struck three with the sound of a hand gently stirring tiny spoons in a drawer. Suspended in an eternal moment, the gilt figures of an old man drawing away the last garment from a plump girl acted out the charade of Time unveiling Truth.

Verney Dacre, sensing rather than hearing a footfall on the broad, thickly-carpeted stairs, swung his long bony legs from the day-bed and crossed to the tall windows which looked down upon Albemarle Street, with a glimpse of St James's. Below him, the carriages drawn by fine bay geldings moved in an unaccustomed silence through the noon sunlight. On the opposite side of the street, in one of the plain but elegant Georgian houses, the Dowager Lady Spencer was dying, a relic of an earlier society. Since early morning her grooms had relaid the cobbles with straw every hour to muffle the cacophony of hooves and iron-rimmed wheels.

He turned from the window, anticipating precisely the moment of the knock upon the door-panel, and the opening of the double doors themselves by his manservant, Oughtram. Dacre's household was small, consisting of the Oughtrams, husband and wife, and a young female drudge whose very name was unknown to him. As servants, the Oughtrams possessed the unquestionable advantages of being content with their position and apparently incurious as to their master's private conduct. They were not hard-worked, since most of Verney Dacre's meals were ordered from the finest cuisine of Stephens' Hotel or the Clarendon in Bond Street, and brought round by a footman. Oughtram and his wife had accepted the addition of Jolie to the *ménage* without comment of any kind. She was not the first of Dacre's mistresses in their experience, nor was she likely to be the last. The girl kept out of their way, as she kept out of Dacre's for the most part, by busying herself in trying on first one costume and then another. It was enough for her to lie like a *grande coquette* before a mirror in one of the finely furnished rooms, enraptured by the reflection of her new beauty. The time would come when such self-caressing admiration would not be enough to satisfy her, but Dacre was confident that by then his need of her would be over. To the Oughtrams, it mattered little what the outcome might be. As James Oughtram remarked, when settling down to steak and porter in the evening, what Mr Verney Dacre did was no concern of his, so long as he himself had the easiest lodging that any servant could have wished for.

On entering Dacre's sitting-room, Oughtram drew himself upright, his sallow cadaverous features suggestive of a professional mourner.

"There's a gentleman downstairs insists he must see you, sir. I asked his name but he wouldn't give it. Said you'd know him when you saw him, and that it was a private matter."

Dacre thought for a moment, sniffed, and then said, as though it hardly interested him,

"What sort of person did he look?"

"Sporting gentleman, might be," said Oughtram expressionlessly.

"This is all a great bore," said Dacre irritably. "Send him away. No—wait—I suppose I must see him. He may have been sent with a message. Show him up before he steals something from the hall."

He had guessed from the first that this must be Ned Roper, and, having guessed that, it was important to impress upon Oughtram that the man was a stranger and that it was a matter of total indifference to Dacre whether he saw him or not. Once Roper had been shown upstairs and the two men were alone together, it was Dacre who spoke first.

"Oblige me, Ned Roper, by never comin' to this house again, and by tryin' not to act like a *cretin* in future."

Roper sat down, uninvited, on the day-bed, lounged backwards a little, crossed one leg over the other, and took a cigar from a leather case. Then he favoured Dacre with the ferret-like smile that he normally reserved for men of Cazamian's type.

"I don't know, Mr Dacre, but what you mayn't thank me for having taken the trouble to step over here. The jacks turned the Langham Place 'ouse inside-out and found nothing. All the same, it ain't the billet you'd like to be found in now, is it?"

Dacre turned his back to the fender and stared coldly down at Ned Roper, despising the coster-boy arrogance and the vulgar clothes which made up Roper's bravery.

"It is inconvenient to me that you should come here," he said at length. "Have the goodness not to repeat this visit."

"Inconvenient?" said Roper, his smile broadening. "Yes, I shouldn't wonder if it was inconvenient, Mr Dacre, seeing as how you're never going to get into the guard's van of the tidal ferry, let alone touch any of the gold."

"Oh?" said Dacre, hardly betraying curiosity.

"Look in the *Morning Post,* if you ain't done already. Where it says, 'Shocking railway disaster at Lewisham.' Eleven passengers was killed, the night afore last, when one train ran slap into the back of another."

Without taking his eyes off Roper for a moment, Dacre opened the thick soft folds of the *Morning Post.* Then he began to read. Presently he looked up again.

"Cazamian?"

"No!" said Roper disdainfully. "He ain't dead, nor wasn't within ten miles of it all."

"Well then?"

"Well," said Roper, "I've had words with Cazamian this morning. The railway company's setting up an inquiry over the accident. 'owever, it seems the passengers is getting worried about all these trains that keep running one into the back of the other. Orders have been issued. From now on the luggage vans at the end of the train is sealed and the guard don't go into them except at the stations. The guard is to travel on the little patform at the back of the van so's he can raise the alarm for any other train he sees coming after him. When the train leaves a station, the guard takes his place at the back, and the railway police close up the van, having first seen that all is as it should be. That's the order of the day."

"When does this start?" Dacre inquired, folding his hands under the tails of his coat.

"It started this morning," said Roper with bitter satisfaction. "Wery inconvenient, ain't it, Mr Dacre?"

Dacre said nothing. He walked across the room to a tall French cabinet, an imitation of the style of Louis Quatorze, the arched panels of the upper doors surrounded by a carved frieze with coloured glass and marble let into the dark, polished rosewood. Taking a key from his pocket, he unlocked the upper cupboard, while Ned Roper watched intently over his shoulder. The three shelves were lined with narrow, though deep, bags made of soft leather and threaded with thin body-straps.

"Courier bags," said Dacre flatly. "If he were to attach them to himself properly, a man might carry half a hundred-weight of gold under his shirt in those."

He stooped down and unlocked the larger doors of the lower cupboard. Six leather carpet-bags lay across the full length of the space.

"Likewise," said Dacre, still talking as if it were a matter of indifference to him personally, "two men who could fill those carpet-bags and the courier bags might carry quarter of a ton of gold between them. Rather, they might carry such a weight with the assistance of the railway company."

From one side of the cupboard, he pulled out a small canvas pouch, open at the top. It tilted a little and a dull grey stream slithered over its edge. Dacre picked up a handful of the hard little pellets which made up the shifting mass.

"Lead shot," he remarked, displaying it for Roper's benefit. "Enough to replace the exact weight of the gold. It can
be bought by the hundredweight from the shot tower in
Southwark. The weighing of the bullion-boxes during the
journey ain't quite the problem it seems, old fellow. Why,
what do they do if the boxes weigh just what they should?"

"Nothing," said Roper hopefully.

"Precisely." Dacre returned the handful of shot to the
canvas pouch. "One thing a man learns from a tour of regimental duty is that the more defences there are, the more
lazy the defenders become. There's nothin' like being certain
you can't be defeated, for making sure that you will be. The
railway police know the bullion can't be robbed, so they
devise the weighing system, which makes robbery almost
certain."

"I don't follow all that," remarked Roper grudgingly. "All
I say is, if you open the safe, which you can do, you must
open the bullion-boxes. You might do that, but you can't
ever replace the bullion merchants' seals. If you was to rob
their vaults to take the seals, you might take the gold then
and there more easily. The railway police 'ull see the boxes
have been tampered with as soon as look at them. And now
you ain't going to get into the guard's van anyhow."

Verney Dacre returned to the far side of the room and
stood with his back to the mantelpiece again.

"You ain't a readin' man, Ned Roper," he said coldly, "so
it's time wasted to talk about Trojan horses. Oblige me by
understandin' one thing, however. I haven't come this far to
be turned back by you, nor Cazamian, nor anyone else. The
plan will be carried into action within a fortnight from now,
the sooner the better."

Roper shrugged, as though Dacre's foolhardiness was
beyond all cure. He tapped the side of his boot with his stick.

"It ain't going to be easy for me, not even though *you* can
spirit yourself through locked doors like a Cock Lane ghost.
Wherever I go, I only have to turn round to find a certain
party following a little way behind. I only come here this
morning a-cos I know his duty took him somewhere else.'

"Very likely," drawled Dacre. "Have the goodness, however, not to frighten Verity by turnin' round and starin' at him too much. I don't care to be waitin' about, any more than you do. Play him on the hook, though, play him, Mr Roper. And oblige me by seein' that when you set out for London Bridge, all tooled up, Sergeant Verity is in attendance."

"In attendance!" said Roper incredulously. "What, me start off on a safe-cracking with a bloody jack walking at my heels?"

"Should y' like to see him come to smash or not?" Dacre inquired with imperturbable patience. He broke off the conversation abruptly as Oughtram brought in the mid-day post on a silver tray. Dacre took up a small blue envelope and then dismissed the man. Roper seemed to forget the problem of Verity for a while as the second object of his visit recurred in his mind."

"When it's all done," he suggested speculatively, "there'll have to be an understanding about the girl you've got 'ere."

"Understand what you please," said Dacre, giving his attention to a sheet of notepaper, "there's nothing for her here."

Roper passed a tongue over his thin lips.

"Suppose you was to buy her off me? Two hundred sovs. Take her where you like, do as you like with her. You could have a worse little doxy, when all's said and done."

Dacre looked up expressionlessly.

"If you suppose anything of the kind, Ned Roper, you are most stupendously mistaken. When I buy, I choose my own goods."

"Meaning?"

"Meaning," said Dacre, "I'll buy Ellen Jacoby and no other, and you shall have five hundred guineas for her without further argument."

Roper smiled wisely and shook his head.

"No, Mr Dacre, nor for a thousand and more. Not even to oblige you."

"Dammit," said Dacre mildly, "how you fellows do take to

a bitch when she whelps. You might be a kennelman with a prime breedin' foxhound."

Roper, having failed to dispose profitably of Jolie, seemed a little downcast.

"You ain't nothin' else on your mind?" Dacre inquired, glancing in the general direction of the door. "It's deuced close to dinner time."

Roper brightened a little at the unintended invitation.

"Well," he said hopefully, "I wouldn't say no to a glass of cham and the wing of a chicken, if that ain't no inconvenience."

Verity and Samson stood shoulder to shoulder in the first rank of the crowd which stretched behind them, twelve or fifteen deep, and extended in a great curve from Hyde Park Gate to the review ground with its large marquees and regimental colours limp in the warm air. In the hazy heat of the June morning, the pale sunlight flashed on the silver helmets of the Life Guards and glowed more deeply on the bronze casques of the Inniskilling Dragoons. Mounted on his horse, at a little distance from the squadrons of the attendant cavalry regiments, the commander of the parade awaited the arrival of the Sovereign and her escort. Even at a distance, however, it seemed to Verity that no soldier of the Crimean expedition could fail to recognise the tall, shaggy-browed, care-worn figure of Sir Colin Campbell whose "thin red line" of Highlanders had held back the attacking Russian cavalry from the port of Balaclava. Behind Sir Colin, the ceremonial squadrons of the 11th Prince Albert's Own Hussars were moving towards their review positions, a pageant of deep, vibrant colour in their tight crimson trousers and short blue jackets with gold embroidery. The band of the Foot Guards concluded the slow march, "Coburg," and the squadrons of Prince Albert's Own moved forward at the trot, in time to "The Keel Row."

Overhead, where the tall elms and horse chestnuts of the park were in full leaf, the branches of the trees seemed alive with boys who had climbed there early in the morning for a view of the parade, and who now defied all efforts of the uniformed constables to dislodge them.

"I dunno," said Samson, directing the words to Verity from the corner of his mouth, "I still dunno what you and Mr Croaker sees in that Langham Place 'ouse. First you and your photographs, then Croaker and his justice's warrant. And what happens? No Joe the Magsman, not a girl who wasn't fourteen at least, and not a tool that would have opened Lady Jane's sewing-basket, let alone a bank vault. Now, as for those two pictures of yours, what came out all black . . . "

"Before another month is out," said Verity bleakly, "you shall have your camera made good."

"It ain't that," said Samson, "but I heard Blackmore say to Meiklejohn he wouldn't be surprised if Charley Wag or Joe the Magsman didn't *want* the 'ouse searched on purpose. Why, they know Mr Croaker won't dare ask for a justice's warrant again, not after his men found nothing. 'e wouldn't get the warrant anyway. That 'ouse is the safest in London now, for Charley and Joe."

"You don't want to take that from Meiklejohn," said Verity sternly, "not from a man that's just been reprimanded in front of the whole detail, and reduced to constable for an assault on a member of the public, for what he did to Tyler on the stairs."

"All the same," Samson persisted, "that Langham Place business was a rum affair."

For an instant, the crowd around them fell silent. Then a murmur of expectancy gathered to a roar of cheering. A distant clatter of hooves grew suddenly louder as the Sovereign's Escort of the Household Cavalry swung into view, the black plumes of their helmets matching the dark gloss of their immaculately groomed horses, their scarlet jackets and white breeches spotlessly smart. In the open carriage with its buttoned upholstery, the plump though still youthful features of the Queen were framed by her fair hair, neatly but severely arranged. The Princes, including the Prince Consort, and George, Duke of Cambridge, rode on horseback in the scarlet and white uniforms of field marshals of the British army. Behind them came a dozen or more riders, all in the plumed cocked hats of the British general staff. The gold-braided headgear and dark blue uniforms of senior officers from the Allied armies of France and Turkey seemed much in evidence. The whole impressive cavalcade rolled past the cheering crowd towards the review ground, where, among the marquees and the regimental colours, Her Majesty was to present the first of the new Victoria Crosses to forty-eight heroes of the Crimean expedition. As the royal carriage spun past them, Verity clutched Samson's arm abruptly and said,

"Look! There!"

"Where?"

"Look at 'im on 'is 'orse!"

"Dook of Cambridge?" said Samson bewildered.

"No, not 'im! The one behind! Frenchie uniform! Touch of the tarbrush! Fat-looking chap!"

"Yes?"

"It's 'im! I'd take my Bible-oath! 'e's the one on those shilling portraits that came to nothing. 'e was the one whose picture I took, twice, standin' on the steps in Langham Place and talking to Ned Roper! I'd know 'im in ten thousand!"

"It's coves like you, Verity," said Samson glumly, "as *starts* wars between people."

"It was 'im, I tell you!"

"And if you'd had his picture, you'd most probably have had him arrested by Inspector Croaker and the whole detail?"

"What of it, if it was 'im and 'e was conspiring with a criminal? Bit of gold lace don't put a man above the law."

"You know what you did?" said Samson, swinging round to face his truculent colleague; "you took a pair of shilling portraits of the nephew of Old Boney himself, cousin to the present King of France, coming out of a common whore-house! And all you can say to that is that you wish Mr Croaker had arrested him while he was here as Her Majesty's guest, just for the fun of seeing little Vic herself stand bail for him!"

"Is that who he is?" said Verity with calm satisfaction.

Sergeant Samson turned to face the procession again.

"If you was to keep your nose out of places where it don't belong, my son," he remarked, "the world might be an easier billet for the lot of us."

3

CRACKSMAN'S MOON

12

The little plot of land was no more than a court, hemmed in by the back walls of mean, dank houses on every side. Only a single archway with an iron gate offered a tunnel to the narrow cobbled street beyond. The turf of this enclosed ground was littered with the paraphernalia of death and burial, accumulated over two centuries. In the crowded earth, it was impossible to bury the newly arrived coffins more than two or three feet below the surface, while in one corner of the little green a pile of old, discoloured bones made up the human debris which the diggers had thrown to one side as they reopened the earth for a new generation of the poor. Even in the hot July afternoon, the poisoned air above the Shoreditch burial ground seemed damp and vaporous.

With the slow, deliberate movements of a mime, the four grave-diggers gently raised the coffin, its wood stained black with damp, from the shallow trench in which it had lain. Moving with the laboriousness of sleepwalkers, they raised it higher still, and slid it into the open back of the glass-sided hearse. If they seemed not to notice the disagreeable vapours which their spades had pressed from the spongy earth, this was the consequence of a generous allowance of "sexton's rum" with which they were supplied. It was an accepted condition of their trade that no man should be expected to endure the stench of a city burial ground while in a state of cold sobriety.

The hearse, with its black-plumed horses, and the black iron scrolling round its glass panels, was a cut above the hand-carts on which the dead were usually trundled to such burying grounds. In more prosperous areas it would have seemed common enough, though in the case of an exhumation great care was taken to keep the coffin decently covered during its journey to a new resting-place. A black velvet pall, fringed with white and set with silver fleurs-de-lys in each corner was draped high above the mortal remains of Major Edward Habbakuk, late of the Honourable East India Company's service.

The major, now the object of so much solemnity, had died six months earlier, a prisoner for debt in the Queen's Prison. After years of service in India, where mess bills were lower and commissions more cheaply bought, he had returned broken in health and spirit. But three months of hopeful trading in Eastcheap as an "East India Merchant" had ruined him utterly, and three months more had brought him to the desolate burial ground behind John's Court. There was hardly room for the major, and as soon as the officials who witnessed the funeral were out of sight, two grave-diggers had danced a macabre minuet upon the coffin to force it down a few inches in the earth.

But Major Habbakuk was more fortunate in death than in life. A brother officer, hearing belatedly of the death of a comrade who had no family or friends to give him decent burial, had paid the entire cost of exhumation and reinterment. On a July afternoon, the major began his last journey, from the courtyard of a Shoreditch slum to the little churchyard of Appleford in Kent, where he was to be buried near his more prosperous ancestors.

Verney Dacre heard and felt every movement and vibration as Major Habbakuk's coffin slid and bumped along the floor of the hearse. The hearse itself had been hired from Pontifex and Jones in Finsbury, though the driver had been persuaded to take a day's holiday and the price of a spree, while Roper's bully, Coggin, deputised for him. In a mews stable near Langham Place it had been a simple matter to remove the catafalque on which the coffin usually rested, and to substitute for it a more lofty one, of the kind which Prince Albert had designed for the Duke of Wellington's funeral car.

Verney Dacre was in no position to admire this "improvement," for he rested in his own coffin, immediately under the lofty pall of black velvet, and not twelve inches above the insanitary remains of Major Habbakuk.

Dacre's was no ordinary coffin. It had been occupied several times before, and never by a corpse. Invaluable in transporting reluctant girls from one country to another, it still had leather anklets and manacles screwed to its inner sides. The manacles retained their uses, since Dacre found that by clutching them he could steady himself a little against the violent bouncing and rocking of the hearse on the cobbled surface of the little streets. For all the buttoned velvet of its interior, there was little padding on the hard, close sides of the box. The base was a laying-out board, with a deep hollow for the head of the corpse to rest in, so that it should be held in position for any final leave-taking. But Dacre had no room to raise his shoulders and the strain of holding his head up from the hollow soon became a slow torture for the muscles of his neck and upper spine. The sweat of exertion and of the airless heat began to gather in pools over his closed eyelids.

He had gambled upon Ned Roper's bewildered loyalty, counting upon the calculation that the man's admiration for Dacre's own gift for strategy would not be overruled by some shortsighted and rat-like cunning of Roper's own. The coffin was so constructed that its left side could be removed, being held in place otherwise by one of two sets of little bolts. One of these was on the inside, but if someone were to close the outside set as well, the man in the coffin was helpless. The exterior bolts were disguised as brass ornamentation and would never be detected. Dacre allowed his mind to run once through the possible horror, the sudden panic of a trap, the half-conscious terror in the swooning heat, and the final thunder of earth, followed by the complete and unspeakable silence of living burial. Then he put the fear resolutely from him and thought of more urgent matters.

After half an hour more, the jolting rhythm began to slacken. The wheels of the hearse still rumbled, but it seemed as though it now rode on air. There was an abrupt jerk, and then a halt. Dacre heard voices and, briefly, the thunder of an engine. He braced himself against the straps, as his little world of darkness lurched and spun. There was a moment of twisting and plunging, the beginning of a sudden drop, and then at last came stillness and the comparative silence of distant activity.

As the hearse had moved sedately from Gracechurch Street into King William Street, rolling towards the river and London Bridge, several other vehicles had stopped to let it pass. One of these, drawn by a pair of grey horses, had the heavy black outline of one of the early horse-omnibuses of the reign of William IV. But it was a plain black van with no windows except for a little grill just behind the driver, and a single door in the downward curve of its back. Two men sat, one either side of the driver, on the high perch above the horses. Their greatcoats and tall hats resembled a uniform without quite being one. As the hearse passed in front of them, they removed their hats, revealing the faces of men whose sense of suspicion had been trained as carefully as their muscles. Their features had the hard, practised anonymity of experienced police officers.

Ned Roper saw them as he paid the driver of the hansom cab and then stood alone for a moment in the forecourt of London Bridge station. His carpet bags had been delivered to the luggage office that morning by Tyler, where they awaited him in the name of "Mr Archer." They were to be despatched by the luggage van of the 7.00 p.m. tidal ferry train for Dover, on which "Mr Archer" would be travelling. Roper himself carried no more than 30 lbs. weight of shot, distributed between the courier bags strapped against his shirt and the leather bag which he carried in one hand.

Before he turned his back and walked towards the station arcade, he satisfied himself that the hansom which had followed his at a discreet distance, all the way from the rank in Regent Street, had drawn up a little way off. The passenger, whom he could only make out as a dark, bulky shape inside the cab, showed considerable reluctance to emerge. It was all that Roper needed to know. He had the jack, Verity, in tow, according to Verney Dacre's instructions. To Ned

Roper's way of thinking, this was not the game to play, but Lieutenant Dacre had never been wrong yet.

At 6.15, according to their arrangement, Roper walked slowly down the arcade of bow-windowed little shops, at the end of which Cazamian stood, apparently taking the air to escape for a moment from the heat and smoke of the glass canopy under which the platforms were built. Cazamian saw Roper, lifted his cap and casually mopped his forehead with a handkerchief. Roper, his attention apparently caught by a display of harness in a saddler's window, stopped, turned so that Cazamian could see the leather bag that he was carrying, and then carefully changed the bag from one hand to another. No further signal was necessary. But as Roper turned, he was momentarily aware of a dark shape behind him which moved suddenly into a shop doorway. He appeared to pay no attention to it. For all that, he felt a slight trembling in his bowels. What if Verity were not alone? But he must be. Verney Dacre swore that the bastard Croaker hated Verity as much as anyone. And Lieutenant Dacre had never been wrong yet.

At 6.30, Ned Roper joined the little knot of travellers by the booking office and took a first-class ticket for Dover. After leaving the vestibule he waited a moment, retraced his steps, and stared at the broad back of Verity, who was handing the clerk a sovereign in exchange for a ticket. Then Ned Roper, with his mind at ease, went to the luggage office and superintended the wheeling of his carpet bags to the tidal ferry train. He did not go straight to his carriage, for Verney Dacre had given him one other instruction. From his pocket he drew an unsealed envelope, and then some nervous precaution made him draw from the envelope a single sheet of blue notepaper and read it for a last time. The block lettering was spidery and in a copperish ink.

ASK MR VERITY WHY HE IS GOING TO FOLKESTONE
TONIGHT

Roper slid the paper in and sealed the envelope, with its penny stamp in the corner. He chuckled as he crossed the station vestibule towards the posting box. Often enough he had taken his oath on the Bow Street testament "to be even with that bugger," and here was the great opportunity. He dropped the letter through the slot and caught a final glimpse of the crude capitals on the envelope.

INSPECTOR H. CROAKER,
PRIVATE DETAIL,
SCOTLAND YARD,
LONDON.

As he walked up the length of the train towards a first-class carriage near the engine, a porter began slowly and lugubriously tolling his little handbell as a five-minute warning of departure. Roper noticed that the luggage van appeared to be bolted from the interior on the side furthest from the platform. On the near side, which would be used for access at Reigate and Folkestone, the sliding door had to be closed from the outside. A railway constable, having just inspected the interior, had closed the door, dropped the iron bar across it, and was now fastening a formidable iron padlock upon it. Grudgingly, Ned Roper admitted to himself that Verney Dacre was right. The railway company believed robbery to be impossible in this case, and that was the best hope of succeeding in it.

He found an empty carriage near the engine, without difficulty. The recent spate of collisions had instilled a prudent choice among railway travellers for carriages near the middle of the train. As he reached for the handle of the door, he heard another carriage door opened and slammed to, very quickly, at a little distance behind him. Ned Roper gave a foxy smile at his reflection in the window glass, then closed the door and settled down against the thick, soft cushioning. In their separate little carriages the passengers were totally isolated from one another. It was true that a lady in distress would sometimes tie a handkerchief to an umbrella and wave it desperately from the window in an attempt to catch the attention of the guard at the end of the train. But even this was usually futile, and there was in any case little that the guard could do.

Roper went to the window and put his head out, as if to observe the scene on the platform but, in fact, to give Verity every opportunity to confirm where he was. Red-faced fathers of families were bellowing at porters to inquire after the safety of their luggage, while children in straw hats and sailor suits sucked impassively at oranges. The shriek of a whistle cut across the pandemonium. With a vigorous snort, the little engine jolted its diminutive carriages forward and the tidal ferry train began to glide clear of the smoky glass dome of London Bridge.

In the little shell of darkness which enveloped him, Verney Dacre's heart seemed to beat with the audible rhythm of a trip-hammer. Even to draw breath cost him an effort. But the first rumble of iron wheels on rail signalled the start of the cracksman's race: twenty-five minutes to Reigate and a fortune to be won. As he shifted his body, reaching for the slender brass bolts of the coffin side, the movement of cramped sinews and the pulse of excitement beating in his throat set up an uncontrollable shaking in his arms and fingers. He gasped, to exhale some of the tension, lay back, calmed himself, and reached out for the bolts again.

Once the side of the coffin was free it opened upwards on a pair of interior hinges. Dacre felt the wood brushing against the black velvet pall which covered it and guessed that he must be lying on some raised surface. Very carefully, he swung his long, thin legs through the gap and tested the drop to the ground. It was no more than two or three feet. The coffin had been laid at the rear of the luggage van on a fixed wooden table, which had once served the guard as a desk.

He straightened up and stood in a dappled twilight. The interior of the van was almost dark, but here and there the sunlight of the summer evening projected spears of dust-filled brilliance between the boarding of the sides. Ghostly outlines of boxes, portmanteaus, trunks, and hampers rose all about him in the gloom. At the far end of the van, he could just make out the broad rectangle of the iron safe, half luminous with its white-painted sides. But for all the weight which it carried, the van seemed to lurch and roll with unpredictable violence, swung by the speeding train as a snake might thresh its tail.

Dacre steadied himself, reached into his pocket for a "Glim" and struck it. After such intense darkness, the flare drew water to his eyes until he could see nothing but a blur. Then, holding the flame to one side, he began to search for "Mr Archer's" carpet-bags. They were all together, four of them, near the closed door of the van. He needed to open only one, which contained his tools: a storm lantern, a hammer, several box-wood wedges, and a balance with a pair of large brass pans. Dacre lit the lamp and hung it from the low, curved roof of the van, close to the iron bullion safe.

In the thick yellow light, he moved about the van again, searching for another cluster of luggage, two leather bags and a "governess" travelling box, the property of Miss Martineau, of Westerham, to be called for at Reigate railway office. The calling would not be long delayed, since "Miss Martineau," *alias* Jolie, had left Langham Place several hours earlier in a hired brougham, driven by Tyler, to be at Reigate before the train.

He found the travelling box and bags, which seemed unusually heavy for the possessions of a pretty young governess, and dragged them over to the safe. Then he set to work, a slender, stooping figure, working intently in the heat of the van, which resembled nothing so much as a chicken shed on wheels. Its interior smelt strongly of sawdust and straw, warmed by the summer air. Dacre's breathing was harsh with the closeness of the day and the exertion of his labours, while even the tallowy light of the lamp still brought the water to his inflamed eyes.

The bright rough keys, which he had filed for the two locks of the safe, were not perfect enough to work in the hands of an amateur. They needed the touch of a virtuoso cracksman to guide them in the locks. Dacre had to stop twice to wipe the sweat from his palms, and to feel more intently the many little pressures of the lock-barrel. Then, the tumblers moved quite suddenly and effortlessly, and the heavy bolts fell back with a ponderous thud. He turned the handle, and raised the weight of the iron lid until it slanted backwards to the full length of the safety chains.

Inside the thick iron walls, the lamplight fell upon a dozen oak bullion boxes, each bound with iron hoops, locked, and sealed by a wafer of red wax across the crevice where the lid of the box closed on the front wall of it. The boxes were almost uniform in shape and approximated in every case to a cube of about twelve to fifteen inches. Dacre judged that the contents of each must weigh about half a hundredweight. The blood pounded in his ears with the strain of lifting the first one clear of the safe and setting it on the floor of the van.

Once the box was firmly placed, with its back against the safe, he set the first wedge in the crevice between the lid and the front. Then, with half a dozen powerful hammer blows, he drove it firmly into place, driving a second one into position on the other side of the lock. He struck the wedges alternately with heavy, rapid blows. The crevice widened, the bolt of the lock jumped and then gave way, wrenched from its socket on the lid. Dacre removed the wedges, inserted them under the iron hoops which still bound the bullion-box, and then drove them in to raise the hoops sufficiently for them to slide clear of the box. Finally, he raised the lid, splintering the unique seal of Messrs Spielmann and Bult beyond any hope of repair.

For all the crudity and force, Dacre thought, it would prove to be a cracksman's masterpiece yet. It was the race to Reigate which had first to be won. The lamplight shone on rich, tawny metal. There must have been a score of small ingots, each weighing two or three pounds, and bearing the stamp of assay.

ROYAL MINT

21 VICTORIA R.

24 CARAT

He touched the cool, smooth metal, fondling it with a pleasure so entirely physical that he wanted to cry out or laugh aloud in the intensity of his triumph. At twenty-four carat, this bullion was gold in its purest form.

A shriek from the engine and the sudden roaring of a tunnel ended his trance of delight. Opening one of "Miss Martineau's" leather portmanteaus, he poured a stream of lead shot from it into one of the brass scale-pans. In the other he set the ingots from the broken bullion-box. When he had brought the two pans into balance, the ingots went into the portmanteau, and the grey mass of shot into the oak box. With his hammer, he beat the iron hoops of the box into place, forcing the lid into position. There was no time to adjust the lock, nor to think about the broken seal. One gamble had to be taken, that the safe and its boxes would not be checked at Reigate. It seemed a reasonable chance to take. Reigate was too soon, at Folkestone it would be a different matter.

As he opened a second box, the train screamed out of Merstham tunnel, crashing and rattling towards Reigate station in the thickening twilight. He judged there was time for a third box, but only at the risk of not being able to replace the iron hoops before the train stopped. With a frenzy that almost paralleled sexual obsession, he raised the stake of his gamble, breaking open the box and exchanging the hastily weighed gold for equivalent shot from the "governess" box. He had just closed "Miss Martineau's" luggage when the train lost speed rapidly and began gliding into Reigate platform. In the final seconds before the door of the luggage van was unlocked by a constable, Dacre swung the broken box into the safe, closed the iron lid, though without time to lock it, and crouched on the floor of the van, under the guard's table, which was enveloped by the folds of black velvet from the pall of the coffin lying upon it. He trusted to an obsequious reverence for the middle class dead, or even plain fear of a six-month-old corpse, to prevent a traffic clerk or porter from disturbing the pall.

Ned Roper swung his oatmeal-suited legs on to the seat and lay, like a grotesque and whiskery male odalisque, observing the passing scene. Evening sunlight picked out the distant cupolas of Greenwich Hospital, or the rusty sails of tall East India merchantmen, and threw long shadows over the broad engine-sheds of the Greenwich Railway Company. Gathering speed, the ferry train flew past little streets of new yellow brick and red tile, past dust-heaps, market-gardens and waste-grounds. With a crash and a rattle, New Cross Station, and the London and Brighton's railway sheds flashed across Roper's carriage window. Then came the Atmospheric Engine House at Croydon, then the tunnel, and then Reigate, with a grinding and screwing of metal brakes, and the smell of water on hot ash.

Taking a silver flask from his inner pocket, Roper unscrewed the top, put his head back, and jerked the remaining dregs into his mouth. Now, he told himself, he was ready for whatever might come his way, from sherry to rum-shrub, as the saying was. He sniffed and wiped his mouth on the back of his hand.

"Thirty-five," he said aloud, "still half a lifetime to come, and the sweetest half at that! Carriage company! Heavy swells on the lark! White ties and pink bonnets!"

As for the girls who came to Langham Place, he'd top and tail 'em once, just for practice as he always had done, but he'd never ditch Nell Jacoby and the "little fellow." Ever since London Bridge, he had wished for her there, to see her stretched out on the carriage seat bucking to the rhythm of the train. Legs like a dancer, thought Roper, bubbies like the statue in the Hyde Park Exhibition, lovely blue eyes and long hair, and an arse like a real young lady of fashion. Once or twice he'd leathered her, but she loved him just the same afterwards.

"No, Miss Ellen," said Roper softly, "there ain't any other would do as well."

At Reigate, he put his head out of the window and caught the dark movement of another head hastily drawn in, several carriages further along the train. There was no escape to the platform without Verity seeing him. It was all as Verney Dacre had predicted. Roper watched a porter cooling a hot wheel with the contents of a watering can, while passengers scurried to and from the crowded refreshment-room. In the twilight, the lamplighter and his boy were going their rounds "putting up" the gas along the station platforms. Roper withdrew his head, so that Verity might resume his vigil on the platform. The five-minute bell rang.

Ned Roper waited two minutes more. Then he gently opened the door which faced away from the platform, taking care not to hold it wider than was necessary. He slipped through the gap and lowered himself almost soundlessly into the shadowy gloom, crouching level with the thick iron wheels of the carriage. He pushed the door to, not slamming it but allowing it to half engage the lock so that at least it would not fly open. He had hardly done this when the whistle shrieked and the engine, with a rapid thunder of preliminary gasps, edged forward, the iron wheels rumbling past him as he crouched there.

By the time that the luggage van at the end of the train came towards him, the wheels seemed to have picked up a terrifying speed. The door of the van was still closed and there was nothing to jump for but the narrow footboard. Roper began to run alongside the moving train. He spurted as the luggage van began to pass him, the flashing iron of the wheels no more than twelve inches from his feet. Then he leapt at the speeding footboard and in mid-leap saw that he had been no judge of distance and seemed now almost to will himself to miss his mark. The iron rims flailed like knives below him, the earth flying away into darkness, as his right foot hit the board and his body fell against the boarding of the van. For what seemed ten or twenty seconds, but could not have been a tenth so long, his nails scrabbled at the wooden side, seeking some hold, and yet knowing that if he found one, death between the wheels and rails would only be postponed a few minutes unless Verney Dacre could open the sliding door.

He felt his body turn, swaying towards the outer darkness

and the horror beneath him. In utter terror he gave one helpless shriek.

"Nell!"

It seemed that he had passed the point of equilibrium and was already falling when a pair of hands gripped him at shoulder and collar, hauling him to safety from the clutch of the winds of death that pulled him outwards. He fell forward at last on the floor of the van, sobbing with mingled exhaustion and terror.

"You killed me!" he said bewilderedly, and then corrected himself. "You almost had me under the wheels, Mr Dacre."

"Oblige me," said Verney Dacre grimly, "by tellin' me in future if you're going to get so drunk that you can't jump two feet on to the running-board of a train."

Nevertheless, he drew out his own cavalry flask, unscrewed it and handed it to his trembling companion. Ned Roper drank long and gratefully.

"It went all right?" he said at length, sniffing and pulling himself together.

"It ain't likely, is it," said Dacre coldly, "that I should be standin' here like this if it had gone all wrong? The box and two bags went off at Reigate, Tyler and the girl had them. They left three more bags for Dover."

" 'ow much?" asked Roper, getting to his feet.

Dacre closed the sliding door of the van on the darkness outside.

"One and a half hundredweight and twelve pounds weight. Say, £10,000, give or take a few flimsies."

He was already raising the lid of the safe again, when Roper, recovering some of his habitual jauntiness, inquired,

"You pitched the major in the river, I take it?"

"No," said Dacre, attending to the safe, "that's what a fool would do, and then bury our own coffin weighted with pure gold! Coggin is drivin' the major smartly to a night's lyin' in state at Appleford church. They expect him about ten o'clock, only they ain't to know he hasn't come from the railway station. Then Coggin drives to Folkestone, announces he's come for the coffin here, and drives it back to town for tomorrow morning. And once the poor major's back in the earth tomorrow, no one will question that it was his coffin the railway company carried in their luggage van. Oh, they may dig him up again, if they please, and see if he got out of his salt-box and robbed their gold. So much the better."

Ned Roper chuckled.

"Oh, my eye!" he said, his happiness entirely restored, "ain't it prime, though?"

"Prime," said Dacre coldly, "since Coggin thinks he's carrying a French doxy back to town in an opium trance, and Tyler and the girl think they've got a load of French prints and figures that came through the customs this morning. Take these boxes and lay them out in two rows. All of them."

With an hour until the train stopped again at Folkestone, there was time to finish the job professionally. Cazamian, on the platform at the back of the train had no access to the interior of the luggage van. He knew only that Verney Dacre was in the van, presumably alone, searching for his "lost diamond." There had been no trouble at Reigate and Cazamian was soon to be richer by four hundred pounds. More than that, he was not to be broken in agony, limb by limb, as one of Ned Roper's welshers.

Dacre's shirt cuffs were twisted and contoured with grime as he settled to the task of emptying the nine bullion-boxes which remained. Squatting at the first of them, he turned to Roper and held a pair of pincers towards him at arm's length.

"Here, old fellow," he said, almost genially, "see if you can't do something about loosening the fastenings of the iron hoops with these. It's the very deuce havin' to beat wedges in with a hammer every minute or another."

Roper, with a job to do, began to recover his self-possession, while Dacre broke open the locks with the wedges and hammer.

"I never could understand bullion coves," Dacre remarked casually, as another bolt was jarred loose from its socket. "Nothing will do but they must have double locks on the door of the safe, and every other sort of nonsense. But their own boxes open easily as a china pig. Uncommon rum, ain't it?"

Ned Roper had put his pincers down and now stood over Dacre, staring down, his eyes wide and his mouth a circle of incredulity at the sight of the little gold ingots laid out in neat rows.

"Sovs!" he said suddenly. "Yellow boys!" and he snatched up a paper tube of coins packed in one of the boxes. Two or We empty each box in turn and keep the weight exact."

"Have the goodness," said Dacre icily, "to put those back. We empty each box in turn and keep the weight exact."

"Eagles!" Roper picked up the coins from the floor. "Yankee Eagles, and all of them gold! Change 'em in Lombard Street in half a minute, and no one'd look twice! Must be five hundred if there's five!"

Dacre's drawl mingled irony and menace.

"If you suppose, Ned Roper, that you will change a single one of them, you are most prodigiously mistaken. Gold ingots can be melted till you couldn't tell 'em from one another. But the man who changes five hundred Eagles, after this dodge comes to light, will have some deep questions to answer. Oblige me by puttin' 'em back."

Roper stood, in the shadows of the van, apparently reproved and acknowledging the justice of the rebuke. He watched as his companion opened every box and every carpet-bag which contained lead shot. One by one, the ingots were measured against the amorphous piles of shot in the brass scale-pans. Then the lead was transferred to the bullion-boxes, and the gold to the carpet bags. Verney Dacre worked with a care which would have impressed many an honest craftsman. The richness of the joke seemed to Roper, in his tipsy state, "good enough for *Punch*." He began to titter.

"Oblige me," said Verney Dacre softly, "by not gigglin' like a ninny, and by handin' the courier-bags from your shirt."

Roper opened his brown frock-coat and began to produce the little wash-leather bags, each with its own individual weight of shot. Dacre added the diminutive streams of pale grey metal to the pile in the brass pan. But when he reached the last of the bullion-boxes, he looked at the row of ingots inside it, and then closed the lid.

" 'ere," said Roper quickly, "what's wrong with them?"

"Nothing," said Dacre coolly, "but that gold stays where it is. We shan't take it."

"Not take it?" Roper looked at him with incredulity, "Three thousand pounds in gold! Not take it!"

Dacre spoke very quietly and with great weariness.

"We've come to the end of the lead shot, old fellow. We can't take any more gold. The boxes would be light at the weighing."

To his disgust, Roper began to whine threateningly.

"But you can't mean to leave it behind, Mr Dacre! You can't. Ain't there something to use instead of the shot? There must be!"

Then he saw something in Dacre's eyes, something which Cazamian had once seen in Ned Roper's, and now Roper was afraid. The whining ceased. Looking at Dacre, he thought that even if the bastard had been kicked out of his regiment for thieving, he had killed men at the battle of Chillian-wallah. To be sure they were black men, but Ned Roper had no intention of trusting to his colour to save him.

"Listen to me," said Dacre, tall and determined. Ned Roper listened.

"These boxes will certainly be weighed somewhere, probably at Folkestone. If the weights don't match the weights at London Bridge, then, by God, the jig is up. The boxes will be open, the hare runnin' loose, and we shall still be on the train. For good measure, you'll have Verity there, too, to put the finger on you."

"Well," said Roper with a half-apologetic smile, "I ain't that keen to have the darbies snapped round my wrists."

"Likewise," said Dacre thoughtfully, "we might take the American Eagles."

Roper's face brightened.

"To throw in the river," said Dacre with a sharp gesture.

"If the coins have gone, you may be sure that the first thing they'll look for is someone changin' them. And they shall still be searchin' for that at the Last Trump."

He hammered down the iron hoops of the bullion boxes and adjusted the locks so that even where the sockets were broken a key would still raise the tumblers in the lock itself. It was not essential to his plan, but a sense of finesse required it. Finally, he began to melt two sticks of red wax in one of the brass scale-pans, holding it above the lamp and using it as a chafing-dish. A smell of warm tallow and incense filled the luggage van as the mixture seethed like a stiff broth. He took four seals from the carpet-bag and lined them up, ready to stamp the molten wax over the crevices of the bullion-boxes.

" 'ow d'yer do it?" gasped Roper, with eyes that reminded Dacre of his beagle's admiration. "Dear God, Mr Dacre! Yer got the bullion merchants' seals!"

"No, I ain't, old fellow," said Dacre flatly, "just four seals bought from a stall in Hungerford Market."

Roper's eyes were suddenly overcast with dismay.

"Hungerford Market? What the 'ell's the use of that? Soon's they come to look at them, they'll know it's wrong. They'll know it, Mr Dacre!"

Verney Dacre finished the sealing of the bullion-boxes. Then he stood up, turned round, and faced his companion with his habitual broken drawl.

"Y'may be a devilish fine bully, Ned Roper, but y'lack observation. These fellows that do the weighin' ain't nothing but well-paid counter-jumpers. Even a man who's Superintendent of Traffic ain't born a gentleman and won't ever be his own master. He'll see the seals are unbroken, but it ain't likely he'll examine them close if the weight of the boxes is right. But suppose he does look close, and suppose he sees a difference. What then? Does he take a hammer and start smashin' open boxes of gold on Folkestone Harbour Pier in the middle of the night? If he does that, he's in no position to show what seal was on the boxes because he'll have broken it to splinters in opening them. But, in any case, Ned Roper, that ain't the way a counter clerk sees his job. First he'd telegraph London Bridge and ask them to please be so good as to discover if the bullion merchants have changed their seals, or whether they mayn't have used the wrong one by accident. There won't even be a reply to that before tomorrow morning, by which time you and I will be back in London. And believe me, Ned, it ain't that easy to tell the difference between seals in a bad light."

Roper seemed unwillingly convinced. They closed the remaining carpet-bags, distributed some of the weight of gold in the sham coffin and carefully closed its bolts. Between them they carried the bullion-boxes to the safe and replaced them in the correct order. At last, Verney Dacre took his two roughly-cut keys and, after a moment's probing, the two heavy bolts in the locks of the bullion safe fell shut with an audible thud.

When there was no more to be done, Roper began a muffled, squittering laugh; and in a spontaneous release of tension, Verney Dacre joined him. Whether it was the thought of the faces of the officials of the Messageries Impériales on opening the boxes, or whether it was sheer relief, neither man could have told. But they sniggered and guffawed and slapped one another on the back until they were beyond Ashford, and beyond Standford, closing fast upon the points between Folkestone upper level and the Harbour Pier.

These points were vital in Dacre's plan. To turn from the main line down to the harbour, the train had first to pass over the points. Then the points were changed and the train, backing over them, turned away from the upper level and down a curved branch of railway track to the Harbour Pier. The tidal ferry train might be advertised as "direct" from Reigate to Folkestone Harbour, but the construction of the permanent way was such that it was obliged to stop for about ninety seconds while the points were changed. According to Verney Dacre's previous observation, it might be more than ninety seconds, it might even be a little less.

Standing close to the off-side door of the van, which faced away from platforms when the train was stationary, Dacre felt the first change in the rhythm of the wheels. The sliding door could not be opened or fastened from the outside, but only by raising or dropping into iron brackets a solid metal bar inside the van. He raised the bar on its pivot and slowly drew the door across, revealing the pale streaks of chalk cliff flashing past them as the train began to lose speed before the points. Of all his tools, the only one which Dacre had not returned to the carpet-bag was a large hammer.

Soon the grinding and screwing of metal signalled that the brakes of the train had been applied, and it passed at walking speed over the points. At the screech which was the prelude to complete braking, Dacre motioned his companion towards the open door, watched him jump and saw him set off along the cutting, running low beside the stationary carriages. Dacre himself remained on the footboard for a moment, gently sliding the door across with as much care as if it had been some delicate mechanism. Once the door was closed, it could be fastened again only if the raised bar inside were dropped into position. Cazamian might do that if he were first to reach the van, but that risk was too great. Dacre judged the point at which the pivot of the bar would be on the inside of the boarding. Then he hit it a hammer blow with all his strength on the outside of the wood. There was no response. He struck it again, and this time heard the fall of metal. How far the iron bar had lodged in its sockets was a mere guess, but now he found it impossible to move the door from the outside.

And then Dacre jumped from his perch and ran with his head ducked below the pale rectangles of light which were cast by the carriage windows. He could see Roper's head and shoulders in dark silhouette, marking a carriage in which no lights were burning. The engine whistle shrieked and the wheels of the carriages began to turn just as he drew level. Roper flung the door wide, Dacre jumped, and as he pulled. himself into the carriage the rhythm of the train grew loud enough to obscure the sound of the door being slammed behind him.

It puzzled Verity that Roper should have travelled so late, unless he were proposing to spend a night or more in Dover, and that he should have come without his doxy this time. At Reigate he was no more than two carriages' distance from Roper, and had kept such a vigil that no man could have entered or left Roper's carriage unobserved. At a little distance from Folkestone, he discovered that he could hear the sound of voices from the other carriages, fragmentarily, by keeping his own window lowered.

Roper was evidently not alone, he caught the strident, bragging tones of the man once or twice, though without being able to distinguish precisely the words that were spoken. Of what was said by one of Roper's travelling companions, he heard little more. The tone of the man's voice was one which Verity had heard often enough before, the languid drawl of the St James's Palace dragoon, still affecting the English of the reign of William IV or even the Regency. Such voices and personalities had come to be thoroughly despised by the riflemen of the Crimea, who compared their own hardships with the easy affluence of the "peacock bastards" in the lancers and hussars.

Verity just managed to hear the voice instructing someone, for God's sake, to "put up some yaller light, or let a fellah have a glim or two," and then to say something about "travellin' on to Paris or Roome and break the Pope's nose." Beyond that, there was nothing.

The wheels of the carriage jolted over the crossing and then ran more evenly alongside the platform of the Harbour Pier. Verity put on his tall black hat, the brim tilted a little over his eyes, and shifted so that he might see if anyone so much as opened the door of Roper's carriage to get down on to the platform. Almost at once, the door opened and Roper stepped out, striding away down the platform. Verity followed him, dodging and peering among the crowd of travellers, until Roper pushed his way into the refreshment room. Through the window, Verity watched him in the brightly lit interior, holding a glass of steaming toddy and favouring the serving girl with a thin, whiskery smile.

With a sense of some relief, he realised that Roper was not leaving the train at Folkestone but travelling on to Dover, as he had expected. A few seconds before the departure whistle, the man left the refreshment room and ran to a carriage in the middle of the train, apologetically pushing himself in among a family party for the last fifteen minutes of the journey. At Dover, Verity was out first, watching for Roper to emerge and carry his luggage from the van. Instead, it was a porter who carried the luggage to the rank, where several hansom cabs still waited in the warm darkness. As usual, a railway constable was in attendance at the rank to take down the number of each cab and its destination. Verity strained to catch the words called out by the porter.

"Number sixteen. Wellington Arms, Walmer!"

The driver cracked his whip and the cab rattled away across the cobbled courtyard. Verity watched it go. There was no hope of carrying out an overnight surveillance at Walmer, since he had to parade for duty before Inspector Croaker the next morning. But though he might not be able to do it, there was one man who could take over the task for him. Julius Stringfellow must now show that he was as good as his word.

"Here," said Verity, clutching at the porter's sleeve, "what time does this train go back to town, my man?"

The porter disengaged himself and looked superciliously at the fat, unkempt traveller, his tall hat askew and his clothes hanging baggily about him. This was no moment for respect.

"Twenty-five minutes," he said grudgingly, and turned away.

Verity stood in deep thought for a while. Then he turned and walked resolutely back towards the harbour station and the telegraph office.

Ned Roper waited until the cab was safely round two

corners, and then he banged with his stick upon the roof. The wheels slowed and the cabman opened the little roof-hatch.

"Were you the one he said 'Wellington Arms, Walmer' to?" Roper inquired.

"Yes, sir," said the cabman firmly.

"Damn the fool!" said Roper in mock-frustration, "that's the other passenger. I'm for the Dover Castle Hotel."

"Ain't that easy sir. Very strict the railway constables is about destinations being entered."

"Look," said Roper ingratiatingly, "set me down at the Dover Castle. Drive on to Walmer or not, as you please. And here's the sovereign for the Walmer fare and another half sov into the bargain. It's worth that much to me for a night's proper rest before I take the shilling sicker for Boulogne tomorrow."

"Right-o, guv'nor," said the cabman cheerily, and turned off towards the Dover Castle.

Five minutes later, Ned Roper and his carpet-bags crossed the vestibule of the hotel.

"Mr Archer," he said to the footman, "travelling from Ostend to London, a private room reserved for dinner, for Mr Archer and one other gentleman."

The footman bowed slightly, turned, and led Roper and the two luggage boys down a broad passageway, brightly lit by the glare of gas brackets.

Verney Dacre sat patiently at the table in the private room, surveying the fine linen, cut-glass, and silverware. He looked up at Roper as the door closed.

"I passed your cab on the way up, standin' idle in the road. As for that jack of yours, damned if he ain't called the dogs off and started back for London Bridge on the ten o'clock."

With that, the two men began to laugh.

"Come on, though," said Dacre at last, "I'm so famished I swear I may die if I don't get a good tightener soon."

The clock of St James's Church chimed the half hour as Dacre and Roper walked down the East Cliff road towards the Harbour station. Ahead of them, the starlit night was blacked out by the mass of the Western Heights. In half an hour more, at 2 a.m., the night ferry train, from Dover to London Bridge, would be on its way.

Each of the two men carried his own carpet-bags, but the weight was much less than when they had contained lead-shot. More than a hundredweight of the gold ingots had been carefully distributed in the coffin and neither man now carried more than half a hundredweight distributed among the leather bags. However, even this was a burden over so long a distance and neither of them spoke as they walked, firmly but breathing heavily, along Townwall towards the harbour.

Just short of the station, Dacre stopped.

"Have the goodness," he said, gasping a little, "to throw away your other ticket and take this."

Ned Roper looked at the proffered slip.

"Ostend to London Bridge?" he said foolishly.

"Take it!" Dacre picked up his bags again. "It's worth a hundred times what it cost. It makes us passengers from Ostend on this evening's boat. If there's a screw loose over the bullion, there's an even chance of showing that we were on the high seas all the time that the ferry train was between London Bridge and Folkestone."

Roper began to cackle with delight, but Verney Dacre ignored him and made for the palely lit outline of the railway office. They had hardly reached it when a dark figure approached them.

"London Bridge, gentlemen? May I find you your carriage, gents?"

Ned Roper showed every sign of clinging on to his carpet-bags unless forcibly parted from them, but Verney Dacre set his down for the porter to carry.

"Tickets, genl'men?" said the porter hopefully. Dacre handed them to him and the man looked briefly at the details.

"Ostend steamer?" he said casually. "Then I fear I ain't able to take you to your carriage. All steamer luggage has to go through the custom 'ouse for opening and inspection by the waterguard before it goes to the train."

It seemed to Verney Dacre that he stood dumbfounded by the impact of this information for a full minute, though it could hardly have been more than a few seconds. Worse still, as he fought for words, he saw Roper reaching inside a pocket for what could only have been a life preserver to strike down the porter in the full light of the station lamps. Dacre took a step to place himself between the two men, and turned his most arrogant manner upon the porter.

"I don't believe," he said contemptuously, "that the waterguard officers would thank us for putting them to the same trouble twice. We came by last night's Ostend steamer and have been stopping at the Dover Castle since. You may see the receipted bill, for that matter."

He reached in his pocket, as though for a sheet of paper, and waited. The porter wavered, judged that a handsome tip was about to elude him if the argument was pressed further, and gave way.

"You need only have said, sir," he murmured ingratiatingly. "There ain't no call for yesterday's passengers to go through the waterguard at all.

Dacre followed him down the platform to a first-class carriage in which the oil lamps were already burning."

"Thank you," he said, handing the man a half-sovereign, "we'll have the bags with us. I don't care to be kept standin' about the luggage van at London Bridge waitin' for them."

He sat back against the cushions, closed his eyes and kept them closed until the train had begun to move. When he opened them again, Ned Roper was holding a gold coin between thumb and forefinger, holding it close to the lamp for admiration. Seeing Dacre's eyes upon him, he hastily put the gold Eagle down and opened his other hand in a little gesture of reassurance.

"It was only two or three," he said reasonably. "They change hundreds of foreign coins at hotels like that. And no one even knows we were there. After all, half of it's mine, ain't it?"

Dacre was too tired for anger, too weary even to feel disgust. He closed his eyes again, and slept.

Daybreak began just before they reached Reigate once more. Dacre looked carefully on both sides of the train and then felt a sudden exultation. In the station yard, beyond the further platform, a pair of black horses, their heads bowed a little, waited patiently in the shafts of an elegant hearse. He saw plainly the outline of Coggin in the driver's seat. The bully had been told to expect a companion who might, or might not, join him from the Dover train at Reigate. It was never Dacre's intention that there should be such a companion. For him, the appearance of Coggin and the hearse at Reigate was merely a signal that the entire plan had operated without fault.

At London Bridge, he and Roper took separate cabs for Euston, and then a single one to the Great Western Terminus, though on the way they gave the driver new instructions to take them to Camden Town. At Camden Town, they walked to Chalk Farm, and there called a cab off the rank for Langham Place.

As they drove through the mean streets of north London, the sky blue with the coming day, Verney Dacre stared without thought or feeling at the shoeless children curled asleep on doorsteps. Already at street corners, the homeless poor and early workers were gathered round breakfast stalls, blowing saucers of steaming coffee drawn from the tall tin cans with their fires glowing underneath. The cries of a little slattern girl screaming watercresses through the sleeping streets made him turn his head. He looked at Roper, whose auburn whiskers were parted in a confident smirk, now that the work was over. Poor mark, thought Verney Dacre, he was not to know that for him only the triumph was over, and the long agony was about to begin.

13

At four o'clock on the following afternoon, at the Gare du Nord, the Chef de Sûreté of the Messageries Impériales turned two keys in the locks of the bullion safe. In the presence of several armed guards of the Banque Impériale and three *négotiants* from the French bullion vaults, the boxes were laid out, unlocked and their lids raised for inspection. The Chef de Sûreté leaned forward and then, without warning, fainted clean away into the arms of the Directeur of the Banque Impériale, who chanced to be standing immediately behind him.

14

"I ain't saying," remarked Stringfellow carefully, "that there ain't no such hostelry as the Wellington Arms at Walmer. And I ain't saying there is. What I am saying is that I have walked the highways of Walmer until I know them as well as I know my own phiz. And I ain't found any such. More than that. I have been into every inn and made careful inquiries about a friend of mine corresponding to the description of your Ned Roper. I'll swear he's never been near Walmer. He never was going there. He must have known you were salting his tail again. It's how you were put down before, Verity. You got no eye for superior numbers."

Verity spat on a boot and rubbed it with a scrap of cloth.

"A soldier ain't to be put down by superior numbers," he said severely, "and I ain't sure I *was* put down. I shouldn't be surprised if Ned Roper wasn't telling me more than he thought when he took that cab for Walmer. *And* I shouldn't be surprised if superior numbers wasn't to be what hung him in the end."

4

SERGEANT VERITY
AT BAY

15

"Sealskin" Kite's fingers played on the table's edge as deftly as though it were the keyboard of a Broadwood or an Erard. The hands were soft and plump as a dowager's, though marked on their backs by a scattering of pale brown freckles. Kite's head, round, plump and bald, the eyes and mouth pouched by ample flesh, reminded Verney Dacre of the old white bulldog curled up on the parlour chair at the Hope and Anchor. Then Kite turned to Dacre.

"You tell me, sir, what man o' business don't suffer the same hardships. Why, let me see, it must be ten years since I was last on a racecourse—me, Sealskin Kite!—and more than that since I saw the inside of a gaff."

He stared at Dacre defiantly, as though inviting contradiction.

Mrs Kite, the third and most grotesque member of the trio, laid a hand on her husband's arm.

"You're a wearing old soul to a 'ooman," she said, winking confidentially at Dacre, "and that's the truth."

Dacre brushed his moustache self-consciously with his right hand and gave a slight, unsmiling acknowledgement of her affability. In her black bonnet and shawl she had a complexion that was brown and wrinkled as a nut by contrast with Kite's pale smoothness. Dacre still stared with amazement that such a dull pair of codgers should be monarchs of the underworld, and the terror of petty thieves, magsmen, or whores alike.

Then Mrs Kite lifted the silver tea-pot and tilted it over a cup. The pot was evidently over-filled, for it spurted hot tea beyond the cup and on to the linen cloth.

"Drat the creetur!" said Mrs Kite ambiguously. She swung round in her chair and gestured towards a servant girl in a plain grey dress, who hovered near the doorway.

"Charity! Work'ouse! Come here this minute! Take this pot off and fill it properly. And p'raps our visitor would like to try a new-laid egg or two. Likewise a few rounds of buttered toast, first a-cutting off the crust in consequence of tender teeth."

She waved the girl away and favoured Dacre with another hideous smile. This time he made no attempt to return the pleasantry. Two days before the bullion robbery had been committed, he had made this appointment with Kite, offering several hundredweight of bullion for sale, and Kite had evasively agreed to the meeting. Now, within twelve hours of carrying the gold back from Dover, Dacre had come to seal the bargain. There was a certain aptness, he thought, in concluding a sale in the very room through which, a few weeks earlier, he had entered Kite's villa as a burglar.

Dacre had not anticipated the ceremonial of the tea table with Mrs Kite present. However, Kite himself seemed indifferent as to whether the matter of the sale was discussed at first, and appeared almost to have forgotten that this was the reason for his guest's presence. Yet Dacre had laid the second part of his plan with even more care than he had prepared the robbery. If he were now to succeed in it, he must work with such speed that his victims had no time to recover from one blow before another was struck.

"That young 'ooman," said Mrs Kite at length, "mayn't come amiss for having her ears boxed about the compass! Nasty charity school creetur!"

As soon as the two men were alone together, Dacre was about to speak, but Kite moved a hand slowly as though asking forbearance.

"I was so glad, my dear young sir, that you were able to honour me by this visit. So glad. Sealskin Kite keeps open house. Always did and ever shall."

He spoke with the deference of a proud man, in the tone of a gamekeeper addressing his young master.

"It ain't nothin' but the need to trade gold for specie that obliges me to call on you in this fashion," said Dacre pointedly.

Kite patted his forehead with a folded handkerchief and pouted his lips in perplexity.

"Gold ain't the spec it used to be, my dear sir, not by 'alf. And there being such a quantity in your hands makes it hard to dispose of in the way of business. Hundredweights! Why, I never knew a man that had *hundredweights* of gold, and I can't think 'ow he should come by them, for the matter of that."

"Five hundredweight, less a few pounds, all at twenty-four carat," said Dacre with flawless arrogance, "but if it's too big a chance, old fellow, you need only say the word."

The faintest flush coloured Kite's forehead and cheekbones at the familiarity and the carefully balanced insult.

"You'd do well, young sir," he said softly, "to recall that nothing you have is too big for Sealskin Kite. You may bring your bullion and whatever else you have, and Sealskin Kite will spend pound for pound with you from here to Jericho. As to five hundredweight of gold, however, you'd do better to sell it to the Bank of England at three guineas an ounce."

"I don't choose to sell it to the Bank," said Dacre flatly.

Kite stroked his chin.

"No," he said, "banks is apt to be fussy about a quarter of a ton of bullion."

"You ain't sayin'," Dacre inquired, "that this may be dishonest gold?"

"No," said Kite.

"You ain't heard of five hundredweight that's been missed anywhere?"

"No," said Kite, "but that's not to say that I mightn't." And with that, the pale dropsical face creased in a smile which indicated that the preliminaries of negotiation were over.

Verney Dacre took a package from his inner pocket, unwrapped the wash-leather and slid the miniature ingot across the table for Kite's inspection. Kite examined the assay mark of the Royal Mint, using an eye-glass for the purpose, weighed the bar in his hand, and then passed it back.

"You'd do best to take it to the Bank," he said finally. "You won't find anyone else to give you three guineas an ounce. It ain't that many that has got thirty-six thousand pounds to give."

"Have the goodness," said Dacre wearily, "to name a price."

Kite pushed his chair back a little from the table.

"Not three guineas," he said firmly. "We must sell abroad. Spain, Egypt, where there's a paper loan to be raised and they want gold to back it. Even they won't pay you three guineas, a-cos there's nothing in it for them if they do. Two pounds ten is their going price. Now, if I must undertake the whole of the transaction, at my own cost and risk, and not knowing or asking where the gold came from, I mayn't go above two pounds an ounce, my dear sir. Really, I mayn't."

It was as much as Dacre had expected and he knew that argument would be useless.

"It ain't far removed from extortion," he said casually, "since you may dispose of it to the Bank in due course and take thirty-six thousand quid for the twenty thousand you give me."

"But I give you twenty thousand, sir," said Kite, "for what may never have cost you near that. And I take the risk and I lose the use and interest of all that money until I can sell the bullion. I can serve you, sir, but a servant must be paid his hire."

Dacre nodded.

"Now, sir," Kite resumed, "you may bring whatever bullion you wish to the Cape and India warehouse in Bermondsey tomorrow afternoon at three. My assayer shall be there. After the assay and weighing, he shall have my authority to pay you two pounds an ounce for whatever you may bring. The sum shall be paid in specie, in notes of a hundred pound denomination. The transaction shall include only gold assayed at twenty-four carat. As to the warehouse, it is a business premises of my own to which you may safely bring your bullion."

Dacre nodded.

"You have my word," said Kite. "Sealskin Kite's word, for good or ill, is never broken."

And then he smiled once more, and, dismissing the subject, resumed the manner of a suburban host at his well-provided table.

Dacre glanced round the room, so that Kite might see him admiring the Regency sofa in banded silk; the elegant chairs; the mahogany or walnut gloss of sideboard and sofa-table; the framed silhouettes, miniatures, and oil portraits in gilt surrounds with which the green velvet of the walls was hung. His heart beat faster but his voice was carefully controlled as he came to the second and more dangerous negotiation.

"Y' have a fine collection of heads," he remarked, nodding at the wall, "uncommon fine."

Kite was on his feet at once, shepherding Dacre towards them.

"Devilish fine, though," said Dacre admiringly, "now ain't these some of the originals of the miniatures you see sold all over town?"

Kite regarded him with a forced smile.

"There you are mistaken, my dear sir, these are my family and my little ones. They were all painted for me by Mr Frost, more than ten years ago. They have never left this house."

Dacre gave a shrug of genial bewilderment.

"Then I have seen some very like," he conceded. "That head of the little girl with blue ribbons in her hair—deuced fine!—I swear I saw the very spit of that not a month ago. The kitten in her arms, too. I wish now I had bought it, so that you might have seen for yourself."

"Was it for sale then?" There was the first note of a tremor in Kite's voice.

"In a manner of speakin'," said Dacre. "A common rough lookin' fellah had it. A pickpocket, an amateur magsman who sells what he can. Seein' he had it, I thought it must be stolen, or else a cheap copy. They tell me he brags of the cribs he's cracked and the trinkets he's found, but I take it for gammon."

"Now, my dear sir," said Kite softly, "this touches me very

close. You may know or you mayn't—it's of no consequence
—but I must see that miniature and your magsman."

Dacre laughed.

"I should not care for you to meet him! He's an uncommon rough sort of cove! He ain't the sort to play at tip and
run. He'd be even with you and even with me, if you were to
press hard on him!"

"If he's got that miniature, as you describe," murmured
Kite, "he won't trouble you after."

"But someone else may," said Dacre evasively.

Kite had sat down again, his face paler than before. He
seemed short of breath, as though even the exertion of talking had been beyond his strength.

"Your meaning?" he said.

Dacre sat down on the far side of the table.

"It don't take the judgment of Solomon to see that you've
been wronged by someone, and that may be our magsman.
It ain't a secret that you suffered a cruel robbery. If I put you
in his way, you may be revenged, and you may thank me for
it."

"I should," said Kite earnestly, "and neither you nor any
friend of mine should be troubled by the man after that."

"Favour for favour," said Dacre smoothly.

"Meaning?"

"You might oblige me by squarin' an account of mine with
a troublesome cove. I know they call you a killin' man, Mr
Kite, and I don't want that. I know you can break a man so
that he never walks straight again. And I shan't want that.
All I want is an affidavit or two, so that a certain party shall
be far enough away from me that I may never hear of him
again."

Kite shrugged.

"Affidavits can be bought," he said amiably. "Only tell me
of your magsman and you shall have a hundred affidavits."

Their conversation, earnest and abrupt, was ended some
minutes later by the return of Mrs Kite. When tea was over,
and Kite rang for his servant to show his guest out, Verney

Dacre took a last look at Sealskin and his wife, nestling side by side on the sofa, like two old mice in a glove.

Ned Roper had slept soundly the length of the hot July afternoon, while Verney Dacre took tea with Sealskin Kite. He had woken only when the jangle of music, two floors below him in the Introducing Room, proclaimed the opening of the evening's business in Langham Place. He got up, dressed, and remembered that since early morning he had been a very rich man. Richer, he thought, than manufacturers and country squires; quite rich enough to have a house in St James's Square, a spanking new carriage and pair, and such an income that would make him a gentleman for life. But that should come later. For the moment he willingly obeyed Lieutenant Dacre's instructions to the very letter. Until half past ten and after, he was to be seen at his post in Langham Place, giving orders to Tyler and Coggin or supervising Ellen's accounts in the little parlour. Just before eleven o'clock, he slipped out and called a cab for Tooley Street.

The hansom set him down a few yards from the dingy, dockside façade of the Green Man. The light from the murky windows fell thickly through the insanitary river mist of the warm night, the outpourings of sewers and gas factories drawn into the very air of the great city. To one side of him, the huge brick arches and buttresses rose like a cliff to London Bridge station. It hardly seemed possible, Roper thought, that it was only the evening before that he and Verney Dacre had set out from there on the bullion caper. Why, it would be hours yet before the shocking news from Paris even reached Folkestone.

Through the steamy windows of the Green Man, he saw Cazamian sitting alone at a settle. Cazamian looked up as Roper pushed open the door and a cracked bell rattled on its spring.

"Thought you ain't coming, Mr Roper," said Cazamian reprovingly.

Roper gathered the skirts of his greatcoat around him and sat down.

"But you got the key, old fellow?" he said anxiously. "You have got it, haven't you?"

"What key might that be?"

"Why," said Roper cheerily, "our gentleman 'as his jewel back! Pleased ain't the word for it. Last night, straight away, he gets me to send a key to your lodgings by penny post. And tonight he sends me 'ere with the money-box what the key fits."

He produced the small metal box, which had carried Dacre's three hundred pounds in sovereigns from London to Folkestone a few weeks before.

"You were to have the box, he said," Roper added, "so soon as you should have finished your day's duty. The key he sent first as a token of good faith."

"I been at work since morning," said Cazamian sulkily, "much chance I've 'ad to get keys in the penny post."

"Then you may break it open, if the key ain't waiting," said Roper, handing the solid weight of the box to Cazamian.

"It was to be four hundred," said Cazamian ungraciously. It seemed to Roper that the man had been drinking for much of the evening and had now convinced himself that he was no mere pawn in cracking a crib, but rather one whose secret knowledge must be recognised.

Roper smiled at him.

"You'll find five hundred in there," he said with studied coyness. "Very pleased the gentleman was to have his diamond back."

Cazamian shook the box and heard the bunched rattle of coins. He stood up, lurched against the settle, and clutched the box under his coat.

"I shall go 'ome," he said thickly, "and there I shall expect to find a key and five hundred quid in the box."

"If you don't," said Roper good-humouredly, "you may call out every jack in the division!"

He watched Cazamian moving slowly through the crowd, towards the door. The door opened and swung to again.

With that, Roper was off, outside and across the street, up the steps to the station forecourt, and into the first hansom cab. He watched with satisfaction as a railway constable took the number and destination of the cab. Then he was whirled away towards the gaslit brilliance of Regent Circus.

Cazamian, still clutching the metal box under his coat, hovered uncertainly on the corner of Tooley Street and Mill Lane, where the ill-lit side streets ran between tall, dark warehouses to the river. In his fuddled mind he hardly knew whether to run to his lodgings in search of the promised key or beat open the box on the flagstones around him. His fingers played with the metal lid as he half-walked, half-ran past Counter Street towards the river and his pathway home.

He had reached the spot where a single gas-jet hissed and flared over the rotten planking of an old wharf, when he heard other footsteps which had been part muffled by his own. As he spun round, the two men were upon him, seizing his arms and alternately dragging and walking him to the wharf steps.

"What do you want with me?" he wailed, uncomprehending still, alone in the remote darkness of the river bank.

At the foot of the steps, which entered the races and eddies of the dark water, two more men sat in a little boat. One held the rudder lines, while his companion had shipped the sculls and was steadying the little craft against the rotten timbers. Both were river men, with ragged hair and weather-beaten faces.

Cazamian's captors pushed him into the boat and jumped in after him. Their companions drove stern foremost into the broad sweep of water until they were in the middle of the great river, the stone pillars of London Bridge and the iron span of Southwark Bridge rising in hard silhouette against the pale glimmer of the city sky. Only then did they take the box from Cazamian. One of his captors broke it open with a deft wrench of a chisel blade and shone a bull's-eye lantern upon the contents. Cazamian watched him pour out a palmful of coins and return them to the box once more. Next he

saw, in total bewilderment, that the man had taken several
sheets of paper and something resembling a cameo brooch
from the box. The man held these out to his companion,
who looked at them and nodded abruptly. The lights of
London Bridge flared more distantly as the little craft drifted
further downstream with the ebbing tide. Away on the far
bank, the paddles of a river steamer beat the foul water to a
phosphorescent foam.

Neither of the two men spoke to Cazamian, from first to
last, as if they wished to conceal all but the inevitable deed
from the lightermen who sculled the little boat. The man
with the box put it down, and seized Cazamian's arms, locking them behind his back in a grip that obliged him to bow
his shoulders rather than dislocate them. In an instant, his
head and shoulders faced over the side of the boat, inches
above the black, foul-smelling water. The second man took
Cazamian's head in the firm but gentle grip of a bone-setter,
forcing his face forward and under the surface of the flood.
The terrible struggle lasted a few moments, Cazamian, suddenly and appallingly sober, tasting the evil, astringent water
at his lips, fighting with bursting lungs against the inevitable intake of breath. The man who held Cazamian's arms
also pressed his knees rhythmically into the back between
the shoulders, and then freeing one of his hands momentarily, struck hard at the back of the neck. Air burst from the
tortured lungs under the impact and, as a cold flood replaced
it, a final brilliant spasm spread before Cazamian's eyes,
fading at the last explosive beat of the heart.

Using a rusty boat-hook, Sealskin Kite's men edged the
limp body out into the stream. The man with the metal box
tossed it into the water, and poured a stream of coins after it.

"Farthings!" he said contemptuously.

From the shadows of the wharf, Verney Dacre watched as
much of the scene as he could make out with the aid of a
military spy-glass. When it was over, he walked quickly to
the house off Southwark Bridge Road, to which he had
followed Cazamian secretly for his own information. What-

ever had happened to Cazamian's wife and child, they were certainly not living with Cazamian. He occupied a single room, which looked down from the first floor of the house on to a cobbled passageway.

A child could have climbed to the room without difficulty. It was one step from the cobbles to a low wall, another from the wall to a wash-house roof, and a brisk pull-up from there to the ledge of the window. The catch opened at the first pressure of a knife-blade. Dacre stepped inside, crossed to a bare wooden table with a drawer at one end. He opened the drawer, inserted two sheets of paper, one of them in an envelope, and closed the drawer again. Then he retraced his steps by fastening the window, and going down the darkened stairs to the street. Whatever else might not happen, as soon as the bullion robbery was known at London Bridge and Cazamian failed to report for duty, the private clothes detail would visit the little lodging-house.

16

Ned Roper looked up from the leather-topped table, where he sat before a sheet of accounts, as Coggin appeared in the doorway of the little front parlour at Langham Place. The mid-afternoon sun fell through the Nottingham lace of the curtains, casting a wavering brilliance across red velvet and green morocco, as though illuminating an underwater world.

"Pair o' swells," remarked Coggin disdainfully, "and they'd be obliged to Mr Roper if he'd take a draft on Coutts Bank."

Roper closed the ledger and beckoned Coggin into the room. Houses in Langham Place or Regent Street, as well as those in Chelsea or St James's, prided themselves on the cheques they took and the celebrity of the names which appeared on them. But there were precautions to be observed.

"What sort of swells?" Roper inquired.

"Regimental, by their look," said Coggin gruffly. "Not a single Victoria in their pockets, I dare say, but ready enough to write their own flimsies for any amount you might name. They've got their own chaise and pair waiting outside, with their own groom to 'old the 'orses.''

Roper brushed his reddish moustaches and gave an undecided sniff.

"What are they paying for?"

"The new blowen, Elaine. She's a-going to take them both on. Seems they want it that way," said Coggin with a broken grin.

Roper thought a moment longer, and then made up his mind.

"Ten sovs a-piece in the best room," he said quickly, "and they may write me the cheque and send their own chaise to Coutts in Piccadilly to bring the money back. That's the usual form, fair and square, ain't it?"

Coggin withdrew, only to return a moment or two later with one of the clients at his heels, a swaggering figure of a guardsman with black hair and moustachios.

"I say, sir, you ain't goin' to keep two warriors standin' to arms while a damned slip of paper goes to Piccadilly and back? Let the man go to Glyn's in Regent Circus."

"Glyn's ain't Coutts," said Roper shortly.

"No, but dammit," said another voice from the hallway, "write the cheque out payable to the fellow. Let it go to Coutts and let the sovs be brought straight back. I don't mind waitin' in turn for a servin' of greens, but I ain't so dashed partial to them when they're off the boil altogether!"

Roper hesitated. He was rich enough now to tell these two bucks and every other that they might go to the devil. But even after two days of wealth, it was hard to break long habit and to turn away a draft for twenty sovereigns. At the worst, he thought, his fifteen-year-old doxy would be topped and tailed for nothing. That would hardly break him. He watched the first client write out a cheque on Coutts Bank, payable to E. Roper, Esquire, in the sum of twenty pounds and against the credit of Charles Scott-Hervey. While the other man went down the steps to call the groom, Roper took the draft into the little parlour and looked it over carefully. Then he slipped it into an envelope and handed it to the groom.

"Take the chaise," shouted the first client, as the man made his way out again, "and cut along to Piccadilly as sharply as you may."

Coggin hovered in the background with the girl beside him, her light brown hair worn loose down her back, framing her snub-nosed sauciness and the slyness of her narrow blue eyes. Then Roper nodded to his bully. The girl ran off up the stairs at once and Coggin, suddenly deferential, approached the two clients.

"This way, if you please, sirs."

As soon as Coggin had come downstairs again, Ned Roper made his way softly up, and gently opened a door adjoining the main bedroom. In the partition wall was a glass, no larger than the lens of a telescope, giving a view of activities in the centre of the bedroom. Being no *voyeur*, Ned Roper made little use of it as a rule, but he felt a professional interest in observing the behaviour of his newly acquired girl. The fifteen-year old had stripped the clothes from her tomboy figure and the degree of excitement shown by the two men, who stood before her in their shirts, reminded Roper of a pair of Smithfield porters rather than two holders of the Queen's commission.

It took only a little while to satisfy him that he had a promising young apprentice in Elaine. While she lay on the bed with the first man straddling her, she flipped and wiggled like a fish in a net with the pleasure of it, striving to impale herself more vigorously. Her eyes closed, her tongue passed rapidly over her lips, and then she turned her face aside to where the other man stood at the side of the bed. When his turn came, he stooped and whispered something to her. The youngster shook back her hair and gave a look of comic fright at the object which menaced her. But she turned over on her belly, her forehead resting on her arms, the muscles of her legs and buttocks showing a visible tension. She kept her face hidden until the tension began to slacken. Then she moved her hips, bucking in time with her lover, and turning her head towards him, pouting for kisses.

Roper walked softly away and down the stairs. The girl had the makings of a professional courtesan. For his successor in the business, she might be another Nell Jacoby. He was sitting in his parlour, elaborating these thoughts, when the girl came hurrying down to take her place in the Introducing Room again. She stood in the parlour doorway in her short, pleated skirts, which revealed a length of bare leg. Seeing that Roper was watching her, she stepped into the room, lifted the skirts to her waist, and spun round and round in front of him.

"Got nice legs, 'aven't I?" she said tauntingly, turning so close to his chair that her bare calves brushed the knees of his trousers. Then she dropped the skirts into place, gave him a careful look, and ran off. It was the same with all of them, Roper thought, they all believed that the keeper of the house could be their own personal protector by a little coaxing and wheedling.

At that moment he heard the front door open and the voices of Coggin and the groom, who had evidently returned from Coutts. But something in the tone of their voices caused Roper to go out into the vestibule and deal peremptorily with the groom.

"Well?" he said impatiently, "where's the cash, then?"

The groom said nothing. He stepped aside and to Roper's complete bewilderment revealed two men, a uniformed police sergeant and a constable, standing in the open doorway of the house.

"Mr Roper?" said the sergeant blandly.

"Yes." Ned Roper tried frantically to anticipate the business which might have brought them.

"Did you hand this person a cheque, payable to you on the account of Mr Charles Scott-Hervey at Coutts Bank?"

"Yes," said Roper with righteous relief. "You don't mean to tell me he was running off with the money!"

"No," said the sergeant quietly.

"Well then?"

"Did Mr Scott-Hervey hand you that cheque himself?"

"Yes."

"And how long might it have been in your possession?"

"Five minutes," said Roper thoughtfully. "Not more than ten, certainly."

"And it passed directly from you to this person?"

"Course it did," said Roper irritably, "why?"

"How long ago was that?"

"Quarter of an hour, p'raps," said Roper. " 'ow the 'ell should I know?"

"A little bother over the sum payable, sir," said the young constable, "some apparent irregularity. Simply explained, no doubt, but being for so large a sum as seven hundred and twenty pounds, Messrs. Coutts naturally wished to take the precaution . . . "

"Seven hundred!" said Roper aghast.

"And wanted in cash," the sergeant remarked. He and the constable regarded Roper with professional scepticism and thinly-disguised contempt. They knew who he was and what he was.

Ned Roper's brain refused to assimilate the fragments of information presented to it. They seemed entirely inexplicable. He had, of course, been prepared for trouble over the bullion robbery, even though the bullion was already disposed of and the resulting banknotes safely hidden. He had rehearsed to perfection every conceivable answer to the deepest questions that might be asked. But the business of a cheque for seven hundred and twenty pounds made no sense at all.

"Perhaps, sir," said the sergeant impassively, "we can now ask you to accompany us to Messrs Coutts in Piccadilly, in order that the matter may be clarified."

Before he could even gather his wits, Roper was sitting in a cab between the two men. Quarter of an hour more, and they marched like a file of infantry into the bank. There Roper saw the cheque. It was still payable to him, but twenty pounds had become seven hundred and twenty pounds by the plausible addition of a "7," and the less plausible addition of "seven hundred and," the spacing of which had been judged in a way that would disgrace the most amateur penman. The script and the ink might otherwise have deceived a counter clerk, but the total effect of the draft was bound to rouse suspicion. Ned Roper needed time to think.

"I can't say nothing," he repeated, "nor I won't."

The sergeant looked at the constable. Roper offered no resistance as, for the second time in his life, the "darbies" were closed over his wrists and he was led, a spectacle for the summer crowds, to the lock-up of "C" Division, Metropolitan Police, off Marlborough Street.

Not far from Mr Hatchard's bookshop, a down-at-heel sporting gentleman, who had been lounging by the shop-front for the past hour, watched the two policemen and their prisoner go by. Then he pulled himself upright and shuffled away towards Pall Mall, where the twopenny buses started for Hammersmith. Sealskin Kite was soon to know that obligations had been discharged on both sides.

"Either Ned Roper forged a draft for seven hundred pounds, which is deuced rum, seein' the money he could make here, or he's been put up, which is more rum still."

As he spoke, Verney Dacre had his hand on the wooden mane of the rocking horse, dipping it rhythmically and letting it rise again. Ellen Jacoby sat on the velvet sofa of the upstairs drawing-room at Langham Place, her blue eyes wider than ever.

"But Ned ain't a penman," she whined, "nor never was."

"If he improved that cove's cheque for him, he was a penman, and no mistake," Dacre stepped away from the wooden horse. "Though why he should do it is a mystery. What matters now, young woman, is that Tyler will drive you to Horsemonger Lane Gaol, where you'll be let speak to Ned Roper in the presence of a turnkey. Now, as it's the only chance you'll have before the sessions come about and he stands trial, use the time well. So have the goodness to listen to what you must say."

The girl checked her whimpering a little and Verney Dacre continued."First, you'll remember never to mention a name, not mine, not yours, nor any other. However, you'll tell Ned Roper that his governor knows it's all a plant and that he shall have the best attorney that can be bought. Tell him that, whatever may happen, his governor will see to it that every farthing of Roper's shall go to you and the little fellow. And then tell him that the friend he used to see at the Green Man has vanished off the face of creation and may have gone to fly a kite."

She watched him like a child learning her lesson.

"Can you remember all that?" Dacre asked sharply.

She nodded.

"Think so."

"And mention no names at all. Ned Roper's done murder in his time and if they were ever to find a noose for him, they'd very likely find a second one for you."

She bowed her head and began to weep silently in her despair.

"Someone has done him wrong this time," said Dacre softly, "and I fancy I know who. You may tell him that his old governor ain't goin' to rest until the man is discovered."

Ellen mopped her eyes.

"What about the boy?" she said doubtfully. "Mayn't his father see him?"

"It ain't allowed," said Dacre firmly. "The child stays safe here until you get back."

Verney Dacre waited until long after Ellen had returned from her prison meeting with Ned Roper. He stood at the window of the room, watching the evening sky above Portman Square turn from flames of vermilion, to plum-coloured dusk, and then to smoke-grey. Within three days of the robbery he had put his two rivals safely out of the way and held bank notes to the value of twenty thousand pounds. He watched the last drunkards go shouting homewards and waited until only an intermittent cab clattered over the deserted cobbles, down the long procession of branched gas-lights which led to Regent Circus. Then he summoned Coggin and Tyler to the upstairs room.

The summons was no surprise to either man. Each had separately concluded many months before that every stick in the house belonged to a bigger fish than Ned Roper. They did as Roper ordered, but never qestioned that their ultimate loyalties had been bought by the man whom Roper served. For several weeks they had known this man to be a slender, fair-haired young swell with the look of a cavalry subaltern. They had heard Roper call him "Mr Dacre."

Now, as the two muscular bullies stood before him, Dacre sat where Ellen had done, on the velvet sofa.

"Should y' like to know what has become of Ned Roper?" Dacre inquired superfluously. "Someone has settled a private account with him. It goes back a long way, they tell me, and it don't touch you or me, or anything in this house."

There was no mistaking the look of relief on the two ham-coloured faces.

"Should y' like to work for me and run the house directly for yourselves?" Dacre tapped his boot with a stick. "For six months there must be great care and no change. Then, if you please me during that time, you shall both have houses of your own, one here and another in Holborn."

The prospect of the means to unexpected wealth brought grins and murmurs of gratitude from the two men. Their heavy torsos seemed to writhe with an almost physical pleasure as they shifted from foot to foot.

"Ain't neither of us'd say no to that sir," remarked Coggin. "We're your men now or in six months' time."

"Very well," said Dacre, "but there's a screw loose, or there will be unless we prevent it. It ain't a man that betrayed Ned Roper in the first place. It was one of two girls, perhaps even both. Until the summer's over and Roper's out of it, one way or the other, neither of the doxies is to leave this building. They can live in one of the little rooms at the top with the barred windows. The door is to be bolted, likewise the gate on the stairs."

"If it's Roper's woman," said Tyler with feeling, "it's no more than she deserves. A spell of breaking-in, in those rooms, does wonders with girls that can't bring themselves to ply the trade."

"Ellen Jacoby," said Dacre softly, "and Jolie."

A smile spread slowly across Coggin's face at the thought of the two pretty prisoners who would be in his care.

"Don't you fret yourself, Mr Dacre, those little shicksters ain't never going to trouble you again."

"Oblige me," said Dacre, "by seein' to it at once."

He waited while his orders were carried out, then he made his way up the broad ovals of the staircase to the attic floor. Jolie was hunched in a corner of the cell-like room, her eyes glittering with a dark animal hatred. Ellen sat stupidly on the edge of a mattress, her dress gone and a glass clutched in her hand.

"See to it," said Dacre to Coggin, "that she has a bottle of 'skyblue' gin fetched up to her every day. Y' need only just wipe it on her lips and she'll suck like a baby at a teat. Keep her in a separate room, and if you want to take turn and turn about with her, you may."

The reference to a "baby" seemed to rouse Ellen a little.

"Where's little Harry Roper?" she said suddenly and wildly. "Bring him to me!"

Verney Dacre looked at her.

"A bawdy house ain't no place to bring up a child," he said sardonically. "And I don't choose to have the keepin' of a parish brat when I pay the poor rate and when the workhouse may bear the cost more comfortably."

He closed the door on her, hearing her hands beat feebly at it as he closed the bolt. A moment later the tall iron gate at the head of the stairs came to with a faint clang. Then, a key rattled in the lock. The footsteps of the three men died away into a deep silence.

17

"Sergeant William Clarence Verity, you are required by order of Superintendent James Gowry, 'A' Division, Metropolitan Police, to attend this investigation and to give such information as may be required of you by your superior officers. The investigation is carried out on the instructions of the Home Office, in consequence of certain allegations which have been made concerning your recent conduct."

Verity stood straight-backed before the long, polished table as Inspector Croaker outlined the procedure of an internal police inquiry, with a voice of unctuous satisfaction.

"Now," Croaker concluded, "you are to answer those questions which will be put to you by the visiting officer, Colonel Hanning, by Mr Bryce, of the Treasury, and by myself."

Verity assessed the two strangers. Colonel Hanning, with the drooping white moustache and sharp grey eyes of a retired regimental commander, might at least have a soldier's sense of fair-dealing. But the beak-nosed man with the smooth face and arched black eyebrows, "Mr Bryce, of the Treasury," was a good deal less welcome. Verity knew that "Treasury" meant "Treasury Solicitor's Office," and that the presence of such a man was a sure sign that they were trying to frame an indictment against him.

In full uniform, Verity stood at attention in what had once been the first-floor dining-room of Whitehall Place. Beyond the heads of the three investigating officers the window opened on a view of the river, sparkling in the light of the summer morning. Penny steamers, their thin black funnels trailing banners of black smoke, and the billowing brown sails of coal barges assured him that the life of the city was running its normal course while the bizarre little drama of Scotland Yard was acted out in this room. At his back, the escort, Sergeant Penzer, belched unobtrusively.

Croaker's eyes seemed small and glittering as he turned them upon Verity.

"Were you, Sergeant Verity, on the tidal ferry train which left London Bridge station for Folkestone at seven p.m. on the sixteenth of July?"

"Yes, sir," said Verity calmly, "but it was London Bridge to Dover, sir."

"Were you acting under orders?"

"No, sir. Rest day, sir. More of an excursion."

"Did anyone know you were going?"

"Never told a soul, sir. Didn't know myself until I got to the station. Spur of the moment, you might say."

"Could anyone else have known of your intention?"

"Don't see 'ow, sir."

It was at this point that Colonel Hanning leant forward and Inspector Croaker sat back.

"Sergeant," said Hanning softly, "before we question you any further, I think it right that you should know of an anonymous note, posted to Mr Croaker before the train left London Bridge. 'Ask Mr Verity why he is going to Folkestone tonight.' It appears that someone must have known your intention."

"Don't see 'ow, sir. Didn't know meself."

"Very well," said Hanning. "But do you now know that the train on which you travelled was robbed of a considerable quantity of bullion?"

"I read what was put in the *Globe* newspaper last night, sir."

"Where were you, and with whom were you, during the journey from London Bridge to Folkestone?"

"In a carriage on my own, sir. Never stirred from it all the way. Near the engine it was, where the train is often quite empty. After Folkestone, I took the train on to Dover and came back on the ten p.m."

Colonel Hanning looked at a sheet of paper in his hands.

"And you have no theory to offer as to the author of the anonymous note?"

"No, sir. No theory, sir."

There was a pause, almost of embarrassment. Then Bryce, the balding Treasury lawyer, took up the questioning.

"Sergeant, when did you first make the acquaintance of Charles Baptist Cazamian?"

"Never," said Verity suspiciously, "first I 'eard of him."

"Did you know that he was guard on the tidal ferry train?"

"No, sir."

"Nor that he has since disappeared and is suspected as a party to the theft?"

"No, sir."

"You never passed confidential police memoranda to him?"

"I never even 'eard of him."

"Answer the question," said Croaker sharply.

"I never passed him anything," said Verity. "How could I, when I never knew him?"

"When his lodgings were searched," said Bryce suavely, "a confidential memorandum, addressed by Inspector Croaker to you, was found in a table drawer."

Verity's heart sank.

"I knew I lost it," he said defensively, "I couldn't say where. But I still never 'eard of this man."

"Lost it!" said Bryce sceptically.

"Yes, sir," said Verity with some irritation, "lost it. It does sometimes 'appen, you know!"

"Not to other officers of the detail," said Croaker with a sniff.

There was another pause, but the Treasury lawyer had not yet finished.

"A second paper was found in the same table drawer. 'This is a duplicate key to the Railway Office at Folkestone pier, removed by me on the thirty-first of May. If it is missed they will change the lock, but won't for a few days. Charles Baptist Cazamian.' Do you recognise that note."

"No, sir," said Verity in his most stolid manner.

"You should do," said Bryce, "it was found in an envelope addressed to you at your lodgings."

"Someone must have put it there," said Verity indignantly.

"Of course someone put it there," said Bryce, with a knowing glance at his two colleagues. "The question is, who put it there, and for what purpose."

Verity stood at attention all this time. He now understood the predicament of men who became wilder and wilder in their search for replies as the questions of a trained mind drove them this way and that at the whim of their interrogator. It was Colonel Hanning who once more intervened on his behalf.

"Sergeant, if you cannot tell us more than this, how are we to help you? Someone knew your intention of travelling by the tidal ferry to Folkestone. You can only tell us that you sat alone in a carriage without a single witness to confirm your statement. It will be alleged by others, perhaps, that you were not in a carriage but, somehow, concealed in the luggage van by Cazamian, who is suspected of being a party to the theft. You admit that you travelled by a train on which he was acting as guard. A confidential memorandum addressed by Mr Croaker to you has been found in the man's room. So has a message, apparently intended for you, which would have involved the man to whom it was written in a criminal attempt against the Railway Office at Folkestone pier. Now, Sergeant, what are we to think unless you can offer us some further explanation?"

Verity took a deep breath and fell back on his last defence.

"One other thing to say, sir. There was a man on that train who is a person of a criminal reputation. His name is Edward Roper. When I lost that memorandum from Mr Croaker, I have reason to believe it was during an assault made upon me. When I recovered consciousness, sir, Roper was not two or three hundred yards distant."

"Yes," said Bryce sardonically, "Mr Croaker has already told us something of your preoccupation with this person. However, we were not aware of your habit of ignoring police regulations by carrying confidential papers away from the divisional office."

"It was pure accident, sir."

"And when a further accident occurred, when the memorandum was lost, it did not occur to you to report its loss to Mr Croaker?"

"No, sir," said Verity, judging humility to be the only answer. "Very foolish, sir. Matter of great regret."

Bryce nodded at Croaker, who took up the questioning once more.

"While you were spying on this man Roper, on the train, what did you see him do?"

"He sat in a carriage between mine and the engine."

"Alone?"

"I think there was other passengers in it."

"Did he get out?"

"Not that I saw, sir."

"Not all the way from London to Folkestone?"

"Not that I saw, sir, though he's clever as a cartload of monkeys."

"But even if he had got out, unseen by you, there was no way of getting into the luggage van, was there?"

"Not unless he was let in by Cazamian."

"Unfortunately, Cazamian would have had no key, sergeant. But even if he could have let this man Roper in, there was no way of getting the bullion off the train, was there?"

"There must 'ave been a way, sir, or it wouldn't 'ave 'appened, would it?"

It was the first time that he had caught Croaker off balance and, despite his own predicament, it did Verity's morale a great deal of good. Bryce, the lawyer, came to Croaker's aid.

"If Roper remained in his carriage, he could not have robbed the luggage van?"

"No, sir."

"And though you, a trained officer, watched the carriage, you did not see him leave it?"

"No, sir. That is correct, sir."

"The evidence, therefore, is that he did not leave it."

Verity made no attempt to answer. In a criminal court, he

reflected, this line of questioning would damn him even more completely than at a police inquiry.

"One final point," said Bryce casually, "if Roper were the man who had stolen thirty-six thousand pounds in gold, including a thousand in gold coins, he would now be a rich man?"

"Yes, sir."

"Not in need of money?"

"Hardly likely, sir, not if he had all that."

"Quite, Sergeant Verity. It is perhaps unfortunate for you that you could not have known that Roper was arrested two days ago on a charge of forging a cheque for seven hundred pounds. Hardly the action of a man who has just made his fortune."

"Likewise," said Verity determinedly, "he may have been arrested but he ain't been convicted yet, sir. Don't always follow."

It was something, at least, not to let Bryce put him down. On the whole, Verity considered him a meaner cove than Croaker himself. He thought that the questioning had finished, when Colonel Hanning leant forward again.

"As a matter of record, sergeant, we understand that you have been advised by Mr Croaker that any attempt by a police officer to allow a crime to be committed for the purpose of subsequently apprehending the criminals may render the officer liable to prosecution as accessory before the fact. You have been so informed?"

"Yes, sir."

Verity had expected better from Colonel Hanning. It seemed for one grotesque moment that they were proposing to try Roper with Verity as his accomplice. Moreover, he might appear to have been an extremely useful accomplice. The search of the house at Langham Place, which he had engineered, had proved so embarrassingly unproductive that the establishment was virtually immune from police interference for months to come. Roper could have turned it into a forger's den or a vault for stolen bullion with more safety than almost any other house in London.

At last he heard Croaker ordering him to withdraw. Verity's flushed jowls trembled as he stamped "about turn" and marched smartly from the room, Sergeant Penzer trotting at his heels.

For an hour, Verity and his escort sat in the Division "schoolroom," where the newly designated "schoolmasters" endeavoured to remedy the illiteracy of the recruits. His gloom seemed to deepen among the distempered walls and bare wooden benches. Sergeant Penzer struck a reassuring note.

"It'll go all right. I seen dozens of these. This ain't nothing, hardly an investigation at all. Strikes me, someone just put you up out of spite."

"Oh, I been put up all right," said Verity, giving the matter deep thought, "and it ain't by Roper, neither. This whole thing is too clever by half for a bawdy-house bully."

When they were called in again, Colonel Hanning and Inspector Croaker watched Verity with great earnestness. Bryce contemplated the cornice of the ceiling. It was Croaker who spoke.

"Sergeant William Clarence Verity, you will be suspended from all active duty pending a fuller investigation of your case. You owe it most of all to Colonel Hanning, and to some extent to your past conduct as a soldier, that you will not be taken into custody this morning. You will, however, continue to parade morning and evening before the duty inspector until the investigation has been completed. You are also under orders to attend the company inquiry to be held by the South Eastern Railway and to answer such questions as shall be put to you there."

After Verity and his escort had been dismissed again, Sergeant Penzer's optimism was undaunted.

"Why," he said, "I only wish I might be suspended and have nothing worse to do than sleep through a Railway Company inquiry."

Within the first half hour of the South Eastern Railway inquiry it was evident to Verity that it would last for two or

three weeks and offer no solution to the mystery. Witness
after witness came before the long table, where Samuel
Smiles, the Company Secretary, sat with his directors like the
officers of a court-martial. Every witness swore that there was
no conceivable means by which the gold could have been
taken. And then every witness admitted that the gold had,
none the less, gone. The press began to lose interest after the
first day and the reports in *The Times* and the *Morning Post*
became increasingly perfunctory.

Every scrap of new evidence seemed only to multiply the
uncertainty. The superintendent of traffic and the chief of
the railway police swore that the weights were correct at
Folkestone. Therefore, it was possible, perhaps even likely,
that the robbery had occurred in France. The directors
clearly liked this idea, since it removed all responsibility
from the South Eastern Railway Company.

On one point there was general agreement. The bullion
had vanished without trace and was unlikely to be seen
again. A guard called Cazamian had also vanished, though
he might yet be found. Beyond that, there was nothing.

The long hall was not unlike a chapel, with benches at
one end and the presiding table on a raised step at the other.
The setting seemed to have been inspired by recent
memories of the Chelsea Board and other inquiries which
had followed the administrative catastrophe of the Crimean
War. As the voices droned and the waiting witnesses dozed,
Verity watched the sunlit sky through the tall gothic windows and considered his loss. The loss was Ned Roper. With
Roper, there had been a trail to follow, a man to shadow.
Now there was none. But, at least, sessions would come on
before the railway inquiry was over. If Roper were to be
acquitted and set free . . . Yes, thought Verity, if the man
were free, his trail might be more clearly marked than ever.

The minor witnesses came and went very rapidly indeed.
But one whole day was given up to evidence concerning the
other articles in the luggage van, including the coffin of
Major Edward Habbakuk. Even this failed to revive the
interest of the newspaper reporters. Official evidence of the

exhumation and reburial was taken. The clerk who had been present on both occasions swore that it appeared to be the same coffin, stained by damp but otherwise sound. It had even been verified that Major Habbakuk occupied it. In order to fasten the brass plate more securely, the lid had been removed, revealing the late major lying there "in an almost complete state of preservation." Clearly there were to be no local legends of Edward Habbakuk lying in his grave with gold bullion all around him.

The brother officer, who had paid the cost of sending the major to his last home, now reluctantly cast aside his anonymity and gave evidence as a benefactor. He proved to be a young ex-subaltern of the 19th Dragoon Guards. His languid replies to the questions showed clearly that if the board of inquiry had had the least evidence of any value, they would not have wasted their time in calling such a witness as this. Why, asked Mr Smiles, had the young man undertaken the reburial of his comrade?

"Major Habbakuk had rendered me a very great service in India," drawled the blond dandy. "I should not care to specify the matter here."

Why had the young man not come forward at the time of the major's death?

"I have been abroad the greater part of the year. I was in Ireland lately and came back a few days since."

On which day had he come back?

"As to the date, I must refresh my mind. But it was the day of the Victoria Cross parade before the Queen in the Park."

And with that, the testimony of Verney Maughan Dacre, late of the 19th Dragoon Guards, and now of Albemarle Street, was concluded.

As the inquiry adjourned for mid-day dinner, Verity found Sergeant Samson in the street outside.

"The news in the Division," said Samson as they trudged towards the Strand, "is that you won't be took in while the railway inquiry lasts. That way you may give evidence there without being in custody."

"And then?" asked Verity indignantly.

"And then Mr Croaker may have you took in and continue his own investigation with you a prisoner."

"Who says so?"

"Most of the detail."

"I been put up," said Verity with a savage grimace. "I been put up by a bugger who's twice the man Ned Roper is. If I bloody well ever get near that fucking . . .

" 'Ere, Verity!" said Samson, outraged, "I thought you was a Wesleyan!"

"So I am," said Verity in anger.

"Wesleyans don't use profanity."

"Wesleyans are 'uman beings," said Verity sharply, "and when tried beyond endurance will speak as strongly as any other man."

They walked for a moment in silence.

"I think," said Samson presently, "as you'd better spare some of your strong speaking for the next subject."

"What's that, then?"

"The guard, Cazamian. His body came up on last night's tide on the river flats near Woolwich. O' course he might have drowned himself. Only when a man drowns himself 'e don't usually tear at his own hair to force his head under, and 'e don't usually kneel on his own back so 'ard that you can see the shape of the knee-bone in the bruises."

"It don't make sense," said Verity, "not yet, at least."

"It makes sense to them that say he met his death after you knew Croaker was on to him."

"You ain't going to say I murdered him!" said Verity with feigned amusement.

"No," said Samson, "*I* ain't. But others may."

"Who?"

"Well," said Samson reluctantly, "there's Constable Meiklejohn, in a way. If there's a brief out for you as accessory to robbery, it'll be accessory to murder as well."

"Meiklejohn says that?"

"No, 'e don't exactly *say* it. He's running a book on it, and the odds are two to one on."

18

Ned Roper's was not a long trial. Indeed, throughout the morning on which it took place, there were courteous exchanges between judge and counsel as to the likelihood of being able to start upon another case that afternoon, a much grander felony, to which Roper's downfall was a poor curtain-raiser.

It was the second time in his life that he had stood in the dock of the Old Bailey, and he admitted ruefully to himself that there had proved to be a sort of fairness in the law's procedures. On the last occasion, when he was guilty to his fingertips, the jurors were persuaded that he might not have known the rings and coins to be stolen property when he bought them. He had duly been set free. This time, the jurors were likely to put him away for a forgery of which he was not only innocent but ignorant. By his own standards, the two errors represented a balance of justice.

In appearance, the courtroom consisted of a deep floor from which rose a number of tall, railed pens, and two boxes of theatrical design on either side. Baron Martin and two brother judges, their faces reduced to flushed and aquiline anonymity by their shabby wigs, sat on their raised bench. Above them on the wall was the lion and the unicorn of England, while an iron rail divided the bench from the rest of the court. In the centre of the room was a large oval pen, from which the attorneys of both sides faced judges or jurors across the heads of the milling, shifting crowds of spectators. Beyond that, at the far end of the court from the judges, was a smaller dais, also railed, where the witnesses appeared in their turn. From the higher boxes on either side, well-dressed young gentlemen looked down upon the creature in the dock, holding handkerchiefs to their noses to dull the scent of the criminal poor with more agreeable perfumes. The humbler spectators pressed around the raised enclosures like brokers at the Exchange.

Roper was not permitted to give evidence, and he knew that no accused person could be a witness. At least, he thought, it protected a man from cross-examination. The witnesses were all called by the prosecution: Charles Scott-Hervey, who proved to be a horse auctioneer, and not a guardsman; Ernest Bullen, his companion; William Stubbs, the groom who had run the errand to Coutts Bank; Thomas Bland, who had driven the chaise, and, to Roper's dismay, the girl, Elaine.

Scott-Hervey and Bullen swore as to the details of the cheque for twenty pounds. Both these men, as well as the girl, described Roper taking the cheque into his little parlour. They described him writing something, which the girl swore was "written on the draft itself." Stubbs and Bland had then taken charge of the cheque in its envelope. Neither of them was even literate, let alone capable of altering the cheque by forgery. When opened at the bank, the envelope revealed a cheque in the sum of seven hundred and twenty pounds.

Shifting from one foot to the other in the dock, Ned Roper cursed them, damned the girl for a treacherous little whore, and damned himself too for not recognising her as a cross-bred young shickster. His attorney, an elderly, bottle-nosed barrister with the appearance and manner of a failed schoolmaster, cross-examined the witnesses in vain. Every question brought an answer which made Ned Roper's case more hopeless still.

Might the cheque not have been tampered with after it had left Roper's possession? But by whom? Surely not by an illiterate coachman or groom? Well, then, might it not have been tampered with, out of malice, by some other person? But for what reason? Roper and the two customers were perfect strangers. What conceivable reason might they have for wishing to injure him? What advantage was there to them in doing so?

The defence went from bad to worse. Ned Roper knew

the answers to some of the material questions, but not all the private-clothes peelers at Scotland Yard, he told himself, could have proved the truth in a court of law. The one thing he did not know was which of his many acquaintances had done him this injury.

During the course of his career, Roper had made so many enemies that it was profitless to speculate as to which of them had paid the witnesses who now appeared against him. There had been rival touts, in his early days, soundly thrashed after race meetings at Epsom or Newmarket as a warning to confine themselves to their own patch. There had been welshers, unable to pay Roper's rates of interest, whose arms or legs had been carefully splintered on his orders and who had been left in the agony of men broken on the wheel. There had been girls, too, abducted, "broken in," and then smuggled abroad in a drugged trance as "invalids," or strapped down inside a sham coffin, for sale to European "houses of joy." A few had even gone to the clandestine "maisons des supplices" in Bavaria or Austro-Hungary, where their torments were ended only by death. Such victims, presumably, had fathers, brothers, or lovers, who might sooner or later discover Roper's part in these transactions.

The arm of justice, when it struck at the command of "the swell mob," was infinitely longer than the arm of the law. Those witnesses who now gave evidence would have no idea of the identity of their employer, let alone of the injured men or women for whom that employer was acting. So many scores were outstanding against him that Ned Roper knew the futility of any attempt to identify this one.

As he listened to the evidence, he admitted to himself grudgingly that this "put up" was impeccable. The two clients, the groom, the coachman, the girl Elaine, were virtually the only witnesses of the transactions and they were all the property of his unknown enemy. On his own side, he might have called Coggin, but it was his counsel's view that, under cross-examination, Coggin would do more damage to the defence than to the prosecution.

When the evidence was finished, his lawyer made an arid

and unimpressive little speech on Roper's behalf, a plea which was no more than a justification of the fee to be paid him. After the counsel for the crown had replied, the jurors seemed inclined at first to put their heads together and reach their decision without leaving the jury box. However, for the sake of apparent decorum, they shuffled out, smoked a pipe in the jury room, and then came back with their verdict. The tone of the proceedings had been so unambiguous that Roper felt no more apprehension than if sentence had already been passed upon him. Yet he was suddenly aware of Baron Martin, looking for all the world like a cantankerous old lady in white wig and red gown, staring directly at him.

"Edward Roper, if you have anything to say to the court before sentence is passed, you will make your statement now."

Roper was not in the least prepared for this. He held the edge of the dock firmly.

"I never altered that draft, your Lordship, and I can't say otherwise. I wish I may be damned if I know why those who have sworn against me have perjured themselves. I 'aven't a good character, I dare say, and there's many other things I wouldn't deny if I was charged with them. But I never was convicted of a crime, and I shouldn't stand here convicted of this one if the truth had been told."

Even as he heard his own words, Ned Roper knew that they sounded like the last desperate plea of a failed trickster. Baron Martin conferred in a whisper with his two brother judges and then turned to face Roper again.

"Edward Roper, you have been convicted of a forgery for which, as the law stood only a few years ago, you might have been hanged. Men are no longer put to death for this felony, but you are not therefore to be deceived into thinking that it is a crime of little consequence. It affronts the royal authority and destroys the very basis of all commercial trust and dealing. It remains in the eyes of the law one of the most heinous items in the calendar of crime I am now to tell you that you will be taken from this place to a prison ship, and thence transported to a convict settlement beyond the seas, where you will be kept in penal servitude for the rest of your natural life."

It was a tribute to Roper's natural optimism that, in all those words, he clung to the fact that he had escaped death. He was to live, if only in a prison settlement in Australia. While they led him down the steps from the dock to the cells, he thought that even in such places there would be men who ruled and men who obeyed. Somewhere in that little world, Ned Roper would still be king.

For Ellen and the little fellow he must now be a dead man. But the loss was easier when he knew that they were better provided for than many a well-born lady and many a gentleman's son. So long as the secret of the bullion robbery was kept they, at least, would never be in want. Ellen had written to him twice since his imprisonment, indicating that she had taken the child with her into the country, for fear that she too might be arrested as Roper's associate and that the child might then be abandoned to the mercies of a Poor Law institution. She spoke of Lieutenant Dacre as though he were a benefactor rather than merely the administrator of Roper's wealth on her behalf.

At first, Roper had fretted over the tone of the letters, wondering if Verney Dacre were not at the girl's tail already. But now it made little difference to him. Indeed, it seemed all for the best if Nell should make a match with the handsome young dragoon whose sole contact with the criminal world had been through Ned Roper.

It was as well for Roper's peace of mind that the prison officers opened letters before they were handed to the prisoners. Thus he had not seen the envelopes which, though posted "somewhere in the country," in fact bore the postmark "London." It was as well, too, that he had not seen the girl in her attic room, writing at Dacre's dictation with the bruises of Coggin's powerful slaps still fresh on her face. Above all, it was as well for Roper that he went into captivity with faith, however misplaced, in Verney Dacre. The alternative was to face hopeless oblivion with a despair that killed most men by its slow but unremitting anguish.

Among the crowd of spectators pressing about the advocates' box was an ill-dressed, decrepit old man, a report-writer for the weekly papers, who attended most of the trials at the sessions house. As Roper was led down, the old man elbowed his way out of the court, hawking and sniffing, and walked to where the pugilistic figure of Coggin was standing a little way off. He spoke to Coggin, who listened, nodded, and handed the old man a half-sovereign. Then Coggin himself hurried away towards Snow Hill, where a hansom cab had stood waiting for the past hour. Coggin opened the door and said,

"Ned Roper goes down to Chatham, to the hulks, next week."

Then Coggin slammed the door and, as Verney Dacre tapped the roof of the cab with the knob of his stick, the driver jerked the reins and the horses jostled forward towards Holborn and Regent Circus.

Verney Dacre's visits to Langham Place were rare, but on the afternoon of Roper's trial it was essential to make certain arrangements there. In all the world, there were only four men and women to be disposed of. In a few months more, it would be safe enough to have Ellen and Jolie delivered into the hands of the keeper of a closed brothel in Marseilles or San Francisco. Jolie with her terror of the noose for her part in McCaffery's death, and Ellen, stupefied by gin, would be in no position to create further problems. Coggin and Tyler, masters of their own "flash houses" in London, would be independent. As for Roper, whom Dacre had already removed from his list, he might as well be in his grave for all that he would ever hear or utter in a convict settlement.

It was a safe afternoon to visit the house in Langham Place, since Verity was attending the railway inquiry on Inspector Croaker's instructions. Verney Dacre had less of an appetite for Verity's destruction than Roper, but it gave a sense of completeness to see the man broken.

Dacre stepped from the cab, went up to the door, and hit it once with the knob of his stick. Tyler opened it and took his master's hat and coat. Dacre handed him the stick as well and said quietly,

"It ain't advisable to have that girl Ellen's brat in the house any longer. See to it that it's taken to the parish union this afternoon. Have it entered in the record as a foundling."

Leaving Tyler to carry out his order, Dacre climbed the stairs, unlocked the wicket-gate, and unbolted the door of Ellen's room. During her imprisonment in the barred attic, she had eaten less and less. The gin, which had been provided as a sedative, was now the sole consolation in her squalid captivity. Her hair was dishevelled, the bones of her face more prominent, and a pale, waxy sheen had replaced the warm bloom of her cheeks. Already the softness of her body had become thin and angular. She sat on the edge of the hair mattress, looking more like a deranged bedlamite in her dirty petticoat than the smart young whore she had been a few weeks earlier.

There was no argument at first. She wrote at Dacre's dictation, the words chosen carefully, for this would be the last letter that Roper ever received from his mistress. There was a reference to a pony for little Harry Roper, and a gentleman's education, all of it under the benign surveillance of Lieutenant Dacre. Dacre was not, of course, referred to by name in the letters but always as "the governor."

It was when he took the paper from her that Ellen roused herself at last, pulling her shoulders back and looking round at him with vacant stupidity.

"Ned Roper'll break you when he's free again!" she sobbed. "Break you bone by bone!"

Dacre looked at her, realising that he had forgotten to allow for her ignorance of the law's technicalities.

"That's what Ned Roper won't do," he said softly. "Whoever put him up is a professional. Most thieves and mobsmen are free again, somewhere or other, but not a penman. When a man is lagged for penning, it's the full stretch, until they bury him in Botany Bay. Ned Roper ain't comin' back, miss. And oblige me by rememberin' that."

By the time her fuddled mind had absorbed this information, Dacre had closed the padded door and bolted it on the outside, so that when the storm of hysterical sobbing broke, it was scarcely audible. It was strange that a few weeks before he had offered Roper five hundred pounds for her. Now, with her wasting body and stupid, lacklustre eyes he would not have given a thousand farthings for her. Of the two, it was Jolie who still preserved her attractions in captivity.

While he was there, it seemed as well to look at the other girl and remind her that she was being kept safe from the constables, who were now pursuing their inquiries into the death of Thomas McCaffery with greater persistence. He opened the heavy bolts at the top and bottom of the stout door, and entered the room. A single sheet lay in disarray on the mattress. A bottle of gin stood unopened on the floor, the remains of the girl's last meal beside it. Of Jolie herself there was no sign. Dacre strode to the window and clutched the bars in his hands. One bar had been worked loose at the bottom. Its lower end could be pulled aside just far enough for a girl of *petite* stature to squeeze out on to the parapet. Dacre cursed aloud. But there was no way down except for a leap to certain death on the cobbles four floors below. From the parapet, however, it was possible to enter those attic rooms which were not barred or bolted.

Without wasting further time, Verney Dacre ran to the two unbolted rooms. As he had expected, the window of one of them was open, indicating that the girl had re-entered the house through it. She could still not have got down the stairs beyond the wrought-iron wicket-gate. And then Dacre realised that he had not locked the gate again on going to Ellen's room. Jolie must have timed her escape so that she crept along the little passageway and down the stairs while he was dictating the letter to Ellen. It would have been child's play for her to get down to the first floor or even the basement and escape from the house by that route.

Dacre leapt down the stairs, two or three at a time, in great crashing strides which brought Coggin out of the little parlour.

"Quickly," said Dacre, "there's a screw loose. That bitch

Jolie has gone. She's got down through the house and on to the street. It must have been since I was up there, so she ain't gone far. But she must be fetched back quick, or she'll do for the lot of us."

Coggin opened the door and he and Tyler raced down the steps to the street.

"Wait a bit!" shouted Dacre, "what's she wearin'? What clothes were in the end attic room?"

"She 'adn't nothing but underthings of her own," said Coggin, hastily excusing himself. "There was only old clothes in the end attic. A page's suit for special evenings, with reddish breeches and a grey woollen coatee."

"Then she'll be wearing those most likely," said Dacre urgently. "Now the worst is that she may try to get to a police office, it ain't likely, but she may do. I shall take a cab for Whitehall Place to see if I can spot her on the way. If I don't, I shall work back again. More likely, she's trying to get shelter from some other girl on the street. Ask any you know, find if they've seen her, and then follow the way I'm going."

While Coggin and Tyler hurried through the crowded streets towards Regent Circus, Verney Dacre called a cab off the rank. The horse ambled slowly through the mass of carriages and twopenny buses, giving him time to survey the street on both sides. In the length of the Regent Street Quadrant there was no sign of her, nor down the Haymarket, nor in Pall Mall. She could surely not have got further than this. He ordered the cab to turn and go back by the same route. If, as he now feared, the girl had run eastward, to the criminal rookery of Seven Dials, she might be anywhere in a warren of buildings and alleyways.

He saw Tyler and Coggin easily enough, at the far end of the Quadrant, ordered the cab to pull up, and waved them towards him.

"Two girls saw 'er," Coggin gasped. "Reckon she must have gone for the Dials. P'raps the gaff in Monmouth Street. Said she was asking about being took into the Holborn refuge."

"Get in, quickly," said Dacre, grimacing impatiently. At

least Jolie was too frightened to go to the police at once, but in a refuge like the Holborn Mission the McCaffery story would be drawn out of her in half an hour.

"If it's the Holborn Mission," said Dacre, "she must cross the Dials to get there. We shan't see her from the road. Cabman! St Giles's Church, and drop us there. Quickly!"

The cab crossed Regent Circus again and clattered away down Oxford Street, bouncing its occupants about with the swaying of the polished coachwork, St Giles's clock was striking three as they approached.

"Look!" said Coggin suddenly, and Dacre saw the strange figure flitting along the paving. The dark hair was hastily pushed up under a little cap, the grey woollen coatee worn open to disguise so far as possible the jut of a pair of trim young breasts. The waist of the maroon breeches was too narrow and their tight seat too softly rounded for the wearer to pass as anything but a girl masquerading in boy's clothes. Dacre flung the cabman a sovereign, shouted at him to wait, and jumped after Tyler and Coggin as the girl broke into a run. She gained the corner and vanished round it into the twisting alleys of Seven Dials.

The three men sprinted after her, turned the same corner, and found a wall facing them. To one side was a narrow passageway. As they veered into it, two men with the figures of Covent Garden porters barred their way, legs astride and arms akimbo. Several more men and women began to sidle from the doorways of tall, dark tenements, their movements furtive and hostile. Coggin and Tyler would have tried to fight their way through, but Dacre called them back. Whether the porters were trying to save the girl from her pursuers, or merely defending their own territory, they would block the path for long enough to enable Jolie to get clear away.

Dacre and his companions doubled back, and took the next opening into the Dials. They ran parallel to the first alley down which the girl had disappeared, and saw her cross a gap at the far end of a long passageway. By the time that they had run the length of it, there was no sign of her.

She must, Dacre thought, be almost out of the Dials by now and within sight of the Holborn Mission. When they turned another corner, they saw her far ahead of them, almost beyond reach. Jolie looked back at her pursuers and swung to one side, disappearing again. Dacre, having outpaced his companions, spurted after her and rounded the last corner.

His heart jumped with relief. She had turned into a long courtyard ending in a high, blank wall. She tried vainly to find fingerholds to pull herself up and over it. There were none. The three men closed upon her, and though she struggled in their clutches, her movements were no more than those of a small trapped animal. They dragged her back to the cab and pushed her inside. At Langham Place, she allowed herself to be led into the back entrance of the house, her eyes bright with defiance but her body exhausted by the frenzy of her attempted escape. Dacre himself was still breathing heavily as he followed Tyler and Coggin into the house and bolted the door.

"Take the bitch to the other attic," he said bitterly. "Strap her wrists to the bed-frame, and see to it that she don't move again!"

In his cold fury, he harboured thoughts of murder. Though he had never killed a girl before, he was almost ready to slip the cord over this one's neck and tighten it with his own hands, while the other men held her. Only the prospect of having Tyler and Coggin as witnesses persuaded him to put aside the temptation.

The two bullies attended their master in the upstairs drawing-room during the rest of the afternoon. Verney Dacre perched silently on the sofa, his face set hard as he meditated thoughts of retribution. That an obscure little street girl should have dared to jeopardise his masterpiece was such an affront that he could hardly think coherently in his fury. From time to time, Coggin and Tyler exchanged uneasy glances. They were growing fearful that their new employer, possessed by rage, would do something to Jolie which would put their necks in greater danger than anything which the girl herself might have had time to do during her brief period of freedom. When the evening had grown dark and the heavy curtains had been pulled across the windows, the hard lines of Dacre's thin face seemed to relax. He sat back against the arm-rest of the sofa and said quietly, "Have the goodness to bring her down to me."

While Tyler fetched Jolie, Dacre gave Coggin his instructions. Presently Tyler returned with his prisoner, who still wore the absurd breeches in which she had escaped.

"Oblige me," said Dacre, "by mounting Miss Jolie over the rocking horse to take her lesson."

Knowing what lay in store for her, she stiffened her body in resistance against Tyler's, as he marched her to the tail of the horse. In the deadened silence of the drawing-room, the bully made her bend over tightly along the wooden back, strapping her wrists and ankles to the carved legs, while Coggin pinioned her at the waist so that her belly was pressed down firmly on the hard surface. Dacre sat on the sofa and lit a cigar. After his earlier fury, he now watched with total calm as the dark, slender beauty was bent forward, the soft, erotic swell of her hind cheeks broadening and stretching the tight seat of the breeches. Her glossy black hair straggled loose from its coiffure as she twisted her head round towards him, her dark eyes shining with anger. But her fierce gaze faltered when Tyler unbuttoned her breeches and eased them down, so that her full rear view was revealed to the three men. Her smooth young bottom had the tint of pale copper and was round as a full moon by contrast with her slim brown waist.

The leather switch was long and tapering. Coggin cut the air in a trial swish, and Dacre smiled as the little doxy's buttocks tightened apprehensively at the sound and the hatred in her eyes was replaced by panic. He was satisfied that the fight would soon be thrashed out of her and that she wasn't the sort to risk such a whipping again. He saw with approval how she flinched from the light touch of the leather as Coggin measured the switch across her rear cheeks. Yes, thought Dacre, the taming of Jolie was well in hand.

The first stroke landed with a report that rivalled a pistol shot and the girl's gasp of pain left no doubt that the quirt must have stung her backside like a scorpion. She twisted her wrists and ankles helplessly in their straps, while her behind jigged desperately with the lingering smart. Coggin shifted his stance, and the room rang with the sharp smacks of leather on flesh, each stroke given before the swelling torture of the last had begun to subside. Even before the whip had marked her seat seven or eight times, her cries had risen to unbridled screams.

On the sofa, Verney Dacre sat and watched expressionlessly. When the cigar was half finished, he raised his hand, and Coggin paused. The girl turned her face again, her nostrils flared, her cheeks wet, and her almond eyes trembling with fresh tears.

"We don't judge by caterwaulin'," said Dacre softly, "but by the speed with which the pupil learns her lesson."

He nodded to Coggin, who passed the switch to Tyler and then pressed the head of the rocking horse down once more. The "pupil" gave a wail of terror as her whipped cheeks were turned upwards again for Tyler's attention. Coggin whispered something in her ear, and Tyler laughed.

When Dacre's cigar had burnt to a dead stub, he stood up, coolly examining the marks of the whip embroidered on the pale gold cheeks of the girl's bottom and on the backs of her thighs. She was sobbing almost hysterically and her legs shook with an uncontrollable convulsive trembling after her ordeal.

"That will do," said Dacre quietly, "for tonight. Leave her as she is, however. I shall be obliged to read her a little curtain lecture to ensure that this distressin' performance ain't necessary on too many future occasions."

The two bullies grinned and withdrew. Dacre resumed his place on the sofa and spoke gently to the girl, who at length managed to calm her sobs and listen. Half an hour later, he left Jolie and the rest of Langham Place to supervision by Coggin and Tyler, according to instructions which he had carefully detailed. As he walked down the steps of the house, he thought it unlikely that they would ever see him again.

19

"Supposing you were to want my advice," said Sergeant Samson hopefully, "you'd stop 'aunting Langham Place and give your mind to Inspector Croaker's investigation. That railway inquiry of yours won't go more than another two or three days. You'd best think what you're going to say then about your ride to Folkestone on the bullion train."

Verity placed one large boot in front of the other, treading stolidly round the kerb as the two men swung into Margaret Street. He remained unmoved by Samson's suggestion.

"If it ain't a inconvenience to you, Mr Samson, you had better keep your advice. One thing I don't need is advice. I've had advice from you, from Mr Croaker, from a young person towards whom I have certain intentions, from her old father as well. Much good has any of it done!"

"Indeed!" said Samson warmly, "seeing you never took any of it!"

They plodded onwards in mutually imposed silence, which was ended at length by Verity.

"Information is more the thing than advice," he said quietly. "Go on telling about what those street girls were saying, about two whores locked up in a bawdy 'ouse somewhere."

"There ain't nothing to go on about," said Samson, "that's all there is. Three or four girls that had been told by another girl of two young blowens locked up by their keepers. They didn't know which girls, nor which whorehouse. It happens in such places all the time. Stories like that aren't worth a pandy's spit."

They turned again, from Margaret Street into the mews which ran along the back of Langham Place.

"However," said Verity, "I never saw rooms quite so convenient for locking up as the attics in Ned Roper's bawdy house. Look!"

Samson followed the direction of Verity's finger and saw the four little windows perched precipitously at the back of the Langham Place house, some fifty feet above the mews yard. Even in the summer heat the windows themselves, behind their bars, were shut tight, and it might be doubted whether it were any longer possible to open them.

"Did you ever see such a prison as that?" said Verity thoughtfully.

"You don't know it is," Samson looked away from the brightness of the sky, "and there ain't no way you could find out if there's anyone in there. They couldn't get out, nor even throw a message down to you, so long as the windows are locked. And while I'm on duty here, you ain't going to scale that back wall, a-cos you'd kill yourself. Nor you ain't going in through the front door, since you ain't got your authority no longer. And you won't trick your way in, because once they see your phiz they'll either break your back for you or else call a constable and have you given in charge for trespass. There ain't nothing you can do, my son, and whatever you may try is going to make matters worse."

Verity nodded.

"I don't say you're wrong, Mr Samson," he said after a pause, "but you ain't a subtle man, are you?"

"Meaning?"

"Meaning," said Verity, "that as I have previously observed, there are men in this great city who believe themselves secure in their wickedness, but I will have them in a sure and inescapable snare."

"I daresay," said Samson sceptically, "but I don't see 'ow."

"Supposing," Verity removed his hat and wiped his forehead, "supposing there was someone in that room who was a prisoner. Now, you couldn't think of any way to ask them except by trying to force messages through glass that don't open, or else fighting your way in through the front door?"

"And you can?" inquired Samson, looking with undisguised amusement at his plump, perspiring companion.

"Today I can," said Verity smugly, "not every day. But today's a good sort of a day. Why, it's a joy to be alive!"

"What the 'ell's that got to do with it?"

"Everything. Watch."

Samson looked at Verity with distrust.

"Now, I hope you ain't going to breach the public peace, my son," he began, "a-cos if you are . . . "

Verity drew from the lining of his hat a little round of mirror glass, no bigger than the palm of his hand.

"There's no knowing what a man can't do, if he's only got a nice bright day," he said cheerfully.

Looking up at the sun, he tilted the glass and caught the light. Samson watched the bright disc of the reflection dance over the stonework until it reached the back of Langham Place. Verity steadied it, and the little blot of light moved gradually upwards to the closed and barred attic windows.

"No one ain't going to notice that," said Samson reasonably, "not even if they're in there. It'll get too faint, for one thing, and, for another, 'ow long do you spend watching the ceiling for secret heliographs?"

Verity trained the reflected light on the first barred window.

"I don't," he said, "but then I've never been a prisoner. Now if you are a prisoner, you ain't got much else to do but watch and listen."

Samson grunted, and Verity played the glass on a dark piece of ceiling just inside the window, which was all that he could reach. For ten minutes he jiggled it patiently.

"Now, see here," said Samson at lengh, "I got duties to perform. *Dooties!* I can't stand about 'ere all day."

"Just carry on, old fellow," said Verity preoccupied, "I'll be all right."

Samson thrust his head belligerently towards his colleague.

"One of those duties," he said firmly, "is shadowing you. Mr Croaker'd have me flayed and salted if I left you to cause more trouble."

Verity nodded and relaxed. He caught the sun again with his primitive heliograph and flickered it across the next barred window. Samson waited for several minutes and then said, "Empty, likewise!"

"No it ain't," said Verity.

"It bloody is!" Samson insisted, looking up. "There ain't nothing but your bit of glass shining on that ceiling."

"Look," said Verity quietly, "look at my 'and. I ain't been flashing my glass for the last half minute."

Samson looked. Verity had turned his little mirror to the ground. Samson looked up again. The brightness on the patch of ceiling was more subdued than Verity's, but it was unmistakeably there.

"Games!" said Samson hopefully, "a child playing games most likely. Why, there ain't been so much as a face at the winder, which there would have been if it was a strapping young doxy."

"You seen inside that attic," said Verity. "It ain't no nursery!"

"Then why don't the girl show herself at the bars?"

"Prisoners," said Verity sardonically, "is sometimes tethered so close that they can't reach the window. I daresay this one may be pushing a mirror about with her feet, for all we know." He flashed the glass again in a flurry of little movements, as if to acknowledge a message. Then he turned to his friend.

"You may be the most honest officer in the Detail, and in time you might learn the art of constabulary vigilance," he remarked, "but you ain't a subtle man, Mr Samson, are you?"

"Don't prose so," said Samson, "just tell me what you want doing."

Verity considered this, folding one large red hand into the palm of the other, behind his back. He kept step with Samson until they reached Great Portland Street.

"Tell Mr Croaker," he said at length, "tell him of the two doxies locked up in a whorehouse and likely to be 'orribly murdered. And then tell him about the barred windows in Langham Place."

"And tell him, I suppose, that I let you flash mirrors into the house?" Samson suggested with heavy irony.

"No," said Verity after a little thought, "tell him *you*

flashed the mirror. He may form a 'igher opinion of you, in consequence."

That evening, Verity reached Samson's room in Great College Street just after eight o'clock. The little window on to the shabby back court was open, but a stale smell of boiled beef lingered in the folds of the dingy curtains and the sagging chairs.

"Well?" he inquired hopefully.

"No," said Samson, "it ain't well. Mr Croaker knew you was at the back of it. I ain't half been roasted! As for the Langham Place 'ouse, you can forget about it. There's a constable on special watch to make certain that people like you don't get the Division into any more complications over it."

Verity's eyes bulged, frog-like, with indignation.

"Look 'ere," he protested, "they ain't going to incriminate themselves with a police officer at the door. Let him be took off!"

"He's there," said Samson, "and that's the end of it."

Verity paused. Then he picked up a brown paper parcel which he had been carrying with him and held it out to his colleague.

"What's this?" asked Samson suspiciously.

"'ave a look and see."

Samson opened the paper wrapping and stared in astonishment. He lifted his face to Verity and it seemed as though his eyes were about to flood with tears.

"A Captain Fowkes," he said, with the faintest tremor.

"I promised to make it good," said Verity, "and here it is."

Samson put the package down and pumped his friend's right hand with prolonged solemnity.

"You didn't have to do that," he said, "bellows and all!"

The camera sat on the table, fully extended, like a black concertina.

"I'm only sorrier than I can say about the old Ottewill," said Verity amiably. "And not one of my portraits came to anything."

"I suppose they didn't" said Samson philosophically.

"Suppose?"

"Well, we only brightened the couple you was interested in."

"Interested!" said Verity hotly. "I was interested in 'em all."

This appeared to displease Samson. He said, "I was thinking of washing them plates with collodion, to use again."

"Brighten 'em!" Verity seemed almost to dance with impatience. "Go on! Brighten 'em!"

"They wouldn't have much on. Not by this time."

"Brighten 'em up and see!"

With the moral obligation of a new Captain Fowkes camera still heavy upon him, Samson gave in. Half an hour later, the first of the twenty undeveloped plates which Verity had exposed in the Ottewill folding camera was drawn from its black sheath and the glass bumped heavily into the bowl of pyrogallic acid. Presently Samson drew it out, held it up, and shook his head.

"Black," he said, "black as your hat. And the salts have dried out quite hard.

"Try another," Verity insisted with undefeated eagerness. Samson tried.

"Hello," he said, "something here! Not much, but something."

A moment later, with a black card behind the glass, Verity was looking at his first shilling portrait of Langham Place, with an anonymous man and girl standing on the steps. Eight plates yielded pictures of some sort. Twelve more were black. Six of the pictures showed men alone, two were of men and girls.

"Could be anyone," said Samson knowledgeably. "You don't always get much of a likeness. Especially not at first."

"They all look like someone or other," said Verity sadly, "but not so that you could be sure. That one looks very like the young subaltern at the railway inquiry that paid for Major Habbakuk's funeral. Only it can't be him."

"Can't it?"

"No. The young gentleman was in Ireland until the day of the Victoria Cross parade. These portraits were took days before that."

"Unless he was lying."

"Yes," said Verity patiently, "but then if he was lying at the inquiry, and this is his portrait, it's plain as a pikestaff why he was lying. Ain't it?"

"Is it?"

"Yes. Well-born young gentlemen with an itch for visiting bawdy-houses ain't in the habit of saying so to their families, nor to public inquiries. Instead, they swear they were in Ireland, or Hindoostan, or Timbuctoo. You ought to know that, Mr Samson."

They cleared away the "brightening" paraphernalia. Then Verity said helpfully.

"I'll lend you a hand to do over those plates that came out black, so's you can use them again."

"Why?" asked Samson, "there ain't no hurry."

Verity shifted his feet awkwardly. He laid a hand on Samson's arm.

"Look, old fellow. I know you only just got your Captain Fowkes camera, but I suppose I couldn't have a loan of it, and a little pyrogallol? Just for tomorrow?"

A great sadness spread over Sergeant Samson's features.

"Can't exactly say 'no'," he remarked bitterly, "can I?"

"You've no notion," said Verity, "how obliged I should be."

Samson nodded gloomily. Then he looked up.

"Only remember," he said coldly, "tomorrow *I* shall be the officer that watches Langham Place, and you ain't going to get close enough to that house to take a portrait the size of a penny stamp."

Under Verity's armpits the thick, camphorated serge seemed to cut like a blade into tender flesh. It had even appeared at first that he would never get his peacetime bulk into his old No. I Dress (walking-out) of Her Majesty's Volunteer Rifle Brigade. At his broad waist, he felt the chronic minor discomfort of a fold of skin which seemed to overlap by an inch or more the white blanco'd belt with its dry chalky surface. Yet for all that, in the scarlet tunic with its gold lace, the forage cap, the white webbing, and the three stripes worn proudly on his arm, he looked the perfect picture of a senior infantry sergeant. And there, on his breast, was the little mark, where the Crimea Medal had been pinned.

Catching sight of his reflection in the window of the cab, Verity seemed to look at the face of a vaguely remembered acquaintance. It was remarkable what change could be brought about by the disappearance of a flat, black moustache, and the addition of a forage cap, worn well down and at a slant.

Throughout the drive from Paddington Green, Bella had edged slowly closer towards him on the buttoned plush of the hansom seat, her blue eyes wide with wonder and her plump little hands clasping and unclasping as she almost cooed with excitement at what lay ahead. Verity, huffing and puffing from time to time, managed to keep himself disengaged until they reached the cab rank in Portland Place. There Stringfellow climbed down from his perch and limped round to the door. Bella prudently withdrew to her own corner of the seat.

"Now, Miss Bella," said Stringfellow soberly, "you ain't to forget you're a soldier's daughter and will act as such at all times!"

"Yes, pa," said Bella demurely.

"You may 'ave to defend your honour in a 'ouse of iniquity."

"I don't mind that," said the girl blandly, "not when it's to help Mr Verity rescue a poor, fallen creature from her misery."

Stringfellow cleared his throat huskily.

"Well, miss. You're to do as Mr Verity tells you, and not contradict him."

"Oh yes, pa!"

And then Stringfellow turned to his other passenger.

"Take care of 'er, Verity."

"Trust me, Stringfellow," said Verity with faint reproach. "If the Rifle Brigade can't take care of her, no one can."

Stringfellow adjusted the strap of his wooden leg a little and watched "the soldier and his doxy" amble away towards Langham Place. Verity spotted Samson patrolling the opposite pavement. As a precaution, he put his arm round Bella's waist and turned his face down towards her.

" 'ere!" he said a moment later, "it's only pretending!"

"Oh," she said forlornly, "is it?"

"Yes. Now, pay attention. This is the house. Do just as you've been told and don't fear. There's a man called Coggin inside, but he hasn't ever seen me. Another one, called Tyler, I have met in the course of duty, but it was only once, and in the dark."

At the top of the steps, Bella banged the brass knocker with a resolute little fist. It was Coggin who answered.

"I should like a room for an hour," said Bella coquettishly, "if it ain't a inconvenience."

"Oh, should you?" said Coggin thickly. "And 'oo might you be?"

"A 'igh-conditioned lady," said Bella firmly, "and I ain't particular what I pay."

Though it was not in her instructions, she gave a backward nod of her head at Verity, for Coggin's benefit and winked at the bully. Coggin looked again at the girl with her fair hair, plump cheeks and lively eyes. Perhaps he saw in her a future apprentice of the house, who might be worth a small fortune to her masters.

"Two sovereigns hire," he said ungraciously. "And a sov for the maid to dress you afterwards."

"Much obliged," said Bella. "And I can fasten my own stays."

" 'ave it yer own way," said Coggin. "It's still three sovs."

She handed him the coins and he stood back to let them cross the threshold. They followed him up the oval staircase to the shabby second-floor room, where Verity and the search detail had found the middle-aged man with his two adolescent street girls.

"In there," said Coggin, "and don't overstop the hour, a-cos there ain't a lock."

Then Bella and Verity sat side by side on the soiled counterpane, listening to Coggin's footsteps fading down the stairs. Verity began to unlace his military boots.

"'ave we got to undress in earnest?" Bella inquired innocently.

"Only boots, miss. Make less noise walking."

He tip-toed slowly out on to the landing and looked over the polished banister rail. The house lay in silence, but to have called out to a prisoner in the attic rooms would have roused the echoes and Coggin or Tyler as well.

"Keep watch!" he breathed in Bella's ear, and the girl took his place at the rail. Verity moved in silence up the next oval of the staircase and confronted the wrought-iron wicket-gate at he top. There was no way through it or over it. Unlike the day of the search, it was now firmly locked. He examined the side where it joined the banister rail, which at least offered a possibility of climbing out above the forty-foot drop of the stair well and round the side.

On that side the banister was divided by a smooth pillar of hollow wood, the thickness of Verity's body, which ran from the marble tiles of the vestibule to the very top of the staircase. The iron post of the wicket-gate was bolted to it. It was possible, in theory for a man to climb round by spreadeagling himself, one foot on the sloping banister rail on either side of the pillar and his hands pressed tight to the sides of the polished trunk itself. Then he would have to balance on one foot for an instant, while he slid himself carefully round the vertiginous drop by pressure of his hands. He might do it if he could banish from his mind the thought of the terrible emptiness drawing him backwards to his death on the marble floor which lay like a deep pit below him.

Verity was well aware that his build was ill-suited to acrobatics of this sort. But he took a deep breath and pulled himself up on to the lower side of the banister rail, where he was still able to clutch one of the iron bars of the wicket for support. Then, hugging the smooth wooden pillar with his other arm, he edged his legs towards it. Reluctantly he let go of the iron wicket and saw, as he moved his arm, the tinted light of the glass dome colouring the marble floor that showed between his feet like water at the bottom of a deep well. His left foot slipped a little on the well-polished rail and he clutched the wooden pillar frantically in an attempt to retain his balance. The blood was pounding in his head and his breath was rasping like a saw in the great stillness.

He braced his chest against the pillar and took a wide, sideways stride with his right foot, finding the far side of the banister but gaining no purchase on it. All his holding power was in his arms, yet to move at all he must release his grip on the pillar. He clung tighter, spreadeagled with his back to the dizzy drop of the stair well. He felt suddenly that he dared not move a limb without falling, and then he heard Bella's frightened whisper.

"Go on, Mr Verity! You must go on!"

The sound of her voice restored his determination. For a second or two he must trust to balance rather than to grip. He released the pillar with his left hand, drew his left foot across, and almost threw himself on to the upper part of the staircase. As he got up, he saw with amazement that Bella had shed her lavender-blue skirt and was standing in long white pantelets on the other side of the iron gate.

"Take these," she said urgently, thrusting the discarded skirts through the bars, "I can't climb with them on!"

"I ain't sure you should try it all," said Verity nervously.

"A soldier's daughter not do it?" she hissed. "Gammon!"

With Verity's webbing belt round her waist as a safety harness, and Verity holding her by it, she slipped easily round the pillar. Then, with her skirts over her arm, she followed him softly along the little passageway towards the attic rooms. He stopped at the first of the two bolted doors and slid back the iron fastenings. When the door swung open, Bella gasped in astonishment.

"Oh!" she said passionately, "Oh, the poor creature!"

Putting down the skirts she flew to the naked figure of Jolie on the bed, who was held by a stout strap pinioning her wrists under the bed itself. Verity slid a leather handled knife from his sheath and cut through the strap. As the naked girl turned on her side, Bella stared with incredulity at the raised welts which marked her bottom and thighs. Jolie looked at her visitors indifferently.

"And who might you be?"

"Never you mind introductions, miss," said Verity, "I flashed you a signal yesterday afternoon, and though you mayn't understand the art of the heliograph, it was to tell you you should be got out today."

She curled up against the wall, pulling away from him.

"I tried getting out. Look what I got for it. I'd sooner have me throat cut first than get me arse leathered like that again!"

"You'll get worse than leathered if you don't do as you're told," said Verity, the tone of his voice betraying him.

"Bloody jack!"

She sat upright, covering her little breasts with her hands, she was shivering with fright.

"Private-clothes detail," said Verity superfluously.

"I ain't going! I know what you want! Leave me be! Leave me!"

"Don't you find the ghost of Thomas McCaffery walks in this room of a night?" asked Verity gently. Jolie began to weep.

"They'll 'ang me!" she sobbed, "they will! I knew it'd come!"

"You can't be hanged for telling lies in court, miss, 'owever much you may deserve it. And you was only an affidavit."

"Affadavy?"

"You wasn't called as a witness. It wasn't important evidence."

There was a pause.

"Are you sure I couldn't be 'ung?" she asked furtively.

Bella intervened.

"Course you can't!" she said knowledgeably, "anyone knows that! Go on, put on those skirts and things."

While the exchange of clothes was taking place, Verity slipped out of the room and drew back the bolts on the other closed door. When he opened the door itself, the stench from the warm little room was insupportable. Ellen Jacoby lay on the mattress in the ragged petticoat which she had lived and slept in for the past two weeks. She had perspired constantly in the hot attic and the sweat had left thick ridges of grime across her forehead and chin. Her eyes failed to focus on Verity, but she mumbled something and sank back on the mattress again. It was out of the question to attempt to take her from the house. Without touching her, Verity swung the end of the bed round so that an oblong of sunlight through the barred window fell on to the mattress and illuminated the girl's body. She lolled there stupidly, one eye badly swollen. From a white-blanco'd haversack, Verity produced a small black box, which extended to reveal itself as Samson's Captain Fowkes camera. In that one small square of the room, thought Verity, there was just enough light to do the job.

When he had finished, he swung the bed back, bolted the door, and returned to the other room. Bella sat on the bed in her freshly-laundered underclothes, while Jolie appeared in the lavender-blue dress, bonnet, and veil. It was far from a perfect fit but this, to some extent, improved the disguise.

"Now, Miss Bella," said Verity gently, "you got to be left here for a little while, but only for a little while. Take heart and never say die! It won't be long before I come back and the men downstairs ain't likely to come up here before this evening. If they do, you got a whistle. Blow bravely, and our friends down in the mews shall hear you."

"I ain't afraid, Mr Verity," she said softly.

He took her little hands between his own large warm palms. Then he motioned Jolie out, followed her, and closed the outer bolts. He helped Jolie to climb the gate first, and repeated his own hazardous negotiation of the wooden pillar. They walked slowly down the stairs. Tyler stood ox-like in the hall below them.

"Drop the veil," said Verity softly, and the girl obeyed.

Tyler saw them coming down the final curve of the stairs, and he went into the little parlour to seek instructions from Coggin. By the time that Verity and the girl had reached the door, Tyler had reappeared to open it, staring incuriously at the couple as they passed through the arch of it.

" 'appy to see you again, miss, when your sergeant's given you the chuck," he murmured as the girl slipped by him. Then the door closed and they stood in the street. Verity led Jolie round the first corner into Mortimer Street and subjected her to a determined catechism.

"Now, miss," he said, gripping her by the upper arm, "let's have an understanding. You stand here, free, only because a good, brave girl has taken your place in there, so that you might be rescued. If you want to save 'er, in turn, and you want to save Ellen Jacoby, you must act as I say."

"I ain't sayin' I won't," she said softly. "She's the only chum I've got, Ellen is."

"You know what's being done to her in there?"

Jolie nodded.

"She ain't long for this world," she said, "that's why I tried to get out when I 'eard that Ned Roper wasn't coming back, after the sessions."

"Would you tell Ned Roper what's being done to Nell Jacoby?"

"Fat chance of that!"

"Would you tell him if you could?"

" 'e wouldn't believe me!"

"Would you tell him if you had the chance, miss?"

"Not if I've got to be leathered again," she whimpered.

"You won't be leathered again. But Nell may be, if you don't help her."

"All right, then," she said uncertainly.

Verity took her by the arm and led her out of Mortimer Street and across the road.

"Mr Samson!"

Samson paused in mid-stride and turned round. He looked blank at first, until Verity removed the forage cap.

"Verity! You can't go round in them things! You ain't a soldier any more! It's an offence!"

"Mr Samson, do you know this young person?"

Samson eyed Jolie.

"Yes," he said, "sorry to say I do."

"Then you'd best just listen to what she has to say."

Samson listened.

"Now," said Verity, "she must be let speak to Ned Roper."

"Must she?" said Samson sardonically. "Ned Roper is safely locked in one of the old refractory cells at Newgate. He goes to Chatham tomorrow, to the hulks, and he'll be bound for Australia on the next tide."

"She'll have to speak to him today," said Verity undeterred. "There's Bella Stringfellow in there, risking her life and worse, so that you may 'ave all the glory of the thief-taking for every crime these villains have committed. You must take this young person to Newgate. They'll let you through the governor's house and give you a turnkey."

"I can't go to Newgate!" said Samson miserably, "it's Langham Place and you that I'm to keep a watch upon."

"Albert Samson," said Verity sternly, "if you want to watch me, you must come to Newgate. In twenty minutes more I shall be ready. A chemist at Regent Circus will have brightened some plates for me and I shall be in a proper uniform. Now, you ain't got so much of your watch left to go that an inspector is likely to come by here. If he should, why, you may say you saw me acting suspiciously, and you thought it wise to follow me."

"Look 'ere, Verity," said Samson pleadingly, "ain't you supposed to be attending the railway inquiry this afternoon?"

Verity ignored the question. He said, "You may accompany me and this young person to Newgate or not, Mr Samson, just as you choose. However, if I should reach Newgate, and you ain't there, I shall take a walk down so far as Blackfriars Bridge, and there I shall take your Captain Fowkes camera and pitch it in the Thames."

20

"Don't it seem rum?" said Verity conversationally, "to think that all these crowds in the street is walking along free and happy no more than a yard away from poor mortals in irons who may all be on the hulks or the gallows this time tomorrow? Nothing but a few inches of wall between the two."

Samson grunted as, with Jolie almost running to keep pace, the two sergeants plodded up Newgate Street, past the small grated windows set high in the prison wall. They walked quickly towards the main façade of George Dance's famous prison, a classical design built in massive blocks of stone, looking like the fortified palace of some Renaissance prince.

At the door of the governor's lodging, Samson rang the bell and handed the servant his warrant card. Both he and Verity were now dressed in familiar black coats and tall hats, Verity having changed from his military uniform in String-fellow's cab before they left Langham Place. The servant returned, the two men and the girl were admitted to a little room where two clerks on high stools worked away at their ledgers, as though it had been a counting house rather than a prison office. One of the clerks presented a book for the signatures of the three visitors.

After a few minutes' wait, they were joined by a tall man of clerical appearance, dressed in black and wearing a broad-brimmed hat. But for his heavy bunch of keys, he might have been a clergyman rather than a turnkey. As soon as Samson had explained their business, this new arrival led the visitors down a passage, past the prison lodge, its walls hung with sets of leg irons and manacles and casts of murderers' heads. The heavy oak gate beyond, bound with iron and studded with nails, opened into the prison itself. At every turning of the passage after that there seemed to be yet another barred gate, which the turnkey unlocked, and then locked again as soon as the party had passed through.

Verity had never before been inside the famous prison.

He found that it was possible, from the few small windows which they passed, to see down into the old paved yards, where prisoners awaiting trial for lesser felonies spent their days wandering more or less at will. One corner of each yard was walled across and roofed with bars, through which the families of the prisoners were allowed to talk to the inmates. In the women's yard, there was a small crowd of visitors at the bars, but in the men's yards Verity saw only a very young girl, shivering in her thin clothes as she spoke to an elderly man who squatted dejectedly against the wall.

Leaving the yards, they passed several of the wards where men or women lived together in groups of twenty or thirty, their sleeping mats hung upon the walls during the day to make more space. In one of these bare, whitewashed rooms, the men had already sat down to their dinner of stewed beef and coarse bread.

At length, the turnkey unlocked two massive gates, set at a distance of about twelve feet apart, and led them across the famous press yard, where prisoners were prepared for the gallows on the morning of their execution. Then the party entered the condemned ward with its refractory cells. The passage ended with an iron grille from pavement to vaulting. Several yards beyond this was a similar grating, forming part of the wall of a room into which a prisoner could be led from the cells. In the space between the two sets of bars, a prison guard patrolled to and fro. The turnkey who had led them to this point called out to the guard.

"Let Edward Roper be fetched to the attendance room."

They waited for a few minutes and then saw a figure beyond the further set of bars, a man in coarse jacket and trousers, his feet shackled by an iron chain and fetters. He shuffled into view, his shoulders bowed and his hair cropped to a light-coloured stubble. When he raised his head he appeared clean-shaven and the lines of his pale face were deeply etched. It took considerable effort on Verity's part to convince himself that this was Roper.

"Ned!" said Jolie softly, and he stared incredulously at her.

"You!" he said hoarsely. "You little shickster!"

"She ain't a shickster, Roper," said Verity calmly, "she's the best friend you and Nell Jacoby ever had."

Roper clutched the bars like an animal in its cage. He stared stupidly at them.

"What's 'appened to Nell?"

"She's dying," said Verity. "Your friends in Langham Place are killing her, slow but steady. You'd 'ardly know her. She drinks enough shrub every day to pickle a side of bacon, and her face is all swole up from where they hit her."

"You go and suck your inspector's bum, Verity!" roared Roper, "I've seen 'er all right. Don't you come 'ere with your bloody twicer and try them tricks on me! I can take a licking and not squeal! Ain't I seen her letters, blast your eyes?"

"They beat her!" whimpered Jolie. "Oh God, Ned, they beat her till she'd 'ave signed her own death warrant to end it!"

"But I *read* her letters," howled Roper. "She wasn't beaten!"

"Look 'ere! Look!" Jolie turned her back and, in a sudden gesture, scooped up her blue skirt at the back. Roper started, and the turnkey patrolling between the bars hurried forward with murmurs of protest.

"That's what they did to me, Ned Roper! When I 'eard you'd been quodded for forgery, I managed to get out of the attic, where me and Nell is locked up, and run for it. I was going to get help for her, Ned. They caught me and that's what they did! And it ain't the half of what they're doing to Nell!"

Roper turned his back to the bars.

"Go to hell the lot of you," he muttered, folding his arms, "Ned Roper don't peach on his chums!"

"Chums!" said Samson incredulously, but Verity waved him to silence.

"Listen, Ned Roper," said Verity quietly, "you say you never penned that draft for seven hundred and twenty pound. Now perhaps you didn't, but you'll spend the rest of your very unhappy life atoning for it. However, I think you know a lot about quarter of a ton of bullion that went missing. You were on that train. This young person here has told us how she was driven to Reigate to deliver one set of luggage and collect another. In a little while more, your bully boys from Langham Place will be in the lock-up, and I daresay they'll have something to say for themselves too."

"Let 'em," said Roper defiantly, "it don't touch me."

"That's your misfortune," said Verity. "Now, if it did touch you, if you had taken all the bullion, why, you might have been quodded for five years, p'raps seven. You'd lose the gold, but you lost that anyhow, ain't you? And Nell Jacoby never saw a half-sovereign of it. And tomorrow, Ned Roper, you go to the hulks, to a slow living death, for a forgery which you may never have committed. You ain't a match for some of the real swell mob, my son. Sentences for forgery is stiffer than for several bullion robberies rolled into one."

Roper stood in silence, his back still turned on them.

"You ain't half made a mess of it, Ned Roper," said Verity gently, " 'aven't you?"

Roper bowed his head, but said nothing.

Verity beckoned the turnkey and handed him two glass plates.

"P'raps you'd just hold these with the black card behind, so as the the prisoner may see them."

The turnkey took them nervously and held the first up to the other bars.

"Look at it, Roper!" said Verity sharply: "Miss Ellen Jacoby in the Langham Place attic this afternoon. Look at her face, Ned! Look at it, damn you!"

Roper turned and stared at the glass picture.

"Trick!" he said uncertainly.

"Then look at the next one."

The turnkey held it up. Roper looked for a long half-minute. Then he turned away, put his face in his hands, and began to weep.

"Little Harry Roper," said Verity softly, "in the livery of Marylebone Workhouse. Where he is, the children don't usually last out a year. That picture was took this morning. If you don't credit it, I can have the child brought here by the Wesleyan missioners."

"It ain't true!" sobbed Roper.

Verity gripped the near set of bars.

"Listen to me, you poor gull! Did you think that the sort of men that plan bullion robberies were going to let you carry off a fortune in gold, all for yourself? Can't you see what's been done? Is it likely that if your woman was living off the fat o' the land, the child would be in the parish union? Can't you get it into your 'ead? They ain't only robbed her of your share of the gold, they've robbed her of everything else you ever had as well! Now, if you was to peach on them, at least Nell would have back what was rightfully yours before the robbery. At least your son wouldn't die in the workhouse infirmary!"

Roper held out his hand for the plates, wiped his eyes on the back of his fingers, looked at the pictures, and handed them back.

"Take 'er," he said softly.

"Take who?" asked Samson. Verity shook his head.

"It's what McCaffery cried when they shot him. Not 'take her,' but 'Dacre.' Now, his coffin story at the railway inquiry was a rum one. But it wasn't suspicious. Then 'e got too clever and said he wasn't in London until the Victoria Cross parade. It was unfortunate I took his portrait just a few days before, in Langham Place. It wasn't a necessary lie, more of a force of habit. But it started me thinking. I looked 'im up in the Army List. He went on half-pay in 'forty-eight while the Nineteenth Dragoons was in Ireland, in summer camp at Newbridge. Just the time when there was a certain difficulty over the mess funds and two young gentlemen was given the choice of selling out or facing an unofficial subalterns' court-martial. Conviction being followed by marking with a horse iron. And there's something else that makes me even surer, but I ain't going to say it here. For the moment, however, Verney Maughan Dacre, late Nineteenth Dragoon Guards, is our man."

Roper raised his head and looked at Verity in amazement.

"Should I be admitted as Queen's evidence?" he asked fearfully.

"You'd 'ave to be," said Verity: "you an' Nell and this young person 'ere."

"I ain't sure," said Roper, "I still ain't sure."

Verity took off his hat solemnly.

"Then you'd better be sure before we leave this place," he said firmly. "Those that ain't evidences will be accomplices in the murder of Charles Baptist Cazamian, whose body was recovered from the river two days since."

Roper nodded.

"Bring him to a proper room," said Verity to the turnkey, "and bring a stool, so's he can sit. It may be a long story. The girl shall be escorted elsewhere."

In its first version, the story was not too long, about half an hour in all. Moreover, Roper refused to say anything about McCaffery or Cazamian. As he talked, he looked at Verity's pink moon-face, crowned by its flattened black hair, and wondered where it was that Verney Dacre had made his unwitting error of judgment.

The hansom drew up in Albemarle Street in the early summer evening. During the warm hour before dinner, the pavements were deserted and the carriageway empty, but for the occasional cab.

"It ain't right," said Samson for the twentieth time, "it ain't right. You oughtn't to be let in, having been suspended from duty."

Verity was first out of the cab and led the way towards the door.

"The sooner we get it done," he said firmly, "the sooner Miss Bella Stringfellow shall be set free. Anyhow, I shan't interfere with your duty."

Oughtram answered their knock.

"Lieutenant Verney Maughan Dacre," said Samson, demanding rather than inquiring.

"Lieutenant Dacre is not receiving visitors."

"Sergeant Samson, Metropolitan Police 'A' Division," said Samson. "I'm sure Mr Dacre wouldn't want an unseemly incident, but see him I must and will."

Oughtram admitted them to the vestibule of the tall
house, with its pilasters and finely-decorated ceilings. He
went upstairs to the sitting-room and presently returned.

"Mr Dacre will see you, Mr Samson, and he'd be obliged
if you could make your business brief. The Lieutenant dines
at seven sharp."

On the landing, with its ornate vases and turkey carpets,
the two sergeants waited again, while Oughtram entered his
master's sitting-room and closed the door. The two men
listened hard. It was impossible to hear all that was said in
the room, but Verity caught scraps of Dacre's conversation.

" . . . see the fellah ain't late with the cab . . . lay out the
russet suitin' and the west-cut in canary yaller."

"Mr Samson," said Verity softly, "a little while ago in
Newgate, I said there was one other thing about Lieutenant Dacre which I wasn't a-going to explain then. But I
am now. At the railway inquiry, I couldn't think why it was
he seemed to be familiar, for I never saw him before except
once through a camera lens, when I wasn't really looking. It
wasn't what I'd seen of him, but what I'd heard. That voice!
The old-fashioned talk! The way he says 'yaller' for 'yellow'
and 'goold' for 'gold', as though it was still the reign of
George IV. I'd swear in any court in the land that he was
with Roper in the same railway carriage on the night of the
bullion robbery, just before we reached the Harbour Pier
at Folkestone. It ain't just Roper's word against him now,
it's mine as well."

Oughtram reappeared and Samson entered the sitting-
room. Verity stood outside the door and listened. He heard
the creak of the sofa as the tall, blond dragoon got languidly
to his feet and inquired,

"To what may I attribute this visit?"

"To Edward Roper, sir," said Samson bluntly, "a convicted felon, now in Newgate and awaiting transportation.
The man has been questioned as to the bullion robbery on
the South Eastern Railway on the sixteenth of July. He has
confessed his own part in it and has named you as his con-
federate."

Dacre gave an abrupt laugh.

"I wonder he don't name Prince Albert as well, for he has more need of bullion than I have."

"It was you he named."

"See here," said Dacre sharply, "what a convicted felon may or may not say is no concern of mine and ain't likely to be believed."

"Are you acquainted with the man?"

"I have paid for his whores. A man who uses whores, as I do, must expect to suffer ill-usage of this sort, I suppose."

"Then, sir," said Samson stolidly, "you admit to knowing the man."

"Damn it!" said Dacre, "have I not said so? I have spent a good many sovereigns at his house, buying girls for the night. I have paid a small fortune for them to him and his bullies."

"A young person, Ellen Jacoby, was held prisoner and beaten at Langham Place, on your orders."

"Fudge!" said Dacre with another laugh. "You talk as if I ran the house, instead of being an occasional paying guest!"

"Another young woman, Jolie, was whipped."

"Have the goodness," said Dacre severely, "not to tamper with the truth. Miss Jolie was thrashed a few times for the diversion of the customers, and at their expense. I saw it done once. Y' may search that whorehouse through and through. You'll find only one connection with me. I paid in goold sovereigns for whatever was to be had."

It seemed to Verity that Samson was making little progress with this line of inquiry.

"Do you maintain, sir," asked Samson, "that you were not travelling on the tidal ferry train from London Bridge to Folkestone on the evening of sixteenth of July?"

"Lookee," said Dacre, "I don't have to maintain any such thing. It ain't possible that I could have travelled on that train, not even if I had wanted to. I was on the steam-packet from Ostend to Dover at the time, and you may see the ticket if you choose."

There was a pause.

"Well, sir," said Samson doggedly, "Roper has sworn you were there. You have also been identified as a traveller on that train by an officer of the detective police, who heard your voice."

Dacre burst out laughing.

"Then let the jury be told that, and see what they have to say! My dear fellah, you come to me with a story beyond all reason. Now, I ain't got the goold, I ain't got a cracksman's tools, nor lead shot. You may search to your heart's content. I liked the doxies at Langham Place—so did plenty of the fellows in the regiment—and I ploughed 'em good and often. And that's the sum of it. I don't know what your man Roper may have to do with any bullion robbery or what he may have told his bullies and whores to say about it. But so far as I am concerned, the matter ends there. If you ain't got more to say, you'll do me the goodness to leave. If there should be more to be said, then it may be said between your Mr Superintendent and my attorneys, Messrs Marshall and Purvis, of Greys Inn."

Verity's heart sank. Samson might be the terror of the magsman and his poll, but he was no match for Verney Dacre.

"Inspector Croaker must be told, sir," said Samson feebly, "and he must decide whether a warrant will be sought for your arrest this evening. In the meantime, an officer will be put at your door and will be instructed that you are to be detained if you should make any attempt to leave the premises."

"Just be sure," said Dacre coolly, "that you leave an officer who has not had his authority taken away from him."

Samson withdrew, closing the door behind him, and kept step with Verity down the stairs and out into Albemarle Street. As they stood outside, Samson said, "There'll be a warrant all right, and he knows it. But then it's Roper's word against his, ain't it? Roper himself admits to being the only one who knew what Dacre was doing. Take away Roper's evidence, and what is there to connect our man with the robbery? All you can prove for certain is that Dacre is a whore-master. And as for the murder of Cazamian, that ain't anywhere in the running at all."

"Mr Samson," said Verity sternly, "ain't you learned yet what detective investigation is all about? Of course you can't prove it all, not this very minute. But once this man is detained, the circumstantial evidence must be collected. Hotel waiters at Dover; luggage clerks at Folkestone; porters at London Bridge; whores from Langham Place. Weave a snare, Mr Samson, weave a snare! You must have patience to do it. It's what I've done these last few weeks. It ain't been easy, but our bullion thief is done for now, and he knows it. A sure and inescapable snare, Mr Samson, and I have my man in it at last! What he's done will be proved, and proved to the satisfaction of a jury."

"And he won't get more than four or five years," said Samson bitterly.

"But, Mr Samson," said Verity, "imagine the 'orror of it for one who lives as he has done!'"

Samson was just hailing a uniformed constable of "C" Division when he and Verity heard a sharp sound above them, like the snapping of a dry branch. Without waiting for formalities, they set off at a run for the rear of the building, burst through the kitchen and up the stairs. Verity, for all his bulk, gained the landing first and threw himself at the sitting-room door. It was locked but it gave easily under his weight. He stood briefly on the threshold and then withdrew. There was no more to be done. Verney Dacre sat in a green velvet arm-chair, his hand in his lap and his head thrown a little back. No doubt the two pistols on the table beside him were still loaded. The Hudson pistol in his lap, with its long "duelling" barrel, was quite certainly empty. He had apparently put on his nightcap to contain the horror of the wound. But he had placed the barrel of the pistol in his mouth, and that alone had blown the lower part of his face into a grisly pulp. The bullet, bursting from the top of his skull, had carried the nightcap off and thrown it across the room. It lay at a little distance from the chair, weighted by the distorted butt of the bullet, and by two fragments of Verney Dacre's skull.

Verity went down to the street again, feeling no sense of triumph at his vindication, and no pity for the fate of his adversary. On reflection, it was what he would have expected such a man to do. However, there were more important people in the world than Verney Dacre.

He passed by Samson, hardly noticing him, and began to run. He ran into Bond Street, past the hotels and tall houses with flowers at their windows, across the stream of cabs and carriages which ferried the fashionable world of peers and their dependents to an early dinner. He ran north and east towards the fine classical façade of Nash's Regent Street Quadrant. He crossed Regent Circus with several waggish urchins crying "Stop thief!" after him, and came within sight of Langham Place. The last notes of seven o'clock had just died away from the steeple of All Souls' church.

At first he could hardly make out what was going on. A crowd of men, with the appearance of the survivors of some military disaster, pushed and heaved about the doorway of Ned Roper's bawdy house. They wore long coats and, in some cases, shabby hats. Most of them carried whips and cudgels. As Verity ran towards them, he heard the shattering of glass, and above that the shrilling of a whistle which fell suddenly silent.

Before he could push his way into the crowd, a group of men broke away from it, led by a man who moved at something between a rapid hobble and a slow gallop.

"Stringfellow!" roared Verity.

He caught up with his friend.

"Miss Bella," said Stringfellow determinedly, "blew the whistle. Couldn't wait no longer. Front door won't budge. Try the back."

" 'oo are all these men?"

"Off the cab rank. Every driver there, when he heard what was 'appening to a cabman's daughter in a 'ouse of iniquity."

"It ain't a job for cabmen!" said Verity in reproof.

"Gammon!" said Stringfellow. "Coal chute, lads! There's the way, my boys! There's your chance!"

"Wait!" shouted Verity.

"What for?" Stringfellow settled himself on the chute,

holding the strap of his leg carefully, and then disappeared with great acceleration towards the basement of the house. Verity clutched his hat and followed. The interior of the house was a pandemonium through which a score of cabmen were attempting to force their way up the narrow stairs from the kitchen. With Stringfellow still in sight, Verity followed the general surge, fighting his way across the vestibule in the direction of the oval staircase. Far above him, under the coloured glass of the dome, he could see Coggin—or possibly Tyler—locking the wicket-gate, as the defenders of the house withdrew to the attic floor.

Verity paused briefly on the stairs at the sound of a female scream.

"Miss Bella!" he roared.

As he ran upwards, it occurred to him that he had never before heard Bella scream and could not have identified her voice at that pitch. It might equally well have been Ellen Jacoby. He reached the wicket-gate at the same time as a group of seven or eight sturdy young cabmen. Stout harness straps were secured to the upright which was screwed to the wooden pillar, and traces were led down from the straps. Soon, a dozen men or more were hauling with all their strength, straining the iron post away from the ornamental wood to which it was bolted. The screws started from the split wood and then, with a sudden wrench and a splintering of the varnished surface, the entire upright was torn free and the gate swung on its hinges, carrying the iron post still locked to it.

The defenders of the upper floor were taken entirely by surprise at the speed with which their iron barricade had fallen. Stringfellow galloped to the doorway of the first room, in time to find Tyler still crouched over Bella, as the girl lay spreadeagled on the bed. It was probable that Tyler was more concerned to fasten her there, or even to take her as a hostage, but in Stringfellow's mind the scene was synonymous with imminent rape. His heavy stick rose and fell once. Verity saw Tyler slither forward on the floor without even a cry.

In the next room, Ellen Jacoby still lay in her stupor, and

247

the two rooms beyond were empty. Still searching for Coggin, Verity ran for the skylight and pulled himself through it. The tiled roof sloped steeply and the only way along it was a path some eight or nine inches wide between the slope of the tiles and the gutter. From the gutter, the façade of the house dropped fifty feet to the street below. At first, Verity thought that he must be alone on the roof. Then he saw Stringfellow and Coggin acting out a grim drama round the chimney stack. Verity had had no idea that Stringfellow could even get through the skylight.

Coggin had brought a stout rope with him, using the thief's favourite technique of escape by gaining the roof, looping the rope round the chimney stack, and then shinning down behind the house. Before he could complete this, Stringfellow had evidently appeared, half standing and half leaning against the slope of the roof. The old cabman was weaving his long whip about in a manner which would have done credit to a regimental riding-master. Coggin was utterly dismayed at his failure to get to grips with his apparently crippled adversary. Indeed, the razor cuts of Stringfellow's lash were now driving the bully back, a foot at a time, towards the precipitous edge of the roof. Coggin had dropped his rope, in trying to defend himself, and it now lay far beyond his reach.

"Touch 'er, would yer, you brute?" said Stringfellow savagely, as Coggin drew back again to avoid a cut of the whip aimed at his head. The next lash caught him across the face, drawing a long welling of blood like a sabre cut. Fifty feet below, a crowd of pale indistinguishable faces were turned upwards to watch the conclusion of the grotesque struggle.

"Twenty pounds to the man who shall take him alive!" shouted a well-dressed man from the crowd. But Stringfellow muttered something to himself and struck again at Coggin. The bully, now completely demoralised by the pain and the appalling death that awaited him, began to scream for assistance.

"Stringfellow!" shouted Verity, "leave him be!"

Stringfellow's answer was to cut Coggin acrosss the chin,

making him stumble backwards and sway, so that Verity thought for an instant that he had gone. But Coggin was still there, on his hands and knees, blinded by the blood running into his eyes from a cut on the forehead and howling for mercy. Verity managed to pull himself up the tiles, level with Stringfellow.

"Leave him, Stringfellow!"

"He touched 'er! Touched Miss Bella, inside 'er clothes! That filthy hog!"

"Leave 'im! For my sake! If you let him die now, there'll be no trial. One of the others has destroyed himself, and the other's got to be an evidence."

"That son of a whore!" said Stringfellow.

"And there's a gentleman has offered twenty guineas to whoever shall take the man alive. You shall have every farthing of it."

Stringfellow thought for a moment, while Coggin bowed his head and whimpered.

"No," said the old cabman at last, "you and Miss Bella shall 'ave it. I wouldn't take a brass button to save this creature!"

To Verity's relief, another head, that of a uniformed constable, appeared through the skylight, and Stringfellow allowed himself to be helped down. Verity and the constable took Coggin, handcuffed him, and lowered him into the custody of two other officers inside the house. Bella, wrapped in a blanket, frightened but unhurt, had been taken to her father's cab. As Verity hurried after her, he came face to face with Inspector Swift on the steps of the house.

"How's this, sergeant?" said Swift quietly. "Suspension from duty ended, has it?"

"No, sir," said Verity, stiff at attention, "not ended, sir. Obliged to take two persons into custody for their own safety, sir. Couldn't see no other way of averting a tragedy, sir. 'ad to use initiative, sir. Very sorry, sir."

"Ah," said Swift, waving him away, "so that was it!"

And when Verity had gone, Swift permitted himself a smile, for he detested Inspector Croaker quite as much as any other man in the detail might.

21

After the events of July 1857, the trial of Coggin and Tyler as accomplices in the Great Bullion Robbery was an anti-climax. They were very minor accomplices, and the testimony of the Crown's "evidences," Roper, Jolie, and Ellen Jacoby, was pale enough by comparison with the garish colours in which the morning and evening papers had depicted the "Shocking Incident in Albemarle Street," or the "Dramatic Apprehension in Langham Place." The inquest on Verney Dacre had, of course, preceded the trial by some weeks and its verdict of "suicide while insane" was the stock finding in such cases. To Verity, at least, it seemed that Dacre had acted in a moment of terrified lucidity.

At the trial, it was learnt that Sergeant Samson, who was on duty under confidential orders from Inspector Croaker, had interviewed Roper in Newgate gaol, and skilfully extracted from him the entire story of the bullion theft. Samson had then gone to Albemarle Street and apprehended Lieutenant Dacre. But even while Samson was fetching a constable to stand guard on the house, Mr Dacre had shot himself. Within an hour, Constable Tucker of "C" Division, attracted by a disturbance in Langham Place, had entered a house and apprehended Coggin and Tyler.

Much was made by the solicitor-general of the manner in which the investigation had been carried out by officers of the private clothes detail under the command of Inspector Henry Croaker. Croaker, in his evidence, accepted such praise gracefully, modestly suggesting that if it had not been for the loyalty and unquestioning obedience of such subordinates as Sergeant Samson, all his carefully prepared plans for the solution of the bullion robbery might have come to nothing.

At noon on the second day of the trial, verdicts were returned against the two defendants. Coggin was sentenced to seven years' penal servitude, and Tyler to five. Ned Roper, as he himself insisted in his evidence, had been "promised nothing" in return for his testimony, and he received nothing. With the trial over, he was to be taken at once to Chatham for embarkation on the convict hulks. There were still unsolved mysteries in the case, but those who might have provided the solutions were either dead or inaccessible, or even protected by the law. The cause of McCaffery's death might be an open secret, but the death of Cazamian remained unexplained. As for Roper's forgery, most of those who saw him give evidence were sufficiently impressed by his blunt dishonesty to believe that he had been quite properly convicted and sentenced for that crime. No good would come of meddling with the matter now.

Verity, whose sole evidence had been that of finding Lieutenant Dacre's body, sat in court throughout the remainder of the Old Bailey trial. He was there, after sentences had been passed, when Baron Pennistone asked Inspector Croaker to step forward.

"It must be said," remarked Pennistone slowly, "that the matters which have been brought before the court in this case have only been revealed by detective investigations of the utmost skill and persistence. It is the duty of this court to ensure that those officers who have brought such ingenious and resourceful conspirators to justice should be publicly commended. In particular, Inspector Henry Croaker, of the private clothes detail has shown a degree of determination and professionalism which is almost beyond praise. Faced by a crime whose enormity and complexity almost baffles belief, his own pertinacity has inspired a loyalty and zeal among his men which is in the finest tradition of the constabulary service. His alertness and vigour have ensured that what might have been one of the most notorious criminal triumphs of our age has, instead, become a vindication of the detective police and of the power of law."

Then Baron Pennistone made a little sign to show that his panegyric was over. Croaker bowed and withdrew. The court rose and Verity, in company with Samson, walked out into the mid-day sunshine of Old Bailey.

"Well!" said Verity, his face glowing as though fresh from a steam-bath, "well! did you hear that?"

Before he could expand his view of the matter he heard a dry cough behind him.

"Sergeant!"

"Sir?"

"Sergeant," said Croaker, "I do not believe it was intended that you should spend the entire morning sitting about in court, once your evidence was given."

"No, sir? No contrary instructions, sir."

"No," said Croaker sceptically. "However, it may not come amiss that you should have heard his lordship's remarks at the conclusion of the proceedings."

"Yes, sir."

"You may find them beneficial."

"Yes, sir. Very instructive, sir."

"Sergeant Verity, you have behaved very foolishly in the past few weeks. You have endangered yourself and the reputation of the entire Division. Your conduct has been wilful and often insubordinate. You need not congratulate yourself on having escaped disgrace and probable imprisonment. You owe your freedom to the efforts of your senior officers and to certain strokes of good fortune."

"Yes, sir. Just so, sir."

"In time, sergeant, you may learn to master your deficiencies and become a good detective officer."

" 'ope so, I'm sure, sir."

"In the meantime, I shall seriously consider what is to be done with you. I understand from Colonel Hanning that Sir Colin Campbell is anxious to have a number of constables available to him to assist, in a civil capacity, in pacifying the native mutiny in India."

" 'indoostan, sir?"

"India, sergeant. Hindoostan has been dropped as a name since the rebellion broke out. It may be that a spell of duty under strict discipline there would materially improve your attitude."

"Couldn't say, sir. Never was in foreign parts, only for the Rhoosian war, sir."

"No," said Croaker thoughtfully, "but fortunately it will not be for *you* to say."

He turned and marched away, in frock coat and silk hat, as smartly as though he had been on the drill square at Woolwich once more.

"Sour as vinegar and mean as a stoat," said Verity softly.

"In-jer!" said Samson respectfully.

It was while they were watching Croaker's impressive departure that a smart spring-green Pilentum came bowling past, drawn by a pair of bay geldings. The carriage would have caught the eye in any case, but all heads turned to admire the girl who held the reins. Jolie, in her pink dress and bonnet, drove with more confidence than she had done with Dacre at Folkestone. Beside her sat Ellen Jacoby, her fresh blonde beauty considerably restored. She was nursing Ned Roper's child.

"Ain't it odd," said Samson, "what that doxy 'as to thank Lieutenant Dacre for? A-cos the Lieutenant took all Roper's share of the bullion, the railway company ain't got no right to all the other stuff. The court made all Roper's goods over to his woman and his son. Nell Jacoby must be a considerable rich young woman."

"If so inclined," said Verity, "she may lead an easy and virtuous life. Let us 'ope she does, Samson."

Samson nudged him.

"So inclined! Constable Meiklejohn says those two doxies have taken a house down in Surrey, to live like spinsters. Ellen Jacoby don't miss Roper's loving any more. Why, you and I wouldn't even think of doing some of the things to a girl that those two does to one another. What Meiklejohn says . . ."

"Much obliged," said Verity in his most magisterial manner, "but I ain't particular to 'ear what that heathen says. On Saturday, at Paddington Chapel, I shall become the 'usband of a young person who *does* need a man. There ain't nothing better than that!"

In the warm darkness of the little room, Verity lay on his back, holding Bella against him with his left arm. Passion being temporarily exhausted, his mind began to run on other things. So, apparently, did Bella's.

"Mr Verity," she said softly, playing with her fingers on his chest, "why was you called William Clarence Verity?"

"On account of the ballot," said Verity gruffly.

"What ballot?"

"The reform—eighteen thirty-two. All the Wesleyans in Cornwall were very strong for the ballot. You can't break the power of the Established Church and the squires any way but by extending the vote."

"But why was you called William Clarence?"

"On account of the old king," said Verity with great patience. " 'is Majesty was very strong for reform too, at the time. And he was King William and he'd been Duke of Clarence. So it was William Clarence."

"Oh," she said, as though rather disappointed.

They lay in silence for a few minutes more, Bella pushing closer towards him.

"It may be," said Verity, "that I shall have to go away for a few months, if Mr Croaker sends me."

"Where to?" she asked quickly.

"India, but only for a few months."

At first Bella seemed forlorn at the prospect.

"All those heathen," she said, "and black women. I've heard what goes on between the sojers and the native women."

"You've no business to listen to such stuff!" said Verity indignantly. "And it'll only be for a little while."

Presently she said, "Will it be like the camp before Sebastopol?"

" 'ow d'yer mean?"

"Will it be for Old England and the Queen?"

"Oh," said Verity, "oh, yes, it'll be that all right."

Bella snuggled closer to him and slid one bare leg over his.

"Oh, William Clarence Verity," she said happily, "I'm no end proud of you!"